"I've never seen anything like it," Annarita said truthfully. "Where do all the games come from?"

"We have crazy people locked up in a psychiatric hospital who make them up," Eduardo told her.

She blinked. He really did like to see how close to the wind he could sail. Everybody knew the Party put trouble-makers in psychiatric hospitals. Getting into one of those places was easy. Coming out? Coming out was a different story.

Everybody knew that, but hardly anybody talked about it. If you talked about it to the wrong people, you might wind up inside a psychiatric hospital yourself. But Eduardo didn't seem worried. He grinned at her.

Annarita wondered if he was a provocateur. Maybe the whole store was a front, a trap to catch dissidents. Would everybody who played games in here end up in a psychiatric hospital or in jail or in a labor camp or dead? She didn't like to think so, but the authorities could be sneaky. Everybody knew that, too.

She walked over to the shelves. There were titles like *Making Your Corporation Profitable* and *Economics of Club Ownership* alongside others like *Greece and Rome at War*. "You sell . . . interesting books," she said.

"Well, if they weren't interesting, who'd buy them?" Eduardo spread his hands and answered his own question: "Nobody, that's who. Then I couldn't make my living having fun. I'd have to do something honest instead."

Tor Books by Harry Turtledove

Between the Rivers
Conan of Venarium
The Two Georges (by Richard Dreyfuss and Harry Turtledove)
Household Gods (by Judith Tarr and Harry Turtledove)
The First Heroes (edited by Harry Turtledove and Noreen Doyle)

Darkness

Into the Darkness
Darkness Descending
Through the Darkness
Rulers of the Darkness
Jaws of Darkness
Out of the Darkness

Crosstime Traffic

Gunpowder Empire
Curious Notions
In High Places
The Gladiator

Writing as H. N. Turteltaub

Justinian
Over the Wine-Dark Sea
The Gryphon's Skull
The Sacred Land

The Gladiator

Crosstime Traffic—Book Five

Harry Turtledove

A Tom Doherty Associates Book

New York

This is a work of fiction. All of the characters, organizations, and events portrayed in this novel are either products of the author's imagination or are used fictitiously.

THE GLADIATOR

Copyright © 2007 by Harry Turtledove

Edited by Teresa Nielsen Hayden

A Tor Book
Published by Tom Doherty Associates, LLC
175 Fifth Avenue
New York, NY 10010

www.tor-forge.com

Tor® is a registered trademark of Tom Doherty Associates, LLC.

ISBN-13: 978-0-7653-5379-5
ISBN-10: 0-7653-5379-2

First Edition: June 2007
First Mass Market Edition: October 2008

Printed in the United States of America

0 9 8 7 6 5 4 3 2

The
Gladiator

One

Annarita Crosetti didn't want to get up in the morning. She didn't want to get up most mornings, but today was especially bad. After she killed the alarm clock, she just wanted to roll over and go back to sleep. But she couldn't. She knew it. She had a Russian test first period, and a Young Socialists' League meeting after school. That meant she'd be up late with school-work tonight, too, and sleepy again tomorrow morning.

Even so, she didn't want to get up.

When she didn't start moving fast enough to suit her mother, she got shaken and pushed out of bed. She muttered and groaned in protest—she had trouble talking till she was re-ally awake, which took a while.

Her mother showed no sympathy . . . and no mercy. "Come on. Get dressed," she said. "Breakfast will be ready by the time you are."

"*Sì, sì,*" Annarita said. By then she was standing up. Her mother went away, knowing she probably wouldn't lie down again.

Because there was a meeting, Annarita put on her Young Socialists' League uniform. It made her look ready to change a tire: marching boots, khaki trousers, dark green blouse. But all the Young Socialists—the up-and-comers— would be wearing the same thing today, so what could she do? Not much. Not anything, really.

She put on the crisscross sashes, one with the badges of Marx and Engels, Lenin and Stalin and Putin, the other with badges of Moroni and Chiapelli and other Italian Communist heroes. The badges of the Russians and the founders were edged in gold, those of the Italians in silver. Annarita didn't know how many times she'd put on the sashes, but she'd never even thought about that before. It was as if her own countrymen were runners-up in the race for fame.

She shook her head. It wasn't as if. Italian Communist heroes were heroes only in Italy. Other Socialist people's republics had their own national heroes. You saw them, grim and unsmiling, on foreign postage stamps. But the founders and the Russians were heroes all over the world. *They should be*, she thought. *If not for them, Marxism-Leninism-Stalinism might not have won. And then where would we be?*

"Annarita!" her mother yelled.

"Coming!" She knew where she needed to be: the kitchen.

It was crowded in there. The Crosettis shared the kitchen and bathroom with the Mazzillis, who were also eating breakfast. Everyone muttered good morning. Annarita grabbed a roll, tore it, and dipped it in olive oil. A cup of cappuccino was waiting for her. Her mother and father poured down espresso instead, thick and sweet and strong. If two or three of those little cups wouldn't get your heart started in the morning, you were probably dead.

Sitting across the table from her was Gianfranco Mazzilli, who was sixteen—a year younger than Annarita—and went to the same school. He just had on ordinary clothes, though. He didn't belong to the Young Socialists, which made his parents unhappy.

His father used espresso to knock back a shot of grappa, and then another one. That would get your heart started, too. Of course, after a while you might not remember *why* you got it started, but Cristoforo Mazzilli didn't seem to care.

Annarita's father eyed the bottle of distilled lightning and said, "I wish I could get going like that."

"Why can't you, Filippo?" Cristoforo Mazzilli said. "Doesn't hurt me a bit."

"I should keep a clear head," Annarita's father answered. "The patients need it."

"'From each according to his abilities, to each according to his needs,'" the elder Mazzilli quoted. He reached for the grappa bottle. "I need this." He was a midlevel Party functionary in one of the provincial ministries. No one would get hurt if he came to work a little tipsy, or more than a little tipsy, or if he didn't come in at all. Knowing that might have been one reason he drank.

As soon as people finished eating, they started jockeying for the bathroom. There were apartments—some right here in this building—where families fought like cats and dogs over the tub and the toilet. The Crosettis and the Mazzillis didn't do that, anyhow. Both families had to use the facilities, whether they got along or not. Easier when they did, so everybody tried. It worked pretty well . . . most of the time.

Going down the stairs, Annarita carried her books in front of her. Gianfranco carried his under one arm. Girls did the one thing, boys the other. Annarita didn't know why, or how long it had been that way. Maybe, if she remembered, she would ask her mother. Did it go back further than that? She shrugged. She had no idea.

"Spring," Gianfranco said when they got outside.

"Spring," Annarita agreed. Spring here in Milan was a lot more hesitant than it was down in Rome, let alone Naples or Sicily. It stayed cool and humid. It could rain—it could come down in buckets. The sun was out right now. But clouds floated across the sky. If the sun hid behind one of them, it might not feel like coming out again.

Other students were coming out of the building, and from the identical concrete towers to either side. Stalin Gothic, people called them—when they were sure no informers were listening, anyhow.

Not far away stood the Duomo. The great cathedral was Gothic, too, only it was the genuine article. Every line of it seemed to leap for the sky, to point toward the heavens. Officially, the Italian People's Republic was as atheistic as the Soviet Union or any other Socialist state. Officially. In spite of Stalin's cruel joke—"The Pope? How many divisions has he got?"—His Holiness Pius XIV still presided over St. Peter's. Some churches stayed open. You weren't supposed to believe any of that stuff, but a lot of people did.

Annarita glanced from the Duomo to the grim, square apartment blocks and back again. The apartments looked as if they'd been run up in six weeks. They probably had, judging by the plumbing. The elevator in her building hadn't worked for years. She and Gianfranco had come down the stairs. They would climb them in the afternoon, too.

The Duomo . . . They'd started building it in the fourteenth century, and hadn't finished till the twentieth. That seemed— that *was*—an awfully long time, but they got it right. Yes, it glorified superstition. So her teachers said, at least half a dozen times a day. But glorify it did.

In the square in front of the Duomo stood a statue of General Secretary Putin *Old Pointy-Nose*, people called him. Not counting the base, he stood four meters tall—twice the height of even a tall man. All the same, the cathedral had no trouble making him seem like a midget.

At the moment, a pigeon perched on his outstretched right forefinger. Gianfranco pointed to it. "Looking for a handout," he said.

"Good luck," Annarita said. "The bird better hope that fist doesn't close." Even though Gianfranco grinned and nodded, she wished she had the words back the second they were out of her mouth. Vladimir Putin was seventy years dead, yes, but making any kind of joke about him to a Party man's son wasn't smart. But *everybody* knew the Russians were so much better at taking than giving.

Fiats and Russian Volgas and smelly German Trabants and Workermobiles from the USA crowded narrow streets that hadn't been built with cars in mind in the first place. A century and more of Communism hadn't turned Italians into orderly drivers. Annarita didn't think anything could. A Volga stopped in the middle of the street to wait for an old woman on the far curb. It plugged traffic like a cork in a bottle. A trolley had to stop behind the Volga. More cars jammed up behind the trolley. The motorman clanged his bell. The drivers leaned on their horns. The man in the Volga ignored them all.

The old lady tottered over and got in. The Volga zoomed away. The trolley got moving, too. The swarm of cars behind it would take longer to unknot.

"There ought to be a law," Gianfranco said.

"There *are* laws," Annarita said. "People don't pay any attention to them."

"That trolleyman should have photographed the guy's license plate," Gianfranco said. "When they found out who he was, they could have fixed him good."

"Maybe the trolleyman did," Annarita said.

"Yeah, maybe." Gianfranco sounded as if he liked the idea. Annarita wasn't so sure she did. They already had so many ways to keep an eye on you. Who needed a motorman with a camera? Even typewriters were registered. As far as the Italian People's Republic was concerned, they were more dangerous than assault rifles. And computers . . . Her school had a couple, which made it special, but only the most trusted teachers and the very most trusted students got to use them.

She thought the progress to real Communism, the kind where the state withered away, would come faster if people could more freely use the tools they had. No matter what she thought, she kept her ideas to herself. What you didn't tell anybody, you couldn't get in trouble for.

While she was thinking dark thoughts, her feet kept walking. She turned right and then left and then right again. She hardly noticed the apartment blocks and shops she passed.

"We're here," Gianfranco said.

"*Sì*," Annarita said. "We're here. Oh, boy." Gianfranco laughed. He was more likely to say something like that. She was the good student—he just squeaked by. But she couldn't make herself get excited about school today.

Enver Hoxha Polytechnic Academy was named for a Communist hero, but not for an Italian Communist hero. Hoxha had ad-

ministered Albania for most of the second half of the twentieth
century. A lot of Italians laughed at Albanians, their neighbors
across the Adriatic Sea. Few did it it where Albanians could
hear them, though. Albanians were supposed to have nasty
tempers, and to be fond of carrying knives.

Students from other schools jeered Hoxha Polytechnic's
soccer and basketball teams because the academy bore a foreigner's name. "Odd jobs!" they shouted. "Odd jobs!" Despite
a century and a half of Socialism, Albania remained the poor-
est country in Europe. Young Albanians sometimes crossed
the Adriatic in small boats. Working as farm laborers or
handymen—or thieves—in Italy seemed better to them than
going hungry back home.

A big black-and-white photo of Hoxha stared down at Annarita and Gianfranco from over the entrance. He didn't look as
if he approved of them. He didn't look as if he approved of anybody. Considering what he'd had to do to drive the Fascists out
of Albania during the Second World War and then rule the
country for so long afterwards, he probably didn't.

"See you," Gianfranco said, and hurried off to his first
class.

"*Ciao*," Annarita called after him. She didn't want to go to
Russian. It drove her crazy. Everybody who wanted to be anybody had to learn it. It was the most important language in the
world, after all. When the Soviet Union sneezed, the rest of the
world started sniffling. But still . . .

Annarita had had a couple of years of Latin. She understood
the idea of cases, of using endings instead of prepositions to
show how words worked in a sentence. *Homo* was a man as the
subject of a sentence. If a man thanked you, he was *homo*. But
if you thanked him, if he was the object, he was *hominem*. In the

possessive, he was *hominis*. A man's dog was *canus hominis*—or *hominis canus*. Word order mattered much less in Latin than in Italian. The same was true in Russian, only more so.

But if Latin's grammar was weird, an awful lot of the vocabulary looked familiar. *Man* in Italian was *uomo*, while *dog* was *cane*. You didn't need to know any history to see that Latin and Italian were related.

Russian's vocabulary, though, seemed even weirder to Annarita than its grammar did. *Man* in Russian was *chelovek*, and *dog* was *sobaka*. Worse, the Russians used a different alphabet, so everything looked funny. *Man* looked like человек, and dog looked like собака. Some of the letters were recognizable, but others would fool you. C was sounded like "s," P was "r," and H was "n." If you weren't careful, if you absentmindedly thought the way you usually did, Russian could really bite you.

"*Dobry den*," the teacher said when Annarita walked into the classroom.

"*Dobry den, Tovarishch* Montefusco," she answered. *Good day, Comrade Montefusco*. That was polite, but she wondered if she really meant it. How could a day with a test in it be a good day?

He waited till the bell, and not an instant longer. "And now, the test," he said, still in Russian. His accent was very good. He'd spent a long time studying in Russia. Some people whispered that he'd spent some time in a camp there. Annarita had no idea if that was true. Nobody'd ever had the nerve to ask him.

He handed out the mimeographed sheets. Mimeograph machines and copiers were kept under lock and key. Annarita understood that. Counterrevolutionaries could use them to reproduce propaganda harmful to the state. As far as she was concerned, this test was harmful to her state of mind.

It was hard. She'd known it would be. They wanted to find out who was just good and who was the very best. The very best—and the ones with the very best connections—would run things when they grew up. The ones who weren't quite good enough for that would get more ordinary jobs instead.

The ones who didn't measure up would miss out on other things, too. They wouldn't be able to travel abroad. They wouldn't get the best vacation houses by the ocean or up in the mountains. They wouldn't get the best apartments in the city, either. And they would spend years on the waiting list for a tiny, miserable Trabant, with a motor that sounded like a tin can full of rocks and angry bees, instead of getting a fancy Zis or a Ferrari or a Mercedes.

So Annarita knew what was at stake every time she wrote her name—Аннарита Кростти—on a test form. The privileges and luxuries that went with being the very best didn't drive her all that much, though they were nice. But the idea of being at the center of things, being where the action was—*that* pushed her. So did the idea of proving she really was the best to a world that didn't care one way or the other.

She got to work. Even counting in Russian was complicated. Numbers changed case like any other adjectives. And the nouns that followed them changed case, too, with strange rules. One house stayed in the nominative—the case for the subject. Two, three, or four houses (or anything else) went to the genitive singular—the case for the possessive. *Three of house*, it meant literally. Five or more houses and you used the genitive again, but the plural this time. *Seven of houses* was the literal meaning.

"*Bozhemoi!*" Annarita muttered to herself. That meant *My God!* It wasn't good Marxist-Leninist-Stalinist doctrine, but it was perfectly good Russian. Comrade Montefusco said it when somebody made a dumb mistake in class. Annarita had heard real Russians say it on TV and on the radio, too. From everything she could tell, Russians were less polite than Italians, or polite in a different way.

She fought through the test. She was still in the middle of rechecking when the teacher said, "Pass them forward, please." She sighed and did. She wasn't sure about a couple of things, but she thought she'd done well.

Analytic geometry next. It was interesting, in a way. Annarita didn't know what she'd ever do with it, but it made her think. Her father kept telling her that was good all by itself. Of course, he didn't have to do the homework and the studying. (He'd done them years before, but Annarita didn't think about that.)

She settled into her chair in the new classroom. Analytic geometry had one thing going for it. No matter what happened, no matter which Party faction rose and which one fell, the answers wouldn't change. Ideology could change history. It could change literature. It could even change biology. But math? Math didn't change. In a world where everything else might, that was reassuring.

Gianfranco bombed an algebra quiz. He'd studied. He'd even had Annarita help him get ready for it, though she was rushed—she had her own Russian test to worry about. He'd thought he knew what was coming and how to do it. But when he looked at the questions, his brain turned to polenta.

And when his father found out, he probably *would* get pounded into cornmeal mush. Not that his old man had been any great shakes in school. He would be something better, something more *interesting*, than a mid-level paper shuffler if he had. He wanted Gianfranco to do what he hadn't been able to.

No matter what he wanted, chances were he wouldn't get it. Gianfranco cared more about basketball and soccer than he did about schoolwork. He was better at them than he was at schoolwork, too. He wasn't great or anything, even if he wished he were. He wasn't tall enough to be anything special as a basketball player, either. He enjoyed the games, though, where he felt like a caged animal in the classroom.

He was shaking his head and muttering to himself when he trudged off to history. He knew he would have trouble paying attention. He was still worrying about that stupid quiz, and about why he was too stupid to get things right. And who cared what happened back in the twentieth century, anyway? It seemed as far from his own life as Julius Caesar did.

Besides, Comrade Pontevecchio was a bore.

"Let's get to work!" the history teacher barked as soon as the bell rang. "Let's all be Stakhanovites in our quest for knowledge!"

He said the same thing every morning. Gianfranco didn't yawn—you got in trouble if you showed you wanted to go to sleep. But he thought this particular Party slogan was dumb. Doing more than your assigned quota made sense if you worked in a factory and made bricks or brushes or something like that. How could you learn more than was in your book, though?

Of course, Gianfranco hadn't learned all of what was in the book, let alone more than that. "In the nineteen sixties, what two events showed that the corrupt, capitalist, imperialist

United States was only a paper tiger?" Comrade Pontevecchio asked. His finger shot out. "Mazzilli! Yes, you! Recite!"

Gianfranco jumped to his feet. "Yes, Comrade Teacher!" But it wasn't yes. "Uh . . ." His wits seemed frozen. "The Vietnam missile crisis?" There was something about Vietnam in the chapter, and something about missiles. He remembered that much, anyhow.

It wasn't enough. Titters ran through the classroom. Some of the laughter was probably relief. Not everybody would have known the answer. Gianfranco could tell it was wrong. He stood there, waiting for the teacher to put him out of his misery—or to give him more of it.

Comrade Pontevecchio made a production of taking a red pen out of his shirt pocket and writing in the roll book with it. "No," he said coldly. "Be seated. If you don't care about the past, how can the present matter to you?"

I'm living in the present, Gianfranco thought. *The past is dead*. But the history teacher didn't want an answer. He wanted Gianfranco to sit down and shut up. Miserably, Gianfranco did.

"What is the real answer? What is the right answer?" the teacher asked.

Teobaldo Montefiore threw his hand in the air. He did everything but sing it out, which would have got him in trouble. *Yeah, show off how smart you are, you little suck-up*, Gianfranco thought scornfully. *If you were really smart, you'd be in the advanced track, not stuck here with me.*

When the teacher called on Teobaldo, he jumped to his feet. "The Vietnam War and the Cuban missile crisis!" he said, squeaking with excitement.

"Very good—so far," Comrade Pontevecchio said. "Why are they important?"

All of a sudden, Teobaldo didn't look so happy. "Because they showed capitalism was doomed?" You could hear the question mark in his voice. He wasn't sure he was right any more, even if he gave an answer that was almost always safe.

"Sit down," the teacher snapped, and wrote something in the roll book in red. Comrade Pontevecchio looked out over the class. "Anyone?" His scorn grew by the second when nobody took a chance. "Knowing what is only half the battle, and the small half at that. You have to know why. Do you think Marx could have invented dialectical materialism if he didn't understand why?"

Nobody said anything. When Comrade Pontevecchio got into one of these moods, keeping quiet was the safest thing you could do. Gianfranco stared down at his desk. People had been trying to drum dialectical materialism into his head since he was five years old, but he still didn't get it.

"When the United States backed down and let the Soviet Union keep missiles in Cuba to balance the American missiles in Turkey, what did that show?" the teacher demanded.

Gianfranco thought he knew, but he wasn't about to stick his neck out. Luisa Orlandini cautiously raised her hand. Luisa was pretty. Even if she got it wrong, Comrade Pontevecchio probably wouldn't bite her head off.

Probably.

He nodded to her. She stood up. "It showed the American capitalist regime was only a paper tiger, Comrade Pontevecchio," she said.

"That's right," he agreed —he'd called the USA a paper tiger himself. "And what does the Vietnam War have to do with this?"

"The Vietnamese were trying to liberate the south from a

neocolonialist dictatorship, and the Americans tried to prop up the reactionary elements," Luisa answered.

"Yes, that's also right." Comrade Pontevecchio warmed all the way up to chilly. "And what happened then, and why?"

"Well, the Americans and their reactionary running dogs lost. I know that," Luisa said.

"*Sì*. They lost. But how? Why? How could America lose? In those days, it was very rich. It was much bigger and richer than Vietnam. What happened?" Luisa didn't know. Comrade Pontevecchio waved her to her seat. He looked around for somebody else. When no one volunteered, he pointed at somebody. "Crespi!"

Paolo Crespi got up. "The Americans stopped wanting to fight, didn't they, Comrade Pontevecchio?"

"Are you asking me or telling me?"

"Uh, I'm telling you, Comrade."

"Well, you're right. When the United States brought its soldiers home from Vietnam in 1968, that was another signal to progressive forces around the world that not even the heartland of capitalism would go on defending an outdated ideology anymore. And so the cause of Socialism advanced in Asia and Africa and South America. One war of national liberation after another broke out and triumphed. Meanwhile, what was happening here in Europe. Does the term 'popular front' mean anything to you?"

It was in the textbook. Gianfranco remembered that much, but no more. Comrade Pontevecchio frowned when no hands went up. "You haven't been studying as hard as you should have." He pointed at a girl. "Sofia! Tell me about popular fronts!"

She got to her feet. "I—I'm sorry, Comrade Teacher, but I don't know."

"And what excuse do you have for not knowing?"

"No excuse, Comrade Teacher." That was the only right answer. You were supposed to know. If you didn't, it was your fault, nobody else's. That was how teachers and the rest of the school system looked at things, anyhow. If the textbook was boring and the teacher hated students . . . well, so what? Textbooks had been boring ever since they were written on clay tablets, and teachers couldn't wallop kids the way they had in the old days.

Comrade Pontevecchio picked on a boy. He didn't know what a popular front was, either.

"This will not do," the teacher snapped. "Get out your books. Write me a fifteen-minute essay on what popular fronts were and why they were important. Anyone who does poorly will have more work assigned. These are your lessons. You *will* learn them."

Gianfranco almost hadn't brought his textbook. The miserable thing was thick as a brick and weighed a ton. But he would have been in big trouble if Comrade Pontevecchio caught him unprepared. He opened the book and looked in the index. There they were—popular fronts. *Oh, boy*, he thought. He flipped to the right page and started scribbling as fast as he could. If he parroted the text, he couldn't go wrong. And he didn't have to think while he wrote, either. Comrade Pontevecchio didn't care what he thought or if he thought, as long as he ground out the right answers.

Popular fronts, he rediscovered, combined Communists with non-Communist Socialists and other fellow travelers. The first one came along in France before World War II, to try to rally the country against Fascism. It didn't work. But later popular fronts swung France and Italy and Scandinavia away from the weakening USA and toward the USSR.

Without these fronts, he wrote, *the victory of Socialism in Europe, while it still would inevitably have come, would have been slower. It might even have required warfare to eliminate reactionary forces from the continent.* That was what the textbook said, and the textbook had to be right. If it was wrong, the authorities wouldn't use it—and what would they do to an author who was wrong on purpose? Send him to a camp? Kill him? Purge his whole family? Gianfranco wouldn't have been surprised.

Was everybody in the class writing the same ideas in the same words? Everybody with any sense was. Why stick your neck out when the answers were right there in black and white? How many times would Comrade Pontevecchio read the same sentences? How sick of them would he get?

Serve him right, Gianfranco thought. The teacher called for the essays. The students passed them forward. Comrade Pontevecchio grudged a nod. "Now, at least, you know what popular fronts are."

He was right. Gianfranco didn't think he would forget. He still didn't care, though. But Comrade Pontevecchio didn't care whether he cared.

After what seemed like forever, the bell rang. Gianfranco jumped up much more eagerly than he had to recite. Escape! But it wasn't escape from school, only from history. Literature didn't interest him, either. Nothing in school interested him a whole lot. He felt as if he were in jail.

And his father and mother got mad because he wasn't a

better student! How could you do well if you didn't care? All he wanted to do was get out. Because afterwards . . .

But he couldn't think about afterwards yet. If he did, he would start thinking about how long it was till he got out. And that would hurt, and then he would pay even less attention than he usually did.

He sighed. Off to literature.

This year, literature covered twentieth-century Socialist writers who weren't actually Communists. Fellow travelers, Comrade Pellagrini called them. A light went on in Gianfranco's head. History and literature were talking about some of the same things, but coming at them from different angles. That was interesting. He wished it happened more often.

All the same, the class itself wasn't that exciting. Right now, they were going through Jack London's *The Iron Heel*. Gianfranco had read *The Call of the Wild* and "To Build a Fire" in translation the year before. Those were gripping stories. London plainly knew about the frozen North, and he was able to put across what he knew.

The Iron Heel was different. It was a novel about the class struggle, and about the ways the big capitalists found to divide the proletariat and keep it from winning the workers' revolution.

"Marx talks about how, in the last days of capitalism, the bourgeoisie are declassed and fall into the ranks of the workers," Comrade Pellagrini said. "You all know that. You started studying *The Communist Manifesto* when you were still in primary school."

Gianfranco found himself nodding agreement. He would have nodded agreement to almost anything Comrade Pellagrini said. She didn't look much older than the girls she was teaching, but she made them look like . . . girls. She was a woman herself, more *finished* than the girls, and prettier than almost all of them, too. She carried herself like a model or a dancer.

She was *so* pretty, Gianfranco almost thought it would be worthwhile to study hard and impress her with how much he knew. Almost. She treated students the way a busy doctor treated patients. She was good at teaching, but she didn't let anybody get personal. And Gianfranco knew that if he tried to impress her and failed, he'd be crushed. Better not to try in that case, wasn't it? He thought so—and it gave him one more excuse not to work too hard.

"How does London take Marx's dynamic and turn it upside down, at least for a while?" the literature teacher asked.

Gianfranco looked down at his desk. He couldn't answer the question. If their eyes met, she was more likely to call on him. He thought so, anyway. Most of the time, he looked at her when he thought she wouldn't be looking at him.

She called on someone else—a girl. The student made a hash of trying to explain. Comrade Pellagrini called on a boy. He botched it, too.

The teacher let out an exasperated snort. "How many of you did the assigned reading last night?" All the students raised their hands. Gianfranco had . . . looked at the book last night, anyway. Comrade Pellagrini scowled. "If you read it, why can't you answer a simple question?"

No one said a word. People looked at one another, or at the clock on the wall, or at the ceiling, or out the window— anywhere but at Comrade Pellagrini. Maybe she thought it was a simple question. Gianfranco didn't. You couldn't just copy from the book to answer it, the way he had in history. You had to recall what you'd read and make that fit the question. It all seemed like too much bother.

"All right. *All right.*" The teacher still seemed angry. "You need to know, so I'll tell you—this once. Doesn't London show the bosses raising some workers to the bourgeoisie with what amounts to bribes to turn them against their natural class allies?"

"*Sì*, Comrade Pellagrini," everyone chorused. Once the teacher gave the answer, seeing it was right was the easiest thing in the world.

"I want you to finish *The Iron Heel* tonight," Comrade Pellagrini said. "We'll have the test on Friday, and then next week we'll start *1984*. You'll see how Orwell shows the tyranny of capitalism and Fascism."

A girl raised her hand. "I had to read that book in another class," she said when the teacher called on her. "He calls the ideology in it English Socialism." She sounded troubled, feeling there was something dangerous in the book that she couldn't quite see.

But Comrade Pellagrini brushed the question aside, saying, "Well, so what? The Nazis' full name was the National Socialist German Workers' Party. They weren't real Socialists, and they weren't for the workers. They used mystification to confuse the German people, and it worked."

That seemed to satisfy the girl. It didn't matter to Gianfranco one way or the other. He hadn't read *1984* yet, and hoped it would be more interesting than *The Iron Heel*. But how interesting could a book be when even its title lay more than a hundred years in the past? And how interesting could it be when you had to read it for school?

The dismissal bell. Well, it was the dismissal bell for most people, anyhow. Annarita knew Gianfranco would be leaving now. But she had the Young Socialists' League meeting. She didn't really want to go—nothing would happen there. Nothing ever did. And she'd get back to the apartment an hour and a half later than usual, and still have a whole day's worth of homework to do.

People in the same boring uniform she was wearing filed into the auditorium. Most of them looked as unenthusiastic as she did. For them, this was something you did because you were in the League. Being in the League put you on the fast track to joining the Party. And getting your Party card was a long step towards a prosperous, comfortable life.

But there were a few eager faces, too. Some kids really believed in the stuff the grown-ups who ran the League shoved down their throats. Annarita felt sorry for them—they were the kind who couldn't see their nose in front of their face. And there were kids who liked to run things, too. She didn't feel sorry for them. They scared her.

Filippo Antonelli was one of those. He banged the gavel. "The meeting will come to order!" he said loudly. He would graduate at the end of the year, and she wouldn't be sorry to see him leave. He intended to study law and go into politics. She thought he would go far if he didn't get caught in a purge. As long as he went far from her, that suited her fine. He turned to the girl sitting next to him. "The general secretary will read the minutes of the last meeting."

Stalin had been general secretary, too. He'd used that innocent-sounding post to run the Soviet Union. Isabella Sabatini didn't have ambitions like that—or if she did, she hid them where Filippo couldn't see them. She was in Annarita's year, so maybe she'd show her true colors once he was gone. For now, she just read the minutes. They were boring, and got approved without amendment. They always did.

"Continuing business," Filippo said importantly.

"First item is preparation for the May Day holiday at the school," Isabella said. "The chairman of the May Day celebration committee will make his report."

He did. There would be a celebration. They had money taken from the Young Socialists' League dues. They would spend some of it on ornaments and propaganda posters, and some more on a dance. The school administration had given them a list of approved bands. They would choose one.

Annarita looked at her watch and tried not to yawn where people could see her do it. The May Day celebration was the same every year. Preparations for the celebration were the same every year, too. Only the band at the dance— sometimes—changed. Everything would go more smoothly if the people in charge didn't take it so seriously.

"The celebration of the victory over Fascism will be the next piece of business," Isabella said.

That was the same *almost* every year. Two years earlier, in Annarita's first year at Hoxha Polytechnic, it had been bigger than usual. That was the 150th anniversary of the end of the Second World War—the Great Patriotic War, the Soviet Union called it. But it got back to normal last year, and would be normal again this May.

After the committee for the celebration of victory over Fascism reported, Filippo asked, "Any new business?" There hardly ever was. Annarita hoped there wouldn't be. Then they could get on with talking about the curriculum. They were going to send the administration a report. The administration wouldn't read it—the administration never read student reports. But it would go on file, and show the Young Socialists' League was doing its job.

To Annarita's surprise and dismay, Marco Furillo raised his hand. "I move we investigate a shop that may be selling students subversive literature."

"What's this?" Filippo said.

"It's true," Marco said. "Have you ever been to the place they call The Gladiator?"

"That's the gaming shop, isn't it?" Filippo said, and Marco nodded. Filippo went on, "I know where it is, but I haven't been inside. Why?"

"Because they skate close to the edge, if they don't go over it," Marco answered, his face and voice full of sour disapproval.

That name . . . Annarita had heard somebody mention it before. Gianfranco, that was who. Did he realize the place might be dangerous to him? Filippo did the proper bureaucratic thing: he appointed a committee to look into what was going on. And Annarita surprised both him and herself by volunteering to join it.

Two

The dismissal bell. Gianfranco exploded out of the seat in his biology class. If Comrade Pastrano thought he cared about the differences between a frog's circulatory system and a mouse's, the teacher needed to think again.

Gianfranco wished he didn't have to lug so many books home. His old man would come down on him like a landslide if he didn't at least make a show of doing his homework, though.

But before he went home . . . Before he went home, he went to the Galleria del Popolo—the People's Gallery. Once upon a time, it had been named for a King of Italy, not for the people. Once upon a time, too, it had been the most stylish and expensive shopping center in Milan. A glass roof covered a crossed-shaped district of late nineteenth- and early twentieth-century buildings crammed with shops and restaurants of all sorts.

Fashion had long since moved on, as fashion has a way of doing. The expensive shops and the first-rate restaurants went elsewhere. The places that took over were the ones that didn't pretend to be up-to-the-minute or first-rate. That didn't mean you couldn't have a good time at the Galleria del Popolo. It did mean the good time you had wasn't the same as it would have been a hundred years earlier.

Now the Galleria del Popolo was where the people

gathered—the strange people, that is. Old men looking for older books prowled the secondhand stalls. People who played music that wasn't in favor with the cultural authorities played it in little clubs there. Gianfranco wouldn't have been surprised if the men and women at those clubs who smoked cigarettes and drank espresso or wine while they listened were political unreliables. If the Security Police needed to make a roundup, they would start there.

He walked past a shop selling clothes that only people who didn't care about getting ahead would wear. Flared trousers and tight-fitting shirts for men, short skirts and gaudy stockings for women . . . They seemed more like costumes than real clothes to Gianfranco. He imagined what his father would say if he came home in an outfit like that. Slowly, he smiled. The look on his father's face would almost be worth the price of the clothes and the price of the trouble he'd get in.

And there was The Gladiator. It had a license in the front window, the way any shop had to. Somebody in the Ministry of Commerce had decided the place could do business. As Gianfranco walked up to the door, he made money-counting motions. He couldn't believe The Gladiator ever opened up without bribes of some sort. Communism should have made corruption a thing of the past. He was only sixteen, but he knew better.

A guy coming out of the shop nodded to Gianfranco as he went in. The other guy looked to be two or three years older than Gianfranco was—he really needed a shave. But he looked to be the same kind of person: somebody who couldn't get excited about most of the life he was living. The knowing grin on his face said he got excited about The Gladiator.

So did Gianfranco. So did all the people who came in here, looked around, and decided they liked what they saw. There were others. Gianfranco had seen them. They'd walk in, go to the back room and stare at the people playing games, eye the games and the stuff that went with them, and walk out shaking their heads. They were fools. They proved they were fools by not getting what was going on right in front of their noses.

"*Ciao*, Gianfranco," called the fellow behind the counter.

"*Ciao*, Eduardo. *Come sta?*" Gianfranco said.

"I'm fine," Eduardo answered. "How are you?"

"I'll live. I made it through another day of school," Gianfranco said. Eduardo thought that was funny. Gianfranco wished he did. He went on, "Is Carlo here yet?"

"*Sì*. He just got here a couple of minutes ago," Eduardo told him. "He thinks he's going to clean your clock—he said so."

"In his dreams!" Gianfranco exclaimed. That touched his honor—or he imagined it did, anyhow. A lot of people called honor an outdated, aristocratic idea. Maybe it was, but plenty of Italians still took it seriously anyhow. Gianfranco set ten lire on the counter: two hours' worth of gaming time. "I'll show him!"

"Go on into the back room," Eduardo said. "I may have to give you some of your money back—I don't know if Carlo can stay till six."

"I'll worry about that later," Gianfranco said. He had money—more money than he knew what to do with. Even if his father wasn't a big Party wheel, he was a Party member. That all by itself just about guaranteed you wouldn't come close to being broke. The trouble was finding anything worth buying for your lire. Cars and apartments had waiting lists years long. TV sets kept you waiting for months. So did halfway decent sound systems. You could get cheap junk right away—but you got what you paid for if you spent your money like that.

A couple of hours of fun? Cheap at the price.

Other people—almost all of them guys from a couple of years younger than Gianfranco up to, say, thirty—sat bent over tables in the back room. They studied game boards with the attention they should have given to schoolwork. Carlo looked up and waved when he saw Gianfranco. "*Ciao*," he said. "Watch what I do to you."

"You can try," Gianfranco said, and sat down across from his gaming partner. Carlo was nineteen, just starting at the university. His father wanted him to be a pharmacist. He didn't know what he wanted to do with his life—anything but push pills, probably. Gianfranco felt the same way about being a bureaucrat.

For now, they both forgot about the real world. Here, they were railroad magnates building rival lines across Europe. They had to lay track, buy engines, and move passengers and goods from one city to another. Dice and the quality of locomotives controlled how fast they could go. Cards told them what to take where and added disasters and blizzards and floods. But there was still a lot of strategy. Getting your line through the mountain passes, picking the shortest or the safest route (the two weren't always the same) between two towns, building here so the other player wouldn't . . .

The Gladiator didn't just sell games and offer a place to play. It also sold books, so players who got interested could learn how things *really* worked. Gianfranco knew much more about nineteenth-century railroads than about twentieth-century history. He'd learned this stuff because he wanted to, and because the more he knew, the better he did in the game.

"Goal!" somebody three tables over shouted. He was running a soccer club. Gianfranco had tried that game, too, but he didn't like it as well as railroading. Playing soccer was great. Running a team? Paying and trading players, keeping up the stadium, getting publicity so your crowds would be large and you could afford to pay better players—that all seemed too much like work.

Carlo was building his own rail line into Paris, an important center where Gianfranco was already operating. Carlo offered lower shipping rates than Gianfranco was charging. Gianfranco lowered his even more so Carlo couldn't steal his business. He cut rates as low as he could while still making money. Then Carlo cut his so he was losing money on that route but trying to make up for it other places.

"Is that in the rules?" Gianfranco asked.

"It sure is." Carlo brandished the rule book, a thick pamphlet. "It's called a 'loss leader.' And it's going to ruin you."

"We'll see about that," Gianfranco said. He built toward Vienna, where Carlo had been operating by himself. Even before he got there, Carlo cut shipping rates. Gianfranco cut them even more. If Carlo wanted to keep him out, he would have to start taking a loss in Vienna, too. He tried it. It didn't work— losing money on two major routes, he couldn't make enough on the others to stay in the black. His whole operation started hemorrhaging money. He had to give up the Paris line.

Gianfranco didn't gloat—too much. "I think you got a little too cute," he said.

"Maybe," Carlo said unhappily. "I didn't expect you to get back at me so fast." He tapped the rule book with his forefinger. "I saw this loss leader thing in here, and it looked so cool I had to try it out."

"I've done stuff like that," Gianfranco said. "I think that one can be good, but you pushed it too hard. The game will bite you if you go with any one thing too much. You've got to stay balanced. That's how you make money."

"You old capitalist, you," Carlo said. They both laughed.

Annarita didn't say anything about The Gladiator to Gianfranco at supper or at breakfast the next morning. She didn't feel like getting worried questions from his parents—or from her own. Right now, all she knew about the place was that Marco Furillo thought it was politically unreliable. That didn't prove much.

So she waited till the two of them went down the stairs together and started for Hoxha Polytechnic before asking, "You've been to The Gladiator, haven't you?"

"Sure!" He sounded enthusiastic.

"What do you do there?" she asked.

"Play games, mostly. I get books sometimes, too." He started talking about a complicated coup he'd pulled off against somebody named Carlo. It didn't make much sense to her. Then he started talking about how railroads really operated in the nineteenth century. Some of that made even less sense, but he knew a lot about it.

"How did you find out about all that stuff?" Annarita asked.

"I told you—they've got books there. The more you know, the better you can play," Gianfranco answered. Playing well mattered to him—she could see that. He didn't care much about school, so he didn't work any harder than he had to there.

"Do you ever do anything . . . political at The Gladiator?" she asked.

He looked at her as if she were crazy. "I play games. I talk with the other guys who play games. What could be political about old-time railroads or soccer teams or hunting dragons?"

"Dragons? You're confusing me," Annarita said.

"Some of the games are in this pretend world," Gianfranco explained. "They're all right, I guess, but the railroad's my favorite."

"How come?" Annarita asked.

"I don't know. I just like it," Gianfranco answered. She made an exasperated noise. He carried his books in his left hand, which kept his right free for gesturing. "Why do you like a song or a movie? You just do, that's all."

"I know why I like a movie," Annarita said. "The actors are good, or the plot is interesting, or it's funny, or *something*."

"All right, all right. Let me think." Gianfranco did—Annarita could watch him doing it. That impressed her all by itself. He wasn't stupid or anything. They'd been living in each other's pockets since they were little, so she knew that. But he hardly ever wanted to do more than he had to do to get by. At last, he said, "When I'm playing, it's like the railroad is really mine. I'm in charge of everything from paying the workers to fixing the track if a flood washes out a stretch to figuring out how much to charge for hauling freight."

He'd talked about that when he was trying to explain what he'd done to Carlo. Carefully, Annarita said, "It sounds like a very, uh, individualistic game." People in the Italian People's Republic weren't supposed to be individualists. They were all supposed to work together for the eventual coming of true Communism, when the state would wither away.

The state hadn't done any withering lately. It still needed to be strong to guard against reactionaries and backsliders and other enemies. So it insisted, in films, on radio and TV, in the newspapers, and on propaganda posters slapped onto anything that wasn't moving.

Gianfranco understood that *individualistic* was a code word for something worse. You'd have to be dead not to. "It's no such thing!" he said hotly. "It's no more individualistic than chess is. You run a whole army there."

Annarita knew she had to back up. You couldn't say anything bad about chess, not when the Russians liked it so well. She tried a different approach: "Well, maybe, but people have been playing chess for a long time. I've never heard of a game like this before. Where does The Gladiator get it? Where does the shop get all its games? I don't think other places have any like them."

"*I* don't know." Gianfranco's shrug, a small masterpiece of its kind, showed that he didn't care, either. Then his eyes narrowed. "How come you're so curious about all this?"

She wondered if she should tell him. After a moment, she decided to—if she said something like *I just am, that's all,* it would only make him more suspicious. She realized she should have had a cover story ready. She wasn't much of a secret agent. "Don't get mad at me," she said, "but somebody at the Young Socialists' League meeting yesterday said they were politically unreliable."

Gianfranco said something that should have scalded the gray tabby trotting down the street. But it just kept going—cats were tough beasts. Then Gianfranco said, "Whoever thinks so is nuts. We sit. We play. We talk. That's it."

"You don't talk about politics?" Annarita asked.

"Of course not. The guys who play the railroad game talk about railroads. Some of them build model railroads, but I don't think that's interesting. The other guys talk about soccer—we all do that sometimes, 'cause soccer's *important*. And the others go on about dragons and ogres and using zoning laws to get orcs out of a pass they need to go through and stuff like that."

"Zoning laws?" Annarita hadn't thought she could get more confused. Now she discovered she was wrong.

Gianfranco only shrugged again. "I don't know, not really. Like I said, I don't play that game much. Stuff like that, though. Politics?" What he said about politics was even hotter than anything he'd come out with before. He went on, "Why don't you come and see for yourself what we're up to? Then you won't have to listen to nonsense." That wasn't exactly what he called it.

"All right, I will," Annarita said. "Do I need to have you along, or can I go by myself?"

"You can go by yourself if you want to. It's a shop. It's looking for customers," Gianfranco answered. "People might talk to you more if you come in with somebody they know. It's like a restaurant or a bar—it has regulars."

She nodded. "Fair enough. Will you take me this afternoon, then?"

"Why not?" he said. "I'm going over there. I've got to finish Carlo off—you just see if I don't. Meet me at the entrance right after classes get out."

"I will. *Grazie*, Gianfranco. The sooner we get this settled, the better off and the happier everybody will be."

"See you then," Gianfranco said. By that time, they'd just about got to school. He hurried on ahead of Annarita, something he hardly ever did. She didn't think he was that eager to learn things from his teachers. No, more likely he was excited about showing off The Gladiator to her.

Annarita was curious. Gianfranco sure didn't think the place was subversive—but then, he wouldn't. Well, she'd find out . . . something, anyway. She could report to the Young Socialists' League. And that, with any luck, would be that.

Because she was curious about The Gladiator, she didn't pay as much attention in class as usual. She messed up a Russian verb conjugation that she knew in her sleep. Comrade Montefusco clucked and wrote what was probably a black mark in the roll book. She almost complained, but what could she complain about? Even if she knew better, she did make the mistake.

She kept doing silly little things like that all day long. She wondered if Gianfranco was doing the same thing. From what she'd heard, he did that kind of stuff all the time, so how was anybody supposed to tell? *She* didn't, though. Whenever she fouled up, her teachers looked surprised. She kept on being surprised herself, not that it did her any good.

After what seemed like forever, the dismissal bell rang. No after-school meetings today. She could just go. Gianfranco was waiting when she got outside. "You ready?" he asked.

She laughed at him. He really was eager as a puppy. "What would you do if I told you no?" she teased.

He just shrugged one more time. "I'd go by myself, that's what."

So there, Annarita thought. But she'd sassed him first, so she had it coming. "I'm not saying no, though. I want to see what got you all excited about this place." And she wanted to see if it really was reactionary and subversive, but she didn't say that.

She liked the Galleria del Popolo. You could find almost anything there—when you could find anything at all, that is.

The buildings that housed the shops were a couple of hundred years old. They might not have been as efficient as the Stalingothic blocks of flats that dominated Milan's skyline along with the Duomo, but they were prettier.

Or was that a counterrevolutionary thought? They'd been built long before the Communist takeover of Italy. If you liked them more than buildings that went up after the takeover, did that make you a reactionary? Could you get in trouble if someone found out you did? She hadn't said anything to Gianfranco. She didn't intend to, either. He *seemed* harmless, but you never could know for sure who reported to the Security Police.

"Here we are." He pointed.

THE GLADIATOR. The sign wasn't too gaudy. The front window also showed a painting of a man in Roman-style armor holding a sword. Under his feet, smaller letters said, BOOKS AND GAMES AND THINGS TO MAKE YOU THINK. She hadn't expected that. "Well, take me in," she told Gianfranco. He nodded and did.

"Hey, Gianfranco!" called the man behind the counter. "*Come sta?*"

"I'm fine, Eduardo. How are you?" Gianfranco said. "This is my friend, Annarita." He didn't say she was there to investigate The Gladiator. That had to be because they *were* friends. He probably would have been more loyal to the shop than to some other member of the Young Socialists' League. *And why not?* Annarita thought. *What's the League ever done for him?*

"*Ciao*, Annarita," Eduardo said, and then, to Gianfranco, "I didn't know you had such a pretty friend."

Gianfranco blushed like a schoolgirl. That made Annarita smile, but she looked away so Gianfranco wouldn't see her do it. She got to glance at what was in the shop. It sold every different kind of game, all in brightly printed boxes. She'd never heard of any of them. *Rails across Europe, World Cup, Swords and Sorcery, Eastern Front, Waterloo, Tycoon, Hannibal . . .* She could figure out what they were about easily enough.

The Gladiator also sold miniatures: soldiers and locomotives and soccer players made of lead or plastic. Some were already painted, others plain—you could buy paints, too, in tiny bottles, and hair-thin brushes with which to apply them.

And there were books about costumes from every period from Babylon to now. There were books about military campaigns. There were soccer encyclopedias. There were books about railroads, and about what stock markets had been like when there were stock markets.

"This is quite a place." Annarita wasn't sure whether that was a compliment or not.

"You'd better believe it." Gianfranco had no doubts. He sounded as proud as if The Gladiator belonged to him. "Is Carlo here yet?" he asked Eduardo.

"No, but I don't think he'll be long," the older man—he had to be close to thirty—said.

"He's not as bold as he was yesterday, though," Gianfranco boasted. "'Loss leader,' was it? He found out!"

"He wasn't very happy when he headed for home. I will say that," Eduardo answered.

Gianfranco set money on the counter. "I'm going to go in there and set up the game," he said. When Eduardo nodded, he went into the back room.

That left Annarita out front by herself, and feeling it. "Can I help you with something in particular, *Signorina*?" Eduardo asked. "Maybe you want a present for a brother or somebody else? Maybe even for Gianfranco?" He looked sly.

She shook her head. "No, *grazie*, I don't think so. I just

wanted to see what it was like. I've heard Gianfranco talk about it a lot. Our families share a kitchen— you know how it is."

"Oh, sure. Who doesn't?" Eduardo replied. "It shouldn't be that way, but it is, and what can you do about it?"

He had nerve, finding anything wrong with the way the world worked with somebody he'd just met. For all he knew, Annarita was a government spy. In fact, she wasn't that far from being one. "So anyway, he's been going on about it, and finally he asked me if I wanted to see it," she said. "And I said *sì*, and here I am."

"What do you think?"

"I've never seen anything like it," Annarita said truthfully. "Where do all the games come from?"

"We have crazy people locked up in a psychiatric hospital who make them up," Eduardo told her.

She blinked. He really did like to see how close to the wind he could sail. Everybody knew the Party put troublemakers in psychiatric hospitals. Getting into one of those places was easy. Coming out? Coming out was a different story.

Everybody knew that, but hardly anybody talked about it. If you talked about it to the wrong people, you might wind up inside a psychiatric hospital yourself. But Eduardo didn't seem worried. He grinned at her.

Annarita wondered if he was a provocateur. Maybe the whole store was a front, a trap to catch dissidents. Would everybody who played games in here end up in a psychiatric hospital or in jail or in a labor camp or dead? She didn't like to think so, but the authorities could be sneaky. Everybody knew that, too.

She walked over to the shelves. There were titles like *Making Your Corporation Profitable* and *Economics of Club Ownership* alongside others like *Greece and Rome at War*. "You sell . . . interesting books," she said.

"Well, if they weren't interesting, who'd buy them?" Eduardo spread his hands and answered his own question: "Nobody, that's who. Then I couldn't make my living having fun. I'd have to do something honest instead." He grinned again.

Even though Annarita grinned back, she still found herself wondering about him and about what the shop sold. "Some of these books look almost . . . capitalist," she said, wondering how he would answer.

"They are," he said simply.

"But—how can you sell them, then?" Annarita asked. Anybody would have—she was sure of that.

"Because they're just for the games," he replied. "Everybody who buys them knows it. If there were real capitalists, that would bring back the bad old days. But these are like books on chess openings and endgames. They help people play better, that's all."

He was as smooth as silk, as slick as olive oil. That only made Annarita wonder about him more. "You can't use books on openings and endgames in the real world," she said. "You could use these. It would be wrong, but you could do it." She had to make sure she said that, in case a camera and a mike were picking up her words. You never could tell. Never. "Somebody who bought one might get the wrong ideas about the way things are supposed to work. How does the state let you sell them?"

"You're smart. Not many people asked questions like that." Eduardo sounded admiring. Then people in the back room started yelling. "Excuse me," he said, and ducked back there. A moment later, Annarita heard him yelling, too. He could call people some very rude things without really cursing. He could make them laugh while he did it, too, which was a rarer talent.

He came out a few minutes later shaking his head. "Argument over the rules. *Dumb* argument over the rules. Where were we, pretty lady?"

Annarita pegged him for the sort who gave out compliments as readily as insults. That meant she didn't need to take them seriously. She said, "You were telling me how you get away with selling books like these."

"That's right." Eduardo nodded. "Nothing fancy about it. We do it the same way the Church gets away with teaching what it teaches."

"This isn't religion. This is economics," Annarita said severely.

"Of course. But a lot of what the Church says goes against science and against dialectical materialism and against Marxism-Leninism-Stalinism. Everybody who thinks about it would say that's so. Why does the state let the Church do it, then?" *Because people would riot if the state didn't*, Annarita thought. Eduardo had a different answer: "Because it's religion, that's why. What the Church says only counts in religion, nothing else. And what we sell here only counts in our games, nowhere else. See? It's simple, really."

He made it sound simple, anyway. How many complications lurked under that smooth surface? Quite a few, unless Annarita missed her guess. But some of what he said was likely true, or the Security Police would have closed this place down. *Unless he belongs to the Security Police*, she reminded herself. She wondered how she could find out.

Gianfranco counted out his latest payment for delivering Russian oil to Paris. "Twenty-three million there," he said, as if the bright play-money bills were real. "That puts me at 509 million." As soon as you went over 500 million, you won. Carlo was still a good sixty million away.

"*Sì*, you got me," he said, and stuck out his hand across the board. Gianfranco shook it. Carlo went on, "When we got into that second price war, that ruined me. You were smart there, Gianfranco. I didn't think you'd do anything like that."

"I'm not always as dumb as I look," Gianfranco said, which made the university student laugh. They got up and went out to the front counter together.

"Who won?" Eduardo asked.

Gianfranco stuck his thumb up. Carlo stuck his down. That was what you did at The Gladiator. The people who ran the shop hadn't started it. The people who played there did. In the ancient Roman arenas, a raised thumb was a vote for sparing a downed gladiator's life. A lowered one was a vote to finish him off. Somebody who knew that must have done it for a joke the first time. Now everybody did.

"Let's see . . ." Eduardo pulled out a chart. "Gianfranco beats Carlo in *Rails across Europe*. Gianfranco, that means you play Alfredo next. Carlo, you go down into the losers' bracket, and you play Vittorio."

"I'll beat him." Carlo didn't lack confidence. Common sense, sometimes, but never confidence.

"Alfredo?" Gianfranco didn't sound so bold. "He'll be dangerous. He studies the game all the time." Alfredo was older than Eduardo. He wore a mustache, and it had some white hairs in it. He was out of school, so he didn't have to worry about homework and projects and things. He had a job, but who took jobs seriously? He spent as much time at work as he could get away with on his hobby, and just about all the time after he got home. He was a fanatic, no two ways about it.

"Hope the dice go your way," Eduardo said. "If you have enough luck, all the other guy's skill doesn't matter. Might as well be life, eh?"

"*Sì.*" That was Carlo, still looking for a way to console himself after losing.

"It's a long game," Gianfranco said. "Most of the time, the dice and the cards even out."

"Well, in that case you'd better pray, because Alfredo will eat you for lunch like fettuccine," Carlo said. "I've got to go. *Ciao.*" He walked out without giving Gianfranco a chance to snap back at him.

"He thought he'd beat you," Eduardo said.

"I know. He figured I was a kid, so I wouldn't know what I was doing," Gianfranco said. "I guess I showed him." Then, cautiously, he asked, "What did Annarita think of the place?" He still didn't want to tell Eduardo she was investigating The Gladiator.

"She seemed interested," answered the man behind the counter. "She's more political than you are, isn't she?"

Gianfranco knew what that meant—Annarita was asking questions. He just laughed and said, "Well, who isn't?" A lot of the time, not being interested in politics was the safest road to take. If you didn't stick your neck out one way or the other, nobody could say you were on the wrong side.

"She seemed nice, though. She's smart—you can tell," Eduardo went on.

"Uh-huh," Gianfranco said. Nobody ever went, *He's smart—you can tell* about him. He got by, and that was about it.

"She really did seem interested," Eduardo said. "Do you suppose she'll come back and play?"

"I don't know," Gianfranco said in surprise. "I didn't even think of it." A few girls did come to The Gladiator. Two or three of them were as good at their games as most of the guys. But it was a small and mostly male world. Some guys who had been regulars stopped coming so often—or at all—when they found a steady girlfriend or got married. Gianfranco thought that was the saddest thing in the world.

"It would be nice if she did," Eduardo said. "People find out pretty girls come in here, we get more customers. That wouldn't be bad."

"I guess not." Gianfranco didn't sound so sure, mostly because he wasn't. One of the reasons he liked coming to The Gladiator was that not so many people knew about the place. The ones who did were crazy the same way he was. They enjoyed belonging to something halfway between a club and a secret society. If a bunch of strangers who didn't know the ropes started coming in, it wouldn't be the same.

Eduardo laughed at him. "I know what the difference between us is. You don't have to worry about paying the rent—that's what."

"You don't seem to have much trouble," Gianfranco said. Along with the games and books and miniatures and models The Gladiator sold, it got all the gamers' hourly fees. It had to be doing pretty well—the Galleria del Popolo wasn't a cheap location.

"We manage." Eduardo knocked on the wood of the countertop. "But that doesn't mean it's easy or anything. And we can always use more people. It's the truth, Gianfranco, whether you like it or not."

"You just want to indoctrinate them," Gianfranco said with a sly smile. "You want to turn them all into railroad capitalists or soccer-team capitalists or whatever. By the time you're done, there won't be a proper Communist left in Milan."

Eduardo looked around in what seemed to Gianfranco to be real alarm. After he decided nobody'd overheard Gianfranco, the clerk relaxed—a little. "If you open your big mouth any wider, you'll fall in and disappear, and that'll be the end of you," he said. "And it couldn't happen to a nicer guy, either."

"Oh, give me break," Gianfranco said. "I was just kidding. You know that—you'd better, all the time and money I spend in this joint."

"Nobody jokes about capitalists. They're the class enemy," Eduardo said.

"Carlo and I were joking about them while we played. We aren't the only ones, either. You hear guys like that all the time," Gianfranco said.

"That's in the game. It's not real in the game, and everybody knows it's not. I was talking with your girlfriend about that."

"She's not my girlfriend."

"The more fool you," Eduardo said, which flustered Gianfranco. The clerk went on, "As long as you know you're only being capitalists in a game, everything's fine. Games are just pretend."

"Not just," Gianfranco said. "That's what makes your games so good—they feel real."

"Sure they do, but they aren't," Eduardo said. "What happens if you go out into Milan and try to act like a capitalist? The Security Police arrest you, that's what. You want to see what a camp's like from the inside?"

"No!" Gianfranco said, which was the only possible answer to that question. But he couldn't help adding, "I've done too much studying for the game. Sometimes I think what they had back then worked better than what we've got now. The elevator in our building's been out of whack for years, and how come? 'Cause nobody cares enough to fix it."

"If I were a spy, you just convicted yourself," Eduardo said. "For heaven's sake, be careful how you talk. I don't want to *lose* customers, especially when I know they'll never come back."

Gianfranco played back his own words in his head. He winced. "*Grazie*, Eduardo. You're right. I was dumb."

"Dumb doesn't begin to cover it." Eduardo shook his head. "In here, it's a game. Out there"—his gesture covered the world beyond The Gladiator's door—"it's for real. Don't forget it."

He was urgent enough to impress Gianfranco, who said, "I won't." But then he couldn't help putting in, "You know what?"

"What?" Eduardo sounded like somebody holding on to his patience with both hands.

"This stuff with working with prices and raising money works really well in the game," Gianfranco said. "How come it *wouldn't* work for real?"

Even more patiently, Eduardo answered, "Because the game has its rules, and the outside world has different ones. The Party sets the outside rules, *sì*? And they're whatever the Party says they are, *sì*?"

"Well, sure," Gianfranco said. "But isn't the Party missing a trick? If it changed the real rules so they were more like the ones in the game, I bet a lot of people would get rich. And what's so bad about that?"

"I ought to throw you out of here and lock the door in your face," Eduardo said. "You're smart when it comes to the game, maybe, but you're not so smart when it comes to the real world. The Party does what *it* wants. If we're lucky—if we're real lucky—it doesn't pay any attention to what a bunch of gamers in a crazy little shop are thinking. You got that?"

"*Sì*, Eduardo. *Capisco*." Gianfranco yielded more to the clerk's vehemence than to his argument. He thought the argument was weak. But Eduardo seemed ready to punch him in the nose if he tried talking back.

"*Bene*. You'd better understand, you miserable little—" Sure as blazes, Eduardo was breathing hard. He was ready for any kind of trouble, all right. Gianfranco couldn't quite see *why* he was getting so excited, but he was. Eduardo wagged a finger at him in a way his own father couldn't have. "You going to do anything dumb?"

"No, Eduardo." Gianfranco didn't want to rattle the clerk's cage. If Eduardo and the other people at The Gladiator did lock him out, he would . . . He shook his head. He didn't know what he would do then.

"*Bene*," Eduardo said. "Maybe you're not so dumb. Not *quite* so dumb, anyhow. Why don't you get out of here for now? Or do you have some other scheme for giving me gray hair before my time?"

"I hope not," Gianfranco said.

"So do I, kid. You better believe it," Eduardo told him. "In that case, beat it." Gianfranco did. Yes, no matter what, he wanted to stay in good with the people here. Next to the games at The Gladiator, the real world was a pretty dull place.

Three

Annarita didn't know what to think about The Gladiator. She didn't say anything at supper—she didn't want to talk where Gianfranco and his family could overhear. She just listened while her father chatted about a couple of patients he'd seen. He never named names, but his stories were interesting anyway. Then Signor Mazzilli went on—and on—about some policy decision that wouldn't mean much either way. Annarita thought he was a bore, but she tried not to show it. The Crosettis and Mazzillis had to live together, so getting along was better than arguing all the time.

After she helped her mother with the dishes, though, she hunted up her father, who was reading a medical journal. "Can I ask you something?" she said.

"Why not?" He put down the journal. "This new procedure sounds wonderful, but it's so complicated and expensive that no one will use it more than once every five years. What's on your mind?"

She told him about visiting The Gladiator. "I don't know what I should say to the Young Socialists' League," she finished.

"Are they hurting anybody?" her father asked. He looked as if he ought to smoke a pipe, but he didn't. He said he'd seen too many cases of mouth cancer to want one of his own.

"Hurting anybody? No." Annarita shook her head. "But they're ideologically unsound."

"And so? I'm ideologically unsound, too. Most people are, one way or another," her father said. "Most of the time, it doesn't matter. You learn to keep quiet about it when you're not with people you can trust—and you learn not to trust too many people. Or it's about something so silly that you can talk about it and it doesn't count, even if you are sailing against the wind. So what's The Gladiator doing that's so awful?"

"They're selling games that make capitalism look good," Annarita answered.

"*Are* they?" Whatever her father had expected, that plainly wasn't it. "How do they think they can get away with that?" he asked. Annarita told him how Eduardo had explained it to her. Her father clicked his tongue between his teeth. "This fellow should have been either a Jesuit or a lawyer. Does he think the Security Police will let him get away with a story like that?"

"The government tolerates the Church. Why wouldn't it put up with something like this?" Annarita asked.

"It tolerates the Church because the Church has been around for almost 2,100 years. The Church is big and powerful, even if it doesn't have any divisions. The Russians let religion breathe, and they don't usually put up with anything." Her father looked unhappy. "A shop that's been open two years at the most just doesn't have that kind of clout. If this Eduardo can't see that, he needs to get his eyes examined."

"Do you suppose somebody's going to start a company or sell stock or exploit his workers because of The Gladiator?" Annarita asked. Those were things capitalists did. She knew that much, if not much more.

"With the laws the way they are now, I'm not sure you *could* start a company. I'm pretty sure you can't sell stock," her father answered. "You'd have to be crazy to try, wouldn't you? Who'd want to stick his neck out that way?"

"What am I supposed to tell the League?" That was Annarita's real worry.

"Well, it depends," her father said. "Do you want to get these people in trouble? If you do, I bet you can."

"But I don't, not really. Most of them are like Gianfranco— a bunch of guys who don't get out much sitting around rolling dice and talking," Annarita said. That made her father laugh. She went on, "What could be more harmless, really?"

She thought he would say nothing could. Instead, he looked thoughtful. "Well, I don't know," he said. "When the Bolsheviks started out, they were just a bunch of guys who didn't get out much sitting around drinking coffee and talking. And look what happened on account of that."

"You think a revolution—I mean, a counterrevolution— could start at The Gladiator?" If Annarita sounded astonished, she had a good reason—she was.

"Stranger things have happened," Dr. Crosetti said.

"Is that so? Name two," she told him.

He laughed again, and wagged a finger at her. He always said that when somebody claimed something stranger had happened. Annarita enjoyed shooting him with one of his own arrows. "What am I going to do with you?" he asked, not without admiration.

"When I was little, you'd say you would sell me to the gypsies," she said. "Is that out?"

"I'm afraid so," her father answered. "If I tried it now, they'd really buy you, and that wouldn't be good."

Gypsies still did odd jobs in the countryside, and sometimes in the city. When they saw a chance, they ran con games or just stole. Not even more than a hundred years of Party rule had turned them into good collectivized citizens. Annarita didn't know how they dodged the Security Police so well, but they did.

"Who's on the committee with you?" her father asked. "Will anybody else go to see The Gladiator in person?"

"Ludovico Pagliarone and Maria Tenace," Annarita answered. "No, I don't think they'll go, not unless one of them knows somebody who plays there."

"Will they listen to you because you were on the spot?"

"Maybe Ludovico will. Maria . . ." Annarita sighed. "Maria will just say to call the place reactionary without even thinking. She always does things like that. If there's any chance it might be bad, she wants to get rid of it."

"More Communist than Stalin," her father murmured.

"What?" For a second, Annarita didn't get it.

Dr. Crosetti explained: "Back in the old days, they would say, 'More Catholic than the Pope,' or sometimes, 'More royal than the king.' They used to say that in France a lot. Only one king there, not a lot of them the way there were in Italy before unification. But we still need a phrase like that for somebody who goes along with authority because it *is* authority."

"Where did you find these things?" Annarita said. "I bet you were looking in places where you shouldn't have."

"And so? Who doesn't?" Her father held up a hand before she could answer. "I'll tell you who—people like your Maria, that's who. They go through life with blinkers on, the way carriage horses used to."

"You have to be careful when you come out with things like that," Annarita said slowly.

"Well, of course!" her father said. "That's part of growing up, learning how to be careful. I don't think you're going to inform on me."

"I should hope not!" Annarita said. In school, they taught about children who informed on their parents or older siblings. The lessons made those kids out to be heroes. Annarita didn't know anybody who thought they really were. No matter what the state did for you after you blabbed, it couldn't give you back your family. And chances were none of the people to whom you informed would ever trust you after that, either. They had to know you would betray anybody at all, even them.

"Good," her father said now, as if he hadn't expected anything else—and no doubt he hadn't. "You can talk to Ludovico, then. Maybe between the two of you, you'll outyell this other girl, and nothing will happen. Sometimes what doesn't happen is as important as what does, you know?"

Annarita hadn't thought about that. It kept cropping up in odd moments when she should have been thinking about her homework for the rest of the night.

Gianfranco opened his algebra book with all the enthusiasm of someone answering the midnight knock on the door that had to be the Security Police. As far as he was concerned, their jails and cellars held no terrors worse than the problems at the end of each chapter.

He groaned when he got a look at these. They'd driven him crazy in middle school. Here they were again, harder and more complicated than ever. Train A leaves so much time and so many kilometers behind Train B. It travels so many kilometers an hour faster than Train B, though. At what time will it catch up? Or sometimes, how far will each train go before A catches B?

They weren't always trains. Sometimes they were planes or cars or ships. But they were trains in the first question.

And, because they were trains, Gianfranco's panic dissolved like morning mist under the sun. This was a problem right out of *Rails across Europe*. There, it involved squares on the board and dice rolls instead of kilometers and hours, but so what? He figured those things out while he was playing. Why couldn't he do it for schoolwork?

Because it's no fun when it's schoolwork, he thought. How could it not be fun, though, if it had to do with trains? He tried the problem and got an answer that seemed reasonable. On to the next.

The next problem had to do with cars. When Gianfranco first looked at it, it made no more sense than Annarita's Russian—less, because everybody picked up a little Russian, like it or not. Then he pretended the cars were trains. All of a sudden, it didn't seem so hard. He got to work. Again, the answer he came up with seemed reasonable.

There was a difference, though, between being reasonable and being right. He took the problems to his father, who was smoking a cigarette and reading the newspaper. "Can you check these for me?" he asked.

"I don't know. What are you doing?" his father asked. Gianfranco explained. His father sucked in smoke. The coal on the cigarette glowed red. People said you were healthier if you quit smoking, but nobody ever told you how. His father shook his head and spread his hands. "Sorry, *ragazzo.* I remember going down the drain on these myself. Maybe you're right, maybe you're wrong, maybe you're crazy. I can't tell you one way or the other. I wish I could."

"I'll find out in class tomorrow." Gianfranco didn't look forward to that. But he still thought he had a chance of being right, and that didn't happen every day in algebra. "Let me go back and do some more."

"Sure, go ahead. Pick up as much of that stuff as you can— it won't hurt you," his father said indulgently. "But you can do all right without it, too. Look at me." He stubbed out the cigarette, then thumped his chest with his right fist.

"Thanks anyway, Papa." Gianfranco retreated in a hurry. He didn't want to spend the rest of his life going to an office and doing nothing the way his old man did. Yes, his father had a medium-fancy title. He'd got it not because he was especially smart but because he never made enemies. But it still amounted to not very much. He'd said himself that they could train a monkey to do his job.

So what do *you want to do, then?* Gianfranco asked himself. He knew the answer—he wanted to run a railroad. How did you go about learning to do that? Figuring out when trains would come in probably *was* part of it.

Gianfranco muttered to himself, pretending airplanes were trains—very fast trains. His trouble was, he didn't just want to run a railroad that had already been operating for 250 years. He wanted to start one and build it up from scratch, the way he did in the board game. How could you do that when it wasn't the nineteenth century any more?

He sighed. You couldn't. He was no big brain like Annarita, but he could see as much. What did that leave him? Two things occurred to him—working at the railroad the way it was now or starting some other kind of business and running it as if it were a nineteenth-century railroad.

He could almost hear Eduardo yelling at him. He could hear the midnight knock on the door, too, and the Security Police screaming that he was a capitalist jackal as they hauled him off to jail. Or maybe they wouldn't bother waiting till midnight. Maybe they would just grab him at his business and take him away. For a crime as bad as capitalism, why would they waste time being sneaky?

But the way things were now, people just went through the motions. Gianfranco's father wasn't the only one. He was normal, pretty much. Everybody knew how things went. People made jokes about it. You heard things like, *We pretend to work, and they pretend to pay us.* That was why you had to wait years for a TV set or a car. That was why crews had to come out to repair repairs half the time. That was why the elevator here hadn't worked for so long, and might never again.

The people owned the means of production. They did here, they did in the Soviet Union, they did in Canada and Brazil, they did everywhere. What could be fairer than that? It kept things equal, didn't it? Gianfranco nodded to himself. He'd learned his lessons well, even if he didn't realize it just then.

Maria Tenace had a face like a clenched fist. "I say we condemn the reactionaries." Her voice said she wasn't going to take no for an answer. "They're trying to corrupt people. The authorities need to make an example of them."

"How do you know? Have you been to The Gladiator?" Annarita asked.

"What difference does that make?" Maria sounded honestly confused.

"Well, if you haven't been there, how *do* you know?" Ludovico Pagliarone said.

"Because that's what was reported at the Young Socialists' League meeting," Maria said. "It must be true."

"If someone said the earth was flat at one of those meetings, would you believe it?" Annarita inquired.

"Don't be silly. Nobody would say such a counterrevolutionary thing," Maria declared.

Annarita didn't understand how saying the earth was flat could be counterrevolutionary. She would have bet Maria didn't, either. Maria just meant saying that was bad. It sounded more impressive when you used an eight-syllable word instead.

"I went over there yesterday afternoon," Annarita said. "Their business license is in order. I looked. They have a bunch of people playing games in a back room, and they sell games and miniatures and books. They seemed pretty harmless to me."

"Miniatures? The kind you can paint?" Ludovico asked.

"*Sì*, that's right," Annarita said.

"Maybe I ought to go over there," he said. "Do they have any from the Roman legions?"

"I think I saw some." Annarita wouldn't have thought Ludovico knew Rome had ever had legions. People could surprise you all kinds of ways. She didn't know how many times she'd heard her father say that. Ludovico didn't seem real smart and didn't have a lot of friends. Maybe he read history books for fun, though. How could you know till he showed you? He sure seemed interested now.

And Maria was getting angrier by the second. "I think the two of you want to cover up antistate activities," she said.

"Like what?" Annarita asked. "Playing games isn't antistate. Neither is painting lead centurions the size of my thumb." She eyed Ludovico. Yes, he knew what a centurion was. You had to be interested in Roman legions to know that.

"Being right-wing deviationist is." Maria sounded positive. She always sounded positive. She probably always was. She was one of those people who thought being sure and being right were the same thing.

The trouble was, Annarita wasn't a hundred percent sure Maria was wrong. Some of the games at The Gladiator did seem to have rules only a capitalist could love. Some of the books they sold there sounded as if their authors felt the same way. And that Eduardo hadn't exactly denied things. He'd just tried to say it was all pretend, not for real. But how true was that? How true *could* it be? Wasn't he trying to dance around the truth?

Annarita remembered a Russian phrase: *dancing between the raindrops without getting wet.* One of Stalin's commissars—was it Molotov or Mikoyan?—was supposed to have been able to do that. He'd dodged all the trouble that came his way . . . and if you worked for Stalin, lots of trouble came your way.

Because of Annarita's own doubts about The Gladiator, she might have gone along with Maria in condemning the place. She might have, that is, if Maria weren't so obnoxious. As things were, Annarita figured anything Maria didn't like had to have something going for it.

Marxism-Leninism-Stalinism might be fine for analyzing historical forces. When it came to looking at how two people got along, or didn't get along, that was a different story.

"I think the shop is harmless," Annarita said. "And denouncing people isn't a game. You don't do it for fun."

Maria did. Annarita could see it in her pinched, angry features. Getting even with anybody who dared act unorthodox in any way had to be her main joy in life. Annarita wondered whether she would denounce her husband if he stepped out of line in any way. She didn't wonder long—she was sure Maria would.

Then she wondered who would marry Maria in the first place. But most women did find husbands, as most men found wives. Somebody else every bit as rigid as Maria might like her fine. When you got right down to it, that was a really scary thought.

And, by disagreeing with her about The Gladiator, Annarita was making her an enemy. That was another scary thought. Still, if you let people like Maria ride roughshod over you, how could you keep your self-respect? You couldn't, and what good were you without it? Not much, not as far as Annarita could see.

"I say The Gladiator is anti-Socialist and needs to be suppressed, and that's what we should report to Filippo—to Comrade Antonelli, I mean." Filippo wasn't a Party member yet, but Maria didn't care. She stuck her chin out—she wasn't going to back down. She had the courage of her convictions. She would have been much easier to deal with if she didn't.

As gently as Annarita could, she said, "You're not the only one on the committee, Maria. We go by majority vote. That's what the rules are." Sometimes reminding her of the rules helped keep her in line. Sometimes nothing did.

This was going to be one of those times. Maria gave her a look that could have melted iron. Then she gave Ludovico

Pagliarone another one. "You're not going to let this—this Menshevik get away with being soft on deviationists, are you?"

"You can't call me that! My doctrine's as good as yours!" Annarita had to sound angry. If she accepted the name of the Bolsheviks' opponents, she gave Maria a stick to hit her with. She wished she'd never, never volunteered for this committee.

And she anxiously watched Ludovico, trying to pretend all the while that she wasn't doing any such thing. He was nice enough, but he had the backbone of a scallop. If Maria could frighten him, he'd go along with her no matter what he thought. Some people just wanted to get along, to stay out of trouble.

She didn't like the way he gnawed at the inside of his lower lip. He was having to make up his mind, and he didn't want to. He would leave somebody unhappy. Maria was meaner than Annarita, but Annarita was smoother. He had to be thinking how dangerous she could be if she set her mind to it.

"Well, Ludovico?" Maria demanded.

"Well . . ." His voice broke, so that he sounded eleven years old at the end of the word. He blushed furiously. "Well . . ." he said again, and stayed on the same note all the way through. That seemed to encourage him. "Well, it doesn't seem to me the place is doing any harm, Maria. Annarita's been there to look it over, and you haven't I think we can leave it alone for now. We can always condemn it if it gets out of line later on."

"Two to one," Annarita said. "So decided. I'll write up the report we submit to the League."

"I'm going to turn in a minority report, and it will tell the truth about you people and your backsliding. You'll see." Maria didn't even try to hide how furious she was. "This isn't over yet, and don't you think it is. I'll get that den of running dogs shut down if it's the last thing I ever do." She stormed out of the classroom where they were meeting. The door didn't slam. Annarita wondered why not.

Ludovico said, "She'll make trouble for us. Maybe it would have been easier to do what she wanted. It wouldn't have hurt anybody we know."

"Yes, it would. I have friends who go to The Gladiator," Annarita answered. "Besides, if you let people like that start pushing you around, they'll never stop. Don't you think we did the right thing?"

"I guess so." Ludovico didn't sound sure—not even a little bit. He *was* a weak reed—he would break and stick your hand if you depended on him too much. But he'd backed Annarita this time, anyhow. And he told her why: "I will have to go over there myself. If they have Roman miniatures, I want to get some."

So principles didn't matter to him. He'd gone along because he didn't want to lose a chance to buy little Roman soldiers. What did that say? That he was human, Annarita supposed. Wasn't it better to let yourself be swayed by something small and silly than to act like Maria, the ideological machine? Annarita thought so. That probably meant she made an imperfect Communist. If it did, she wouldn't lose any sleep over it.

"I'll write up the report for Filippo," she said. "You'll sign it, too?"

"I guess so," Ludovico said again, even more reluctantly than before. "Do I have to?" He didn't want his name on anything that could come back to haunt him later on.

But Annarita said, "Yes, you have to. You're part of the committee. You voted this way. Either you sign my report or you sign Maria's. And what do you think will happen to Maria one of these days?"

"Maybe she'll end up General Secretary of the Italian Communist Party," Ludovico said. Annarita winced, but she couldn't tell him he was wrong, because he wasn't. People with Maria's kind of single-minded zeal *could* rise high. But he went on, "More likely, though, she'll get purged."

"That's what I think, too," Annarita said. Most Communists were people just like anybody else. Maria had a knack for getting everyone around her angry. Odds were she'd end up paying for it—and never understand why nobody liked her, even though she was (in her own mind) right all the time. "So which will it be? Mine or Maria's?"

"Yours." Ludovico wasn't happy, but he saw he couldn't get away with pretending none of this had anything to do with him.

"*Bene.*" Annarita smiled at him, and he lit up like a flashlight. Just acting friendly was one more thing Maria would never think to do.

Comrade Donofrio passed back the algebra homework. When he gave Gianfranco his paper, he said, "Please see me after class for a moment, Mazzilli."

Gianfranco didn't follow him for a second. The algebra teacher spoke a French-flavored dialect of Italian that sounded peculiar in Milanese ears. When Gianfranco did get it, he gulped. Had he botched things again? "*Sì,* Comrade Donofrio," he said, no matter how much he wanted to say no.

"*Grazie.*" The teacher walked on.

Only then did Gianfranco look down to see how he'd done. There was his score, written in red—*100%*. He blinked, wondering if he was seeing straight. He hadn't got all the problems right on a math assignment since . . . He couldn't remember his last perfect score on a math paper. He wondered if he'd ever had one before.

And he wondered why Comrade Donofrio wanted to see him. What could be better than a perfect paper?

He tried to follow along as the teacher went through today's material. It didn't make as much sense as he wished it did. Could he get another perfect homework paper? He had his doubts, but he hadn't expected even one.

When the other students left the room, Gianfranco went up to the teacher and said, "You wanted to see me, Comrade?"

"That's right, Mazzilli." Comrade Donofrio nodded. "You did very well on the last assignment. Did you have any, ah, special help with it?"

A light went on in Gianfranco's head. *He thinks I cheated*, he realized. But he said, "No, Comrade," and shook his head.

"Well, let's see how you do on another problem, then," Comrade Donofrio said.

"All right." Gianfranco didn't know what else he could say. He just hoped he didn't make a mess of this one. If he did, the algebra teacher would be sure he'd had somebody else do the homework for him. *If I got good grades all the time, he wouldn't suspect me.* But he didn't get good grades all the time. He usually didn't care enough about them to work hard. Thanks to the game, he'd got interested in these problems.

Comrade Donofrio pulled a book off his desk. Maybe it was the algebra book he'd used when he was in high school. It looked like an old book, and he wasn't a young man. He flipped through it till he found the page he wanted. "Here. Let's see you do problem seventeen."

Gianfranco looked at it. It was a train problem, so he didn't have to pretend. But it was more complicated than the ones he'd done the night before. *Just a lot of steps,* he told himself. *You've done them in other problems. Now you need to do them all at once.*

Instead of numbers and times, he tried to picture squares on the board and dice rolls. It helped. He also tried not to do anything dumb, like multiplying seven times six and getting thirty-five, which had messed him up for fifteen minutes on one of the homework problems.

If you just kept at it, this problem wasn't that bad. He looked up and gave Comrade Donofrio the answer: "Four hours twenty minutes, 390 kilometers."

The teacher grunted. Then he worked the problem himself on a piece of scratch paper. He was much quicker and more confident about attacking it than Gianfranco was. When he got done, his bushy eyebrows jumped. "You're right!" He sounded surprised. No—he sounded amazed.

Gianfranco grinned like a fool. He wanted to turn cart-wheels, right there in the classroom. "I really *can* do them!" He was telling himself at least as much as he was telling Comrade Donofrio.

"Well, so you can." Yes, the algebra teacher looked and sounded as if he didn't want to believe it. "I gave you a hard one. Let me see your work."

"Here you are, Comrade." Gianfranco gave him the paper where he'd scribbled.

Comrade Donofrio studied it. Still reluctantly, he nodded. "Your method is correct, no doubt about it. If you did so well on the rest of your papers, you would have a much higher mark in this course. Why have you mastered these problems and not the others?"

"I think it's because of *Rails across Europe*," Gianfranco said.

He waited for the teacher to ask him what the devil that was. Instead, Comrade Donofrio looked astonished all over again. "You play that game, too?"

"*Sì*, Comrade," Gianfranco said after he picked his chin up off his chest. "But . . . I've never seen you at The Gladiator."

"No, and you won't," Comrade Donofrio said. "But a friend and I play every Saturday afternoon. We play, and we drink some chianti, and we talk about how to make the world a better place."

"And how *do* you make it a better place?" Gianfranco asked.

Comrade Donofrio actually smiled. Gianfranco hadn't been sure he could. "Well, the chianti helps," he said.

"If—" But Gianfranco stopped. He'd been about to say something like, *If the world ran more the way the game does, that might help*. Eduardo would call him a fool if he spoke up like that, and Eduardo would be right. Why should he trust Comrade Donofrio? Because he got one algebra problem right? Because they both enjoyed the same game? Those weren't good enough reasons—not even close.

"You'd better go," the teacher said. "You'll be late to your next class if you don't hustle." As Gianfranco headed for the door, Comrade Donofrio murmured, "*Rails across Europe*? Who would have imagined *that*?"

Since Gianfranco was at least as surprised about his algebra teacher as Comrade Donofrio was about him, he didn't say anything. *But I got the problem right!* he thought as he hurried down the hall.

———

Annarita had a class with Filippo Antonelli. She gave him her report on The Gladiator, saying, "This is what the committee decided." Actually, it was what she'd decided, and she'd got Ludovico to go along. She was beginning to suspect a lot of things in the world looked that way.

"*Grazie,*" Filippo said, putting the report into his binder. "Maria Tenace already gave me her minority report. She's not very happy with you or Ludovico."

"She's never very happy with anybody," Annarita answered. That was certainly true. "She got outvoted, and she should have."

"I looked at her report," said the head of the school's Young Socialists' League. "She's . . . very vehement."

"She's throwing a tantrum," Annarita said. "If she weren't doing it in committee work, somebody would send her to bed without supper. Just what she deserves, too, if you want to know what I think."

"Well, yes." But Filippo laughed nervously. "Even so, she's dangerous to cross, because she knows other people who think the same way she does."

What was that supposed to mean? Annarita feared she knew—he was saying Maria had connections with the Security Police, or somebody like that. "What should we have done, then? Said this place was corrupt when it isn't?" she asked, thinking, *I hope it isn't, anyway. If it is, I've given Maria enough rope to hang me.* She went on, "That wouldn't be right. Think about what could happen to the people who work there—and to the people who just play there. Do you think they're all right-wing obstructionists who get together to plot how to bring back capitalism and exploit the workers?"

"No, of course not," Filippo said, which proved he was still in touch with reality. "I know some kids from this school go there. In fact, I know a couple of people who do. Don't you?"

"*Sì,*" she said. If he asked her who, she intended to duck the question. What he knew, he might have to report one of these days. Yes, he led the Young Socialists' League. Yes, he would probably end up with a job in the government, and one of the things the government did was make sure the Italian people didn't get out of line. Even so, he understood how the system worked. As long as he didn't officially know something, he wasn't responsible for doing anything about it. And so he stayed away from the question that would have led to knowing.

When Annarita didn't name any names, Filippo just nodded and said, "Well, there you are."

"Do you think this report will be the end of it?" Annarita asked.

"I sure hope so," he answered. "And I hope you're right. If you turn out to be wrong, if people at The Gladiator really are messing with the wrong kind of politics, Maria won't let you forget it. She won't let you get away with it, either."

A nasty chill of fear ran up Annarita's spine. Filippo was bound to be right about that. She didn't let him see that she was worried. If she had, it would have been the same as admitting she wasn't so confident about the report. "What could they be doing there?" she said.

"I don't know of anything. I guess you don't know of anything, either," Filippo answered. "Just hope you're right, that's all. I hope you're right, too, because I'm accepting your report, not Maria's. Don't make the League look bad."

Don't make me look bad, he meant. Once he did accept the

report, his reputation would be on the line with it, too. The person at the top was responsible for what the people in the organization did.

"I won't, Filippo," Annarita told him, responding to everything under the words as well as what lay on the surface.

"I didn't think you would," he said. "You've got good sense. After I graduate, are you going to head up the league yourself?"

"I've thought about it." Annarita knew it would look good on her record. "Maybe I've got too much good sense to want all the trouble, though, you know?"

"*Sì. Capisco.*" He nodded. "I ought to get it. Most of this year's been pretty easy, but when it gets ugly, it gets *ugly*." He smiled a crooked smile. "I'll bet you'd say yes if Maria were graduating with me."

"Maybe I would." Annarita smiled, too. Filippo was acting nicer than he usually did. "But there's bound to be at least one person like that every year, isn't there?"

"Well, I haven't seen a year when we didn't have one," Filippo admitted. "Pierniccolo, two years ahead of me . . ." He rolled his eyes. "His father really is a captain in the Security Police, so he had a head start."

"He'll probably end up with a fancy car and a vacation home on the beach by Rimini," Annarita said. Going to the Adriatic for the summer, or even for a bit of it, was every Milanese's dream. Not all of them got to enjoy it. Her family and the Mazzillis went, but they stayed in a hotel, not a place of their own. A red-hot Communist from a Security Police family was bound to have the inside track for things like that.

"I can't help but think . . ." Filippo Antonelli didn't finish.

That he didn't spoke volumes all by itself. He'd started to say something unsafe and thought better of it. He shook his head. "Let it go."

"I understand," Annarita said. Both their smiles were rueful. People got so they automatically watched their tongues. Most of the time, you hardly even noticed you were doing it. Every once in a while, though . . . Annarita wondered what it would be like to say whatever she had on her mind without worrying that it would get back to the Security Police.

Somewhere in a police file drawer sat a folder with her name on it. Whatever word informers brought on her went in there. Maria might well go to the trouble of writing out a denunciation. All the same, Annarita didn't think the folder would be very thick. She didn't go out of her way to cause trouble. Nothing the authorities had, wherever they got it from (and the informers you didn't know about, the ones who seemed like friends, could be more dangerous than out-and-out foes like Maria), would make large men in ill-fitting suits knock on her door in the middle of the night.

She hoped.

"I wish—" she began, and then *she* stopped.

"What?" Filippo asked.

"Nothing," Annarita said, and then, "I'd better head for home."

As she walked out of Hoxha Polytechnic, she knew she'd been right on the edge of saying something really dumb. She shook her head. That wasn't right. She'd been on the edge of saying something risky. Saying risky things was dumb, but what she almost said wasn't dumb at all. She sure didn't think so, anyhow.

I wish it weren't like this. I wish we could speak freely. I wish

*the Security Police would leave us alone. I wish there were no
Security Police.*

If she did say something like that, what would happen?
She'd get labeled a counterrevolutionary. She'd get taken somewhere for what they called reeducation. If she was lucky, they'd
let her out after a while. Even if they did, though, her chances
for making it to the top would be gone forever.

If she wasn't so lucky, or if they thought she was stubborn,
she'd go to a camp after reeducation. She'd probably only get
five years, ten at the most—she was still young, so they'd give
her the benefit of the doubt. But she'd stay under suspicion, under surveillance, the rest of her life.

Just for saying people ought to be free of the Security Police. For saying people ought to be free, period.

That's not right, she thought. *It really isn't.* She looked
around in alarm, as if she'd shouted it as loud as she could. She
hadn't, of course, but she worried all the way home anyway.
Maybe she really was a counterrevolutionary after all.

Four

"You're helping me in school," Gianfranco told Eduardo the next time he walked into The Gladiator.

"Don't say that." The clerk thrust out the index and little fingers of his right hand, holding the other two down with his thumb—a gesture against the evil eye. "Who'd come in here if he thought we were educational?"

"But you are. What would you call it?" Gianfranco pointed to the shelves full of books.

"That stuff?" Eduardo shook his head. "That's only to help people play the games better. Games are just games. How can they teach you anything?"

Gianfranco might not be sharp in school. But he could hear irony, even if he didn't always call it by its right name. "You're trying to fool me," he said now. "Lots of people have learned lots of things from your books."

"Now you know our secret," Eduardo whispered hoarsely. "And do you know what happens to people who find out?"

"Tell me," Gianfranco said, curious in spite of himself.

Eduardo used another gesture, with thumb and fore-finger—he aimed an imaginary pistol at Gianfranco. "Bang!" he said.

Even though Gianfranco laughed, he wasn't a hundred per-

cent comfortable doing it. Eduardo was joking—Gianfranco
thought Eduardo was joking—but he sounded a little too serious. If The Gladiator had a real secret, he might do everything
he could to keep it.

How much was that? How much could people at a little
shop like this do if somebody powerful—say, the Security
Police—came down on them? Gianfranco's first thought was,
Not much. But after a moment, he started to wonder. The Young
Socialists' League at Hoxha Polytechnic couldn't be the first set
of zealots to notice them. They were still here, though. That argued they had ways of protecting themselves.

But Gianfranco had more urgent things on his mind. "Is Alfredo here yet?" he asked.

Eduardo grinned. "Eager, aren't we?"

"I don't know about you, but I sure am," Gianfranco answered, grinning back. "I know he's tough, but if I beat him, I
make the finals, and I've never come close before. That would
be a big deal, right?"

"If you think it would, then it would." In a sly voice, Eduardo went on, "Would you get that excited about finishing in
the top two in your class?"

"I don't think so!" Gianfranco said. "Are you going to go all
Stakhanovite on me? I thought I could get away from all that
stuff as soon as I left school."

"You're probably working harder here than you are there,"
the clerk said.

"Yes," Gianfranco said, and then, in the same breath,
"No."

"Which is it?" Eduardo asked. "You can't have that one
both ways, you know."

"Maybe I try harder here than I do in school," Gianfranco

said. "I wouldn't be surprised. But this isn't *work*, you know what I mean? I want to come here. I have fun here. Going to school . . ." He shook his head. "It's like going to a camp. You do it because you have to, not 'cause you want to. They *make* you do things, and they don't care if you don't care about them. You've got to do 'em anyway." He eyed Eduardo. "Does that make any sense to you?"

"Some, maybe, but not as much as you think it does," Eduardo answered. "You've never been inside a camp—I know that. But do you know anybody who has?"

"The janitor at our building—he's a zek, I'm pretty sure," Gianfranco said. The word for a camp inmate sounded about as un-Italian as anything could. Just about every European language had borrowed it from Russian, though. There wasn't a country without camps these days, and there wasn't a country without people who'd done their terms.

"Well, ask him whether he'd rather do algebra and lit or chop wood and make buildings and starve," Eduardo said. "See what he tells you."

"I hear what you're saying. But school still makes you do stuff you don't care about and you don't want to do," Gianfranco said. "That's what I don't like."

"Some of that stuff, you end up needing it," Eduardo said. "You maybe don't think so now, but you do."

"Oh, yeah? How much algebra have you done since you got behind that counter?" Gianfranco asked.

Eduardo looked wounded, which made Gianfranco think he'd scored a hit. But the clerk said, "All right, so I don't have to know X equals twenty-seven. Even so, algebra and your languages make you think straight. You need that, especially with some of the other stuff they put you through."

Which other stuff did he mean? Literature? History the way schools taught it? Dialectical materialism and Marxist philosophy? That was how it sounded to Gianfranco. But he couldn't ask Eduardo to say more, not without seeming to want to entrap him. And Eduardo couldn't say more on his own, not without asking to get denounced.

Before Gianfranco could figure out a way around his dilemma, the bell over the front door rang. In walked Alfredo, with his graying mustache. He looked rumpled and smelled of tobacco smoke. "*Ciao*, Eduardo," he said, and then, grudging Gianfranco a nod, "*Ciao*."

"*Ciao*," Gianfranco answered.

"Shall we do it?" Alfredo didn't sound excited or anything. He just sounded as if he wanted to get Gianfranco out of the way so he could go on to something serious. It was intimidating.

After a moment, Gianfranco wondered if it wasn't intimidating on purpose. If it was an act . . . If it was an act, it was a good one. He made his own nod as casual as he could, as if he knew he was a tough guy, too. "*Sì*," he said, sounding almost bored. "Let's."

Eduardo had heard him being all bubbly before. The clerk had to know he was faking his cool now. But Eduardo didn't let on. He played fair—and why not? The Gladiator got the same fee no matter who won.

Gianfranco and Alfredo went into the back room. Other games were already going there. The Gladiator had games going from the minute it opened till the time when the clerks kicked everybody out so they could close up. "Good luck," Gianfranco said as the two of them sat down.

Alfredo looked surprised. He seemed to have to make himself nod in return. "Thanks," he said. "You, too." He couldn't keep himself from adding, "It's a game of skill, though."

"Well, sure," Gianfranco said. "That's what makes it fun." Alfredo sent him a measuring stare. Gianfranco felt under the microscope. Part of the skill in the game was figuring out how the guy on the other side of the board thought.

They rolled for first build. *That* was luck, like seeing who went first in a chess game. Gianfranco outrolled Alfredo, so he got to start. Against some players, it wouldn't have mattered one way or the other. Against Alfredo, he figured he needed every edge he could get.

He would have expanded faster against some players. If some people saw you get a big railroad net in a hurry, they lost heart. Gianfranco played a more careful game against Alfredo. Somebody who knew what he was doing would wait till you got overextended, then attack your weak routes, drive you out of cities where you didn't have a strong grip, and take them over for himself.

Alfredo played as if Gianfranco weren't there. That was intimidating, too. It said he thought he could do whatever he pleased, and that Gianfranco didn't have a chance to stop him.

Their first clash came over Turin. The northern Italian city—Milan's rival in everything from style to soccer—made engines you could ship to Moscow for a nice profit. Alfredo got there first. But Gianfranco had a route from Copenhagen to Turin, and Danish butter did well there. He used the profit from the first load to buy a stronger, faster engine to bring in more. And he built toward Moscow himself.

Alfredo did everything he could to throw Gianfranco out of Turin. Nothing worked. Gianfranco hung on. After a few turns, he started to prosper. Once, when he was deep in thought about whether he could move more tourists through Turin and build up a hotel business there, he happened to catch Alfredo studying him again. The older gamer looked more thoughtful than he had when they started.

I can play with this guy, Gianfranco thought. *I really can, and he knows it, too.* He had no idea whether he would win or lose. It was still much too early to tell. But, in a way, whether he won or lost hardly mattered. Alfredo was one of the best around. Everybody knew that. And Gianfranco was holding his own against him.

If I can play against Alfredo, I can play against anybody, Gianfranco grinned. He'd come as far as he could—he'd come as far as anyone could—with *Rails across Europe*. That made him proud. Then it made him sad. Once you'd taken the game as far as it would go, what else could you do?

"We are lucky today, class," Comrade Montefusco said in Russian. "Two Russians from the delegation in Milan to promote fraternal Socialist cooperation and trade are going to stop by the class. You will get to practice your Russian with native speakers."

Annarita nodded. Talking with someone who'd grown up speaking a language was the best way to learn it. She grinned. It sure was a chance she hadn't had when she was studying Latin!

The Russian teacher looked at his watch, then at the clock on the wall, then at his watch again. "They're supposed to be here now, in fact." He sighed. "But one thing I found when I studied in Moscow—Russians are often late. I know the Germans say the same thing about us. . . ."

Everybody laughed. Germans had made fun of Italian inefficiency even when the two countries were allies against Russia in the Great Patriotic War. The next time an Italian cared about a German opinion would be the first.

"But Russians are often *really* late," Comrade Montefusco went on. "What do you suppose this has to do with the way the Russian verb works?"

Along with the rest of the class, Annarita blinked. *That* wasn't the kind of question they usually got. Almost everything was right or wrong, true or false, yes or no, memorizing. With those questions, deciding what a student knew was easy. This? This made her think in a way she wasn't used to doing in school. Some of the kids looked horrified. They didn't like anything different from what they were used to. A little to her own surprise, she found she did.

Hesitantly, she raised her hand. It was the first one up even though she hesitated. The teacher pointed at her. "Comrade, isn't it because the Russian verb isn't so good at describing when something happened in relation to now or in relation to some other time? There's just finished action or unfinished action. The Russian verb *to be* doesn't even have a present tense. You can't say *I am* in Russian, only *I was* or *I will be*." She'd been amazed and dismayed when she discovered that.

Comrade Montefusco didn't wear a smile very often, but he beamed now. "*Sì*," he said. "Very good! That's just right. Ever since the glorious October Revolution, the Russians have tried to run more by the clock, the way Western Europe and America do. I have to say it hasn't worked too well. Their own language fights against them."

"Comrade, why is it the glorious October Revolution when

it happened in November?" a boy asked. "Did their verbs make
the Revolution late, too?"

The students laughed. Comrade Montefusco didn't. "No,"
he answered. "The Tsars were so reactionary, they were still using the old-fashioned Julian calendar, and it was out of phase
with the sun and with the rest of the world. The Soviet Union
brought in the Gregorian calendar and even improved it,
though no one will see a difference between theirs and ours till
the year 2700." He paused. "Since our distinguished guests
aren't here, let's get on with our regular lessons."

They'd just got well into the homework on prepositions
when the two Russians breezed into the classroom. They
didn't apologize for being late. They didn't seem to notice they
were. They both looked old to Annarita's eyes. The man had to
be past forty, and the woman wasn't far from it. But they had
on Italian clothes not much different from those Annarita and
her classmates wore when they weren't in uniform. It made
him look stupid and her look cheap. She wore too much per-
fume, too.

And the way they talked! Comrade Montefusco taught the
class proper grammar and the best Moscow pronunciation. If
they were going to learn Russian, he said, they should learn it
right. The two real, live Russians couldn't have set things back
further if they were trying to do it on purpose. The man's accent
made him sound like a mooing cow. He stretched out all his O's
and swallowed most of the other vowels. The woman sounded
more like a Muscovite, but her mouth was so full of peppery-
sounding slang that Annarita could hardly follow her. And
some of what Annarita couldn't understand made the teacher's
ears turn red.

"Comrades, do you have any suggestions for students learning your language?" Comrade Montefusco asked. He was careful to keep his own pronunciation and grammar as fine as usual.

Both Russians understood him well enough. "Stoody hard. Woork hard," the man said. "And yoo'll gooo fur."

The woman winked at the Russian teacher. "Dmitri's right," she said. "And having a pal on the left never hurt anything, either."

Annarita did understand that bit of slang, and wished she didn't. In Russian, doing things on the right was the legal way, the proper way. The left was the bribe, the black market, the underworld . . . all the things the glorious Revolution was supposed to have wiped out but hadn't.

These were the representatives of the greatest Communist republic in the world? Annarita knew Russians weren't super-men and -women, but seeing them with such obvious feet of clay still hurt. And they didn't really want to have anything to do with the class. *Why are they here, then?* Annarita wondered. But she didn't need to be Sherlock Holmes to find the answer to that. *Because their boss told them to show up, that's why.*

They'd come late, and they left early. When the door closed behind them, everyone in the class seemed to sigh at the same time. If any of the students had any illusions about Russians left, that pair would have shattered most of them.

Comrade Montefusco sighed, too. "Comrade Mechnikov"—the man—"comes from southern Russia, near the Volga," he said. "That accent is common there. We have different dialects here, too—think how much trouble you can have talking with someone from Naples or Sicily."

He wasn't wrong. Those southern dialects of Italian were so different, they were almost separate languages. Even so . . . Someone else said it before Annarita could: "The way he talked made him sound stupid. I don't know if he is, but he seemed like it."

"I know." The Russian teacher spread his hands, as if to say, *What can you do?* "For whatever it's worth, people in Moscow feel the same way about that accent."

"And what about Comrade Terekhova?" Annarita asked. "Am I wrong, Comrade Montefusco, or did she sound like a zek who'd just finished her term?"

"I'm afraid she did." Comrade Montefusco looked even more unhappy than he had before. "There's a whole other side to Russian—*mat'*, they call it. It's more than slang. It's almost a dialect of its own, and it's based on . . . well, on obscenity." He spread his hands again. "The more you deal with Russians, the more you hear it. And yes, it thrives in camps."

"Can you teach us?" a boy asked eagerly. He wasn't a very good student, but he sure seemed to want to learn how to be gross in Russian.

But the teacher shook his head. "Foreigners shouldn't use *mat'*, or not very much. You almost have to be born to it to do it right."

"What else shouldn't foreigners do?" a girl asked. It was a legitimate question—and it was a lot more interesting than which prepositions meant what with nouns in which cases.

"Don't try to drink with Russians," Comrade Montefusco said. "I know most of you drink wine at home. I know you've been doing it since you were *bambini*. That's fine. Don't try to drink with Russians anyway, not unless you keep a spare liver in your pocket. They have more practice than you do. They have more practice than anybody."

"Why do they need to drink so much?" someone else asked. "They rule the roost."

The Russian teacher looked at the boy as if he didn't have all his oars in the water. "One of the things you'll find out when you get a little older is that everybody has something to worry about. That's how life works."

Annarita had some notion of what he wasn't saying. The Russian security apparatus was even bigger and snoopier than the Italian one. Somebody could be watching you every minute of every day. You never knew which minute it would be, either, so you had to watch yourself all the time. If you were on edge so much, wouldn't you want to dive into the vodka bottle to escape for a while?

"What other things do we need to watch out for, Comrade?" Annarita asked.

"Don't tell a Russian he's uncultured, even if he is—especially if he is," Comrade Montefusco replied. "It's a much worse insult with them than it is with us. We Italians, we know we're cultured." He preened a little. "But Russians have doubts. They always measure themselves against Western Europeans, and they worry they come up short. Some ways, they're like peasants in the big city. Don't remind them of it."

"What else?" somebody else inquired.

Now the Russian teacher frowned. He'd run out of obvious answers—and he'd seen something else that was pretty obvious. "I think you people are trying to waste time till the bell," he said, but he couldn't quite keep from sounding amused. And then something else did occur to him: "When you're talking with Russians, never remind them Marx said theirs would be the last country where a revolution happened. Never, you hear me?"

"Why not?" asked a student who was earnest but naive.

Comrade Montefusco rolled his eyes. "Why not? Because they're sensitive as the devil about it, that's why not. The least that'll happen is, you'll make them angry. If you get a punch in the nose, you shouldn't be surprised. And if you do it in the Soviet Union and there's a knock on your hotel door at midnight, you shouldn't be real surprised about that, either." Two or three people raised their hands then. The teacher frowned. "One more question—and I mean one. Luisa?"

"*Grazie*, Comrade," the student said. "How are Russian camps worse than the ones we've got here?"

"How? I'll tell you how," Comrade Montefusco answered. "Russia has all of Siberia to put zeks in. Everything you've ever heard about Siberia is true, except the real thing is worse—and colder—than you can imagine. And the Russians really, really mean it. Sometimes you'll see security people here going through the motions. Not there. In the USSR, you climb to the top through the KGB. The smart, eager people are the ones who join."

"Do you have fewer rights in the USSR if you're a foreigner?" Luisa asked.

That was another question, but the Russian teacher answered it—in a way. "Don't be silly," he said, and then, firmly, "Now—prepositions."

Annarita followed the lesson only halfheartedly. *Don't be silly how?* she kept wondering. Only one answer occurred to her. *It doesn't matter whether you're a foreigner in the USSR or not. Nobody has any rights there.*

And how was that so different from Italy?

Alfredo rolled the dice—a nine. He moved his train into Athens and unloaded the soft coal he'd carried from Dresden. "That puts me over the top," he said.

"*Sì*, so it does," Gianfranco said. He'd just picked up a cargo that would have given him enough cash to win once he delivered it, but his train was still hundreds of kilometers from where it needed to be. He stuck out his hand across the board. "You got me, all right. Congratulations."

"Thanks." Alfredo shook it. "You played a devil of a game. When I saw you were so young, I thought I'd have an easy time of it. But it didn't work like that. You weren't especially lucky, either. You know what you're doing, all right."

"I gave it my best shot. I really wanted it," Gianfranco said. "But you're good. I knew going in you were. You didn't make any mistakes I could latch on to. Good luck in the finals. I bet you win."

"If you were in the other bracket, I'd probably see you there instead of here," Alfredo said. "When the next tournament starts, you'll be somebody to watch out for."

Gianfranco shrugged. "We'll see what happens, that's all. Some of it's skill, but some of it's luck, too. That's part of what makes it fun, because you can't be sure ahead of time what'll happen."

"I think so, too." Alfredo sent him a curious look. "I don't want to make you mad or anything, but you *are* just a kid. I thought you'd be more disappointed if you lost."

"Part of me is. I wanted to win," Gianfranco said. "But I played as well as I could, so what's the point of getting all upset? And I showed myself I could play in your league even if I didn't win."

"I'm not going to tell you you're wrong, because you're right," Alfredo said. "That was quite a game, and I could see it was no fluke. You've got the right attitude to be a good player, too. You don't get too high when things go well, and you don't get too mad if they don't."

Gianfranco climbed to his feet. Several joints in his back popped like knuckles. He'd been sitting hunched over in a hard chair for a long time. He hadn't noticed till he stood up. Stretching and twisting felt good. "Let's go tell Eduardo," he said.

The clerk eyed both of them when they came out of the back room. "Who won?" he asked. "I can't tell by looking at you."

"He got me," Gianfranco said. "I made him work for it, but he got me."

"He gave me a big scare," Alfredo said. "With a little more luck, he would have beaten me."

Eduardo wrote the results on the tournament chart. "Cheer up, Gianfranco," he said. "You've still got the third-place game. You win that, you get a little trophy and a free book."

"I'm not down," Gianfranco said. "It's like I told Alfredo—I gave it my best shot, and it was pretty good. I know which book I want if I do win the third-place game, too—that one about the way the Prussian Army organized their railroads for war. I bet I can get a lot of ideas out of it."

Eduardo glanced over at Alfredo. "He *is* going to be dangerous."

"He sure is," Alfredo said. "I've got a copy of that one myself. He's right. It gives you all sorts of notions about the best way to put your rail net together."

"So you've read it?" Gianfranco asked. Alfredo nodded. Gianfranco winked at him. "One more reason for me to want to get my hands on it, then."

"You sure don't act like somebody who just lost a big game," Eduardo said.

"I told him the same thing," Alfredo put in.

"Oh, I wish I'd won," Gianfranco said. "But playing against Alfredo helped me take my game up a notch. I've never seen anybody who makes as good a capitalist as he does—in the game, of course." He didn't want to insult the older man.

And he didn't. "I understood you, *ragazzo*," Alfredo said. "Where else can we be capitalists except in games? If we tried to do it for real . . . Well, we'd get in trouble, so we don't."

"Here, look—I have to be a capitalist," Eduardo said. "I have to take money from both of you for sitting at a table in my shop and playing."

"I don't think you're being a capitalist for that," Gianfranco said. "I think you make a perfect Marxist, as a matter of fact."

Both the clerk and Alfredo raised an eyebrow. "How do you figure?" Eduardo asked.

"You have the ability to give us a place to sit, and we have a need to play your games," Gianfranco said. "What could be better?"

Eduardo looked thoughtful, but Alfredo laughed and wagged a finger at Gianfranco. "You've got it backwards, *amico*. It's *from* each according to his abilities, *to* each according to his needs. By that logic, Eduardo ought to be paying us."

"Works for me." Gianfranco held out his hand, palm up.

Eduardo had a can of Fanta on the counter. He made as if to pour some soda into Gianfranco's hand. Gianfranco jerked it away. That set all three of them laughing.

Alfredo said, "I've got a question for you, Eduardo, if I can ask it without getting wet."

"Well, you can try," Eduardo said, but he made a point of keeping his hand near the can.

"Where *do* you get your games?" Alfredo asked. "I've looked all over Milan, and this is the only place that sells them."

"Of course it is," Eduardo said. "This is the only place in town where the elves make their deliveries."

Gianfranco laughed again. He'd got the same kinds of answers when he asked questions like that. But Alfredo frowned and said, "Come on, Eduardo. You can do better than that. What am I going to do, take your answer to the Security Police?"

"Well, you might," the clerk said. That turned Alfredo's frown into a scowl. You couldn't say much worse about a man than that he was an informer. Gianfranco wondered why that was true, when so many people really *were* informers. Memories of days gone by, he supposed. But before Alfredo could say anything everybody would regret, Eduardo went on, "You see, the true secret is that we have a *sharashka* full of zeks down in the basement, and they turn out the games for us."

That was only a little less unlikely than the story about the elves. A *sharashka* was a lab where privileged prisoners went on working for the state. If they came through, they might get their terms cut. If they didn't, they went back to being ordinary zeks. Somebody who knew his Dante once called *sharashkas* the first circle of Hell: they were bad, but you knew there were worse places. That was the kind of joke you could repeat only to the people you trusted most. The USSR had got some good work out of *sharashkas*. The Germans and the Chinese also used them a lot. They weren't so common in Italy and most other fraternal Communist countries.

Gianfranco clicked his tongue between his teeth. "Now I know you're telling us lies, Eduardo," he said sadly.

"Oh, you do, do you?" The clerk stood on his dignity. "And how do you know that?"

"Because The Gladiator hasn't got a basement."

For some reason, that set all three of them off. They laughed so loud, somebody came out of the back room to complain that players there couldn't concentrate on the games. "And that's *important*," he finished, as if they were too dense to know it.

"*Sor*ry," Eduardo said. The irate gamer rolled his eyes and went back to his board and his cards and his dice. Eduardo and Gianfranco and Alfredo laughed harder than ever. That life should get in the way of the games . . . Well, heaven forbid!

As Gianfranco had seen during the game, Alfredo was stubborn. When the laughter faded, the older man said, "You still didn't answer my question."

"Why don't you ask other places why they don't have them?" Gianfranco said.

Alfredo looked at him as if he wasn't so bright after all. "I've done that," he said. "They tell me they can't get them. They say they don't know where to get them."

"See?" Eduardo said. "They don't have the telephone number for the zeks in the basement."

That made Gianfranco laugh again, but Alfredo didn't think it was so funny. "Confound it, Eduardo, how can you have games nobody else can get his hands on? What do you do, bring them down from the moon?"

"Sure," the clerk said. "If you go out to the alley behind the shop, you'll see the launch tower for our rocket ship."

Alfredo gave him a very odd look. "You know, I almost wouldn't be surprised. *Ciao*, Eduardo. One of these days, maybe you'll tell me the truth. *Ciao*, Gianfranco. You played a fine game there." He walked out before either of the other two could answer him.

Eduardo tried to make light of it, saying, "He doesn't like mysteries."

"Neither do I," Gianfranco said, which seemed to startle the clerk. He went on, "I put up with them, though, because I like the games so much. Alfredo's the same way. Now that he's one win away from taking the tournament, you think he'll kick up a fuss?"

"Well, I hope not," Eduardo said slowly.

At supper, Gianfranco was full of all the details of his epic match with Alfredo. Annarita heard much more about the railroad game than she ever wanted to. Trying to shut Gianfranco up, her mother said, "Then you won, did you? Congratulations!"

"Oh, no, Signora Crosetti," Gianfranco answered. "He beat me. But it was a good game. That's what really counts."

Annarita's father eyed Gianfranco over the tops of his glasses. "If you can say that and really mean it—and I think you do—you've taken a long step toward growing up. You deserve more congratulations for that than you would for winning."

"*Dottor* Crosetti is right," Gianfranco's father said. "Things don't always go the way you want them to. You have to learn to roll with the punches."

Comrade Mazzilli was always good for a couple of clichés. An ordinary man, he had ordinary thoughts, and they came out in ordinary ways. The next new idea he had would be the first. But Annarita thought he and her own father were right about this. She wouldn't have expected Gianfranco to lose a game and be as proud as if he'd won. But he was, plainly. The Gladiator had more going for it than she would have guessed.

When they were walking to school the next morning, he asked Annarita, "Did you manage to get that nonsense about The Gladiator being a capitalist plot taken care of?"

"*Sì*," she said. "Ludovico went along with me on the report, so you don't need to worry about that any more."

"*Grazie*," he told her. Then he said, "You know, I almost asked my old man where The Gladiator gets its games. He could probably find out through purchase records and things. Alfredo was pitching a fit about that last night."

It had puzzled Annarita, too. The games and a lot of the books there looked to be in a class by themselves. "Why didn't you?" she asked.

He looked sheepish. "I didn't want to kill the goose that lays the golden eggs, that's why. Maybe they aren't as legit and legal as they ought to be, you know? I just plain don't care. I have too much fun there to want to take any chances about getting those people in trouble. I kept my big mouth shut." He mimed zipping it closed with the hand that wasn't carrying his notebook and books.

"If they are doing something under the table, chances are it'll come out sooner or later, you know," Annarita said.

"Better later than sooner," Gianfranco answered. "Another tournament'll start soon, and I'm going to win this one!"

"You've got it bad, don't you?" Annarita might almost have been talking with a girl friend who had a crush on a boy.

Gianfranco grinned at her—he must have recognized the tone. "I have fun. What's wrong with that?" he said. "I haven't found anything I enjoy more." He grinned again, in a slightly different way. "And if I don't still feel like that once I find a girl . . . well, I'll worry about it then. I've seen it happen with other guys."

"All right," she said, because that was in her mind, too.

And then he looked at her again, thoughtfully. "Eduardo said I was a fool because *you* weren't my girlfriend."

"Did he?" Annarita said. Gianfranco nodded. She wagged a finger at him. "If Eduardo wants to tell you how to run your railroads, that's one thing. If he wants to tell you how to run your life, that's different. It's none of his business, you hear?"

"*Sì*, Annarita." Gianfranco sounded more subdued than usual. "But you know, it might not be so bad."

She almost laughed in his face. Only the thought that she'd keep on seeing him at breakfast and supper every day held her back at first. Her family and the Mazzillis needed to be able to get along with each other if they could. Because they'd shared so much for so long, though, they did have some notion of what made each other tick. Yes, Gianfranco was a year younger than she was. But there was more to him than she'd thought, even if it came out in his game and not in something really important. He might not be her very first choice for a boyfriend, but she realized she could do worse. A couple of years earlier, he would have been an impossible object. These days . . . ? She looked at him with new eyes. No, he wasn't so bad.

She tried not to let any of that show. She didn't want Gianfranco getting a swelled head. That *would* make him impossible. All she said was, "Well, we've both got other things to worry about right now." He just nodded, which was a point in his favor.

Annarita found out how right she was when she came out of Russian that morning. She ran into Maria Tenace on the way to her next class. No, that wasn't how it happened. Maria was lying in wait for her outside Comrade Montefusco's door, and waved a newspaper in her face as soon as she came out.

"Did you see this?" Maria shouted. "*Did* you?"

"If you don't get out of my way, Maria, you'll see stars, I promise," Annarita said.

The other girl paused for a moment, then decided Annarita wasn't kidding and backed up a step. That was smart, because Annarita would have loved an excuse to knock her block off. But Maria kept waving the paper. "Did you see the *Red Banner*? Did you see what's in it?" Her loud, shrill voice reminded Annarita of the noise a dentist's drill made.

"What's in the *Red Banner*, Maria?" Annarita asked resignedly. She paid as little attention to the Party newspaper as she could. Any newspaper was full of propaganda, but the *Red Banner* stuffed it in the way a sausagemaker shoved ground meat and spices into a salami casing.

"Here. See for yourself."

Maria pointed to the story she had in mind. CAPITALIST PLOTTERS ARRESTED IN ROME! the headline screamed. The article said the Security Police had seized seven men and a woman on suspicion of trying to undermine Marxism-Leninism-Stalinism. They were accused of planning to set up a corporation to enrich themselves and grind down their workers. And they were supposed to have got their ideas from playing games at a shop called The Conductor's Cap, a place that sounded an awful lot like The Gladiator.

When the Security Police came to this wicked den of iniquity, they found the proprietor and his henchmen fled, the story said. *Their capture is expected momentarily, for they cannot hope to escape the aroused forces of Socialist justice.*

"You should have listened to me." Vindictive pleasure

glowed on Maria's face. It bubbled in her voice, like noxious gas bubbling up in swamp water.

Even if she knew what she was talking about, her attitude disgusted Annarita. "Why should anyone listen to you, Maria?" she asked.

"Because I was right!" Maria exclaimed.

"A stopped clock is right twice a day. Nobody pays any attention to it anyway," Annarita said.

She got what she wanted—she made Maria angry, too. It wasn't pretty. It *was* scary, because Annarita could see Maria putting her in a mental card file. *Subversive*, the card said. *Reactionary. Capitalist sympathizer.* Those were the cards that spawned denunciations, all right.

"Go ahead. Have your joke," Maria said now. "But they'll come after The Gladiator, too. And do you know what they'll do then? They'll come after *you*. And do you know what else? I'll be glad!"

She stalked off, as well as anyone so dumpy could stalk. People stared from her to Annarita and back again. Annarita tried to laugh it off. But laughter didn't come easy, not this time.

Five

Gianfranco heard about The Conductor's Cap from Annarita the next morning. "It might be a good time to stay away from The Gladiator for a while," she said. "If the Security Police do crack down, you don't want to be there when it happens."

"Why? Do you think they won't get my name?" Gianfranco said. "Not likely, not with the time and money I've spent there. Besides, I hope I know who my friends are."

The look Annarita gave him said she might be seeing him for the first time. "That's . . . brave, Gianfranco," she said after a long pause. "It's brave, but how smart is it? What can you do for your friends if the Security Police are feeding you truth drugs or beating you with rubber hoses or doing any of the other wonderful things they do?"

He shivered. He couldn't help it. Stories about what the Security Police did to people were limited only by the storyteller's imagination. The worse they sounded, the more likely they were to be true. So everybody said, anyway. Gianfranco didn't know whether what everybody said was true, but he didn't have any reason to doubt it here.

Maybe my father could keep me safe, he thought. Plenty of Party officials' children stayed out of trouble when other kids without connections ended up in deep. But if he got arrested on charges having to do with capitalism, would the Security Police care whose son he was? He didn't think so.

And he didn't think he ought to rely on his father here any way. "All I've done is play games and read books," he said. "How bad can that be?"

"As bad as the Security Police want to make it," Annarita said, which was bound to be true. "Don't do anything silly, that's all."

By the way she talked, he half expected to see Security Police vans in front of Hoxha Polytechnic to carry off all the students who ever went into The Gladiator. No vans there. Everything seemed normal. Everything *was* normal. He had an ordinary day. He didn't butcher his algebra quiz, but he didn't think he aced it, either.

As soon as the closing bell let him escape, he headed for the Galleria del Popolo. It had started to drizzle by then, but the glassed-over roof held the rain at bay. He bought a couple of biscotti and a Fanta to keep his own engine steaming while he played at The Gladiator.

Only one thing wrong—the shop was closed. When he tried the door, it was locked. Looking inside, he didn't see anybody. He went to the leather-goods shop next door. "Where is everybody?" he asked a man setting out wallets.

"Beats me," the fellow answered. "They never opened up today."

"It sure looks empty in there." Gianfranco remembered what had happened to people who played at The Conductor's Cap down in Rome. Worry in his voice, he said, "They aren't in trouble, are they? I mean, the Security Police didn't come for them or anything?"

"Not that I know of. What would the Security Police want

with a game shop, for heaven's sake?" The man laughed to show how silly he thought that was. Gianfranco wished he thought it was silly, too. The man went on, "*Scusi, per piacere,* but I have to put these out." He reached for more wallets.

Get lost, kid. That was what he meant, even if he made it sound more polite. "*Grazie,*" Gianfranco said, and mooched out of the shop, his hands in his pockets. He stood there on the sidewalk, staring at The Gladiator. It was as if the place would magically open up if he just stared hard enough.

No matter how hard he stared, The Gladiator stayed dark and quiet. Plenty of people walked past Gianfranco, but nobody paid too much attention to him. Under the roof of the Galleria del Popolo, you didn't have to go anywhere fast—or at all. You could amble along, or you could just stand still.

A couple of minutes later, Carlo came up to him. "What are you doing hanging around out here?" the other gamer asked. "Why aren't you in there playing?"

"Because it's closed," Gianfranco answered mournfully.

"What? You're crazy. The Gladiator's never closed this time of day." Carlo walked over to the shop and tried the latch. It didn't open, of course. He looked very surprised and very foolish.

"You were saying?" Gianfranco rubbed it in.

"Why are they closed? Do you know? Is somebody sick? Is somebody short of money? Can we do anything to help?" Carlo could spit questions faster than Gianfranco could possibly hope to answer them.

But he did have an answer: "I think they're in trouble."

"Of course, they're in trouble. If they weren't in trouble, *ragazzo*, the place would be open," Carlo said. "But what kind?"

"You call me *kid* again and *you'll* be in trouble," Gianfranco growled. "And I know what kind of trouble they're in and you don't, so don't you think maybe you ought to keep your big mouth shut and your ears open?"

He didn't impress Carlo. He might have known he wouldn't. "So what kind of trouble are they in, if you're so smart?" the university student asked.

"Political trouble," Gianfranco said softly.

He wondered if he would have to spell that out for Carlo, but he didn't. The other gamer got it right away. "What happened?" he demanded. "Did some jerk decide he wanted to be a capitalist for real and not just on the game board?"

"Not here. Down in Rome. Guys who play at a place called The Conductor's Cap," Gianfranco answered.

"Ah, *sì*. I've heard of it," Carlo said.

Gianfranco hadn't, not till Annarita told him about it, but he didn't let on. "There must be a connection between that place and The Gladiator," he said. "I hear it was empty when the Security Police came, and now The Gladiator's closed down, too."

"That's not good," Carlo said. "You think the Security Police are going to come after us?"

"I don't know." Gianfranco shrugged. "I don't know what we can do about it if they decide to, either. Do you?"

"Not much you can do," Carlo said gloomily. "You can't even disappear. They'll run you down and catch you. But we haven't done anything wrong."

"No, of course not." Gianfranco would have said the same thing even if he had done something. He didn't *think* Carlo was an informer, but you never knew. He did add, "Will they care, though?"

"Not likely!" Carlo said. That was true, but it also left him vulnerable to Gianfranco. Even if some things were true, you weren't supposed to say them out loud. Carlo went on, "Where are we going to play now?"

There was an important question! "Well, I've got my own copy of *Rails across Europe*," Gianfranco said.

"Sure. Me, too. But so what?" Carlo said. "How many people do you know who play? I mean, know away from The Gladiator?"

"A couple," Gianfranco answered. "Guys who go to my school. Even one teacher."

"Same here," Carlo said. "I know a couple, maybe three, at the university. We can still play, but it won't be the same—not even close. All the tournaments, the fools at the next table going nuts when something exciting happens in their game . . . Won't be the same, trying to have a game in your kitchen."

"Tell me about it!" Gianfranco said. "We share ours with another family."

"Who doesn't? I can't wait to get my own apartment—but even then, I'll be sharing the kitchen and the bathroom." Carlo sighed. "What can you do? That's how they build 'em. That's how they've built 'em for the last hundred years and then some."

Ever since Italy went Communist, probably, Gianfranco thought. Maybe it had to do with keeping people in groups, not letting them be individuals. Or maybe it wasn't that complicated. Maybe the Italians just started imitating the Russians, who'd been building apartments that way ever since the glorious October Revolution.

"You're right. It won't be the same. Better than nothing, though." Gianfranco knew he sounded like someone whistling in the dark. He felt that way. He'd just had a big chunk of his life yanked out by the roots.

"Maybe the people from The Gladiator will turn up somewhere else. We can hope, anyhow." Carlo sounded like someone whistling in the dark.

Another gamer strolled up then, and looked horrified to discover The Gladiator was closed and dark. He and Gianfranco and Carlo went through a conversation a lot like the one Gianfranco and Carlo had just had. Then they all went away unhappy.

Annarita was doing Russian homework at the kitchen table when Gianfranco came in. "Why aren't you at The Gladiator, if you were going to go there?" she asked in surprise. Then she took a real look at him. "And why do you look like somebody just ran over your cat with a tank?"

"Remember what you told me about The Conductor's Cap?" he said. "Well, The Gladiator is closed, too."

"Oh. Well, I'm sorry, but I can't say I'm too surprised," Annarita said. Gianfranco didn't look consoled. "What are you going to do now?" she asked him.

"I don't know!" he burst out, fiercely enough to startle her. "I'll probably go out of my mind."

"Is it really as bad as that?" Annarita said.

"No. It's worse." Gianfranco couldn't have sounded any sadder if he tried for a year. If he was acting, he should have gone out for drama, because he would have grabbed leading roles with the greatest of ease. "How would you like it if somebody took away your favorite thing in all the world?"

"Not very much, I'm sure," Annarita answered. "But can't you still play somewhere else?"

"*Sì*, but it won't be the same." Gianfranco explained why not. He brought everything out so pat, it was as if he'd said it before. "No tournaments or anything like that. I'll be lucky to get a game in every once in a while." He stopped—something new seemed to have occurred to him. "You wouldn't be interested in learning to play, would you? We could have games easier than people who don't live here could come over. It's a good game. It really is. You'd like it, I think."

He was pathetically eager to have her want to play. No—she changed her mind. He was pathetically eager to have *anybody* to play against, and she seemed handy. She almost told him no, which was her first impulse. Then she remembered all the things her folks said about the need to get along with the Mazzillis. Gianfranco would be very unhappy if she turned him down . . . and *Rails across Europe* had looked interesting.

"I suppose we could try," she said slowly. "I'm not going to let it get in the way of my schoolwork, though—and you shouldn't, either." He couldn't afford that as well as she could. His grades were weaker. He had to know it, so she didn't bother spelling it out for him.

The way his face lit up when she said yes convinced her she'd done the right thing. It was almost like feeding a stray puppy you found in the street. "*Grazie!*" he said, and then, "Do you want to start now?"

"Well . . ." Again, she almost said no. She didn't quite. "We won't be able to play very long, because I have to help get supper ready—and I do need to study this Russian, and some other stuff, too."

He hardly heard her—she could tell. "I'll be right back," he said, and dashed from the common kitchen into the Mazzillis' rooms. Maybe he paused to say hello to his mother and father. Then again, maybe he didn't. He sure reappeared in nothing flat, the box with the game in it clutched firmly in his hands. He sat down across the table from Annarita.

"What do I have to do?" she asked, thinking, *It has to be better than Russian.*

It turned out to be more complicated than Russian. As far as Annarita was concerned, that wasn't easy, but *Rails across Europe* managed. Building your railroad and shipping things from here to there were pretty straightforward. After that, though, things got stickier. You could let the other player use your track if he paid you, but how did you know how much to ask for? What happened if you were both shipping the same product into the same town? How did you deal with natural disasters? And so on, and so on.

Gianfranco did a better job of explaining than Annarita would have expected. He knew the game backward and forward and inside out. Sometimes he tried to tell her more than she needed to know. Mostly, though, he stuck with the basics till they ran into something hard. Then he told her how that worked.

As far as she could see, he didn't try to take unfair advantage because she wasn't sure what she was doing. When she thanked him for that, he looked surprised. "It wouldn't be any fun if I did," he said. "Who cares if you win if you've got to cheat to do it?"

"Lots of people would say the point of winning is winning, and who cares how you do it?" Annarita answered.

"But if you know you didn't win square, it leaves a bad taste in your mouth," Gianfranco said. "Or if it doesn't, it ought to."

"*Sì.* I think the same thing. But plenty of people don't," she said.

After about half an hour, her mother called her to help cook. "What do you think?" Gianfranco asked as he marked places and put their cards and play money into separate envelopes.

"It's not bad," Annarita said. "I can see it's not the kind of game where you get good as soon as you've played once. I've still got a lot to learn."

"*I'm* still learning," Gianfranco said. "That loss-leader trick Carlo tried to pull on me a while ago . . . I had no idea that was in the rules, but it is." He held up the rule book.

"It's thick enough," Annarita said. "Probably all kinds of other sneaky things hiding in there, too."

"Do you want to study it?" Gianfranco asked.

"Maybe another time," she said. "If I start looking at it, I *won't* study my Russian, and I've got to." She sighed. "I think Comrade Montefusco's teaching us to speak it better than the Russians do themselves." She told him about the classroom visitors they'd had.

"I don't care if the Russians were the first Communists," Gianfranco said. "Nobody'd pay any attention to them if they weren't the biggest, strongest country in the world."

"That's true, but be careful who hears you say it," Annarita warned. She was glad to get away to help her mother cut up a chicken and chop vegetables.

Quietly, so her voice wouldn't carry over the sound of chopping, her mother asked, "Are you really playing that silly game with Gianfranco?"

"It's not silly. It's kind of interesting, as a matter of fact,"

Annarita answered, also in a low voice. Her mother snorted. "It is," Annarita insisted. "It's complicated as anything, too."

"So is a car's engine. That doesn't make it interesting, not unless you're a mechanic," her mother said.

"It's got to be as complicated as bridge," Annarita said. Her mother loved to play cards. Her father didn't, but he went along to keep his wife sweet. In self-defense, he'd become at least as good a player as she was.

"Don't be silly," her mother sniffed. "You don't know what you're talking about."

Since Annarita didn't care anything about bridge, her mother had a point. But the coin had two sides, whether her mother wanted to see it or not. "Well, you don't know anything about *Rails across Europe*."

"I know most of the boys who play it have thick glasses and funny clothes and never comb their hair," her mother said. "What else do I need to know?"

"You could say the same thing about chess players," Annarita answered.

"That's different. Chess is respectable," her mother said. "Even the Russians take good chess players seriously."

Even the Russians, Annarita thought as she sliced a green pepper into long strips. Gianfranco was right— if they weren't top dogs, nobody would pay any attention to them. Comrade Montefusco had talked about the Russian insult—*nye kulturny*—that meant *uncultured*, and that foreigners shouldn't use against them. The Russians used it against one another, though. If they didn't have soldiers and rockets from Poland to the Atlantic, everybody in Western Europe would have thrown it in their faces. Sometimes, though, saying what you thought came at too high a price.

Following that line of thought, Annarita made her voice as innocent as she could when she asked, "So you want us to act just like the Russians, then?"

"No!" Her mother's knife came down hard on the joint between thigh and drumstick. It crunched through gristle and bone. "I didn't say that. I didn't mean that. But Gianfranco's silly game isn't chess, either."

"I didn't say it was. But it's not easy, and it's not silly, either." Annarita passed her mother the cut-up pepper and squashes. Her mother browned the chicken in olive oil, then put it in a pan with the vegetables, with wine and tomato sauce and chopped tomatoes, and with spices and bits of crumbled prosciutto. Into the oven it went.

As her mother was washing her hands, she said, "I hope you're not playing just to make Gianfranco happy. You can do better than that, sweetheart."

"Maybe." It wasn't as if Annarita hadn't had the same thought herself. But she said, "He's kind of like the game, you know? There's more to him than meets the eye."

"And so? His father's still an apparatchik." Her mother used another Russian word that had spread all over Europe and America. It didn't just mean a petty bureaucrat. It meant someone who was born to be a petty bureaucrat. People who really did things, like Annarita's father, naturally looked down their noses at the ones who made a living by shuffling pieces of paper back and forth.

"Comrade Mazzilli's not so bad," Annarita said. "Plenty worse."

"Well, heaven knows that's true," her mother agreed. "But still . . ."

"You don't need to get all upset," Annarita said. "You and

Father always go on about how I should work hard to get along with Gianfranco. So here I am, working hard to get along with him, and you don't like that, either."

"I didn't expect you to play his silly game." Her mother seemed stuck on the word. "That goes too far."

"I told you—it's not silly," Annarita came back again— and there they were, starting again from square one.

The more her mother argued with her about it, the more interested in *Rails across Europe* Annarita got. She would have angrily denied that any such thing would happen. She didn't like to think of herself as so predictable. But it did work out that way.

When she got to school the next morning, Maria Tenace was gloating some more. "So much for your majority report," Maria sneered. "The reactionary lackeys at The Gladiator must have known the fat was in the fire. They fled yesterday, one jump ahead of the Security Police. Sooner or later, the vanguard of the people's justice will catch up with them. I don't think it will take long."

She could seriously say things even a TV announcer would have had trouble bringing out with a straight face. A TV announcer would have known how silly and stupid they were. Maria didn't. She believed every scrap of Party doctrine. A few hundred years earlier, she would have got just as excited about the Inquisition, and would have been just as sure it was necessary.

She let out one piece of information without even noticing she was doing it. "So the people at The Gladiator did get away?" Annarita asked.

"*Sì*," Maria said reluctantly. "But not for long. The hand of every decent Marxist-Leninist-Stalinist is raised against them in iron condemnation of their wicked and corrupt manipulation of the social order and class structure."

"Did the Security Police catch the people from The Conductor's Cap in Rome?" Annarita made it sound as if she hoped the answer was yes.

"No," Maria admitted, even more reluctantly than before. "But they can't hope to escape revolutionary justice, either."

"How do you know they're really guilty of anything?" Annarita asked. "Rome is a long way from here."

"They must be guilty. If they weren't, the Security Police wouldn't go after them." Maria could even say that and sound as if she meant it. Anyone with the sense of a head of cabbage knew the Security Police did whatever they wanted and whatever their Russian bosses told them to do. Whether you were guilty or innocent didn't matter. Whether they thought you were dangerous to the state did.

"I guess." Annarita didn't say an eighth of what she was thinking, or an eighteenth.

"I"m going to tell Filippo to make sure *my* report on The Gladiator is the official one," Maria said importantly. "I don't want the Young Socialists' League to be seen as out of step with the advance of revolutionary and progressive elements in the state."

"You can't make a majority out of a minority," Annarita said. "You can tell the world I was wrong—though I don't think anybody's proved that yet—but you can't do the other."

Maria looked at her as if she were very foolish to say such a thing. "Of course I can. What do you think *Bolshevik* means?"

Annarita bit her lip. No matter how obnoxious Maria was, she was right. At a Party meeting before the Revolution, the group that became the Bolsheviks found themselves outvoted on some issue or other. So they simply declared themselves the majority—*Bolsheviki* in Russian. Their more moderate opponents were known as the Mensheviks—the minority—forever after. Annarita thought the Mensheviks were foolish to let themselves get stuck with the name, but it was almost two hundred years too late to worry about that now.

"Do you really *want* to get tagged as an unreliable? You're sure working on it." Maria went off shaking her head before Annarita could even answer.

At least half in a daze, Annarita sat down in her Russian class. She made a bunch of careless mistakes. "Are you feeling all right?" the teacher asked her, real worry in his voice—he knew something had to be wrong.

"Yes, Comrade Montefusco. Please excuse me," Annarita said.

"Well, I'll try," he answered. "I know you're a better student than you're showing. Is everything at home the way it ought to be?"

"Yes, Comrade," she answered truthfully. If the authorities had left The Gladiator alone . . . If Maria had let her alone . . . But none of that had anything to do with what went on in her apartment.

Comrade Montefusco still didn't look as if he believed her. "Try to keep your mind on the grammar and the vocabulary, then," he said.

"Yes, Comrade," Annarita repeated. "I'll do my best." And she did. But her best that morning just wasn't very good. Shaking his head, Comrade Montefusco got out the roll book and made a couple of notes in it. Annarita didn't think they were the kind of notes that would help her grade.

Things were almost as bad in her other classes. They got a

little better, because she wasn't in such a state of shock as she had been to start the day. Even so, she had a lot more on her mind than the rest of the students did.

She went looking for Filippo Antonelli at lunch. He found her first. One look at his face told her he'd already talked—or, more likely, listened—to Maria. "You're not going to change the report, are you?" Annarita asked in dismay.

"Well, I don't know," Filippo answered. "If we're on the wrong side here, it makes us look bad. We shouldn't do that, not if we can help it."

"We still don't know the authorities raided The Gladiator. All we know is, it's closed." Annarita was grasping at straws, and she knew it.

And Filippo broke the straws even as she took them in her hand. "The Security Police *did* raid the place," he said. "They didn't catch anybody, though."

"How do you know?" Annarita asked.

Filippo looked smug. "I know because I've got friends I can ask," he answered. "And I'll tell you something else funny— some of the fingerprints they found there don't match any on file in the records."

"What's that supposed to mean?" Annarita said. "Do they think they're foreigners? The one I talked to didn't just sound like an Italian. He sounded like somebody from Milan."

"No, not only in the Italian records. That's what my friend says," Filippo told her. "Not in anybody's records, even the Russians'."

"That's impossible," Annarita blurted. Maybe it wasn't quite, but it sure struck her as unlikely. The Security Police had files on everybody in Italy. The Russians had files on everybody in the world, except maybe people from China and its satellites. Whatever, whoever, Eduardo was, he wasn't Chinese.

"I thought so, too, but that's what I heard," Filippo said. "And they found a big secret room under The Gladiator."

"What was in it?" Annarita asked. "It sounds like something out of a spy story."

"It does, doesn't it?" Filippo said. "There wasn't anything in it. It was just a room with a concrete floor. There were yellow lines painted on the floor, lines that might warn you to stay away from something, but there wasn't anything to stay away from."

"That's . . . peculiar," Annarita said, and he nodded. She went on, "It all sounds like the little man who wasn't there."

"Well, he must have been there once upon a time, or the Security Police wouldn't have raided the place," Filippo said, which proved he believed what his friends in high places told him.

"I guess so." Annarita didn't want to argue with him. "What would the Security Police do with one of those people if they did catch him?"

"Question him, I suppose." Filippo sounded as if he didn't want to think about that. Even the way he answered said as much. It was true, but it didn't go far enough. The Security Police didn't just question. They drugged. They tortured. They did whatever they had to do to find out what they wanted to know. Everybody understood that. But nice people—and Filippo *was* a nice person—didn't like to dwell on it.

Annarita didn't like to dwell on it, either. Did that make her a nice person? She could hope so, anyhow. She could also hope everybody at The Gladiator had a hole and pulled it in after himself. Not rooting for the Security Police was slightly subversive, or maybe more than slightly. She knew she wasn't the only one who did it just the same.

Gianfranco went back to the Galleria del Popolo after school hoping for a miracle. Maybe he'd just had a bad dream. Maybe The Gladiator would be open and everything would be fine. Maybe pigs had wings, and they'd built the roof on the Galleria because of that.

The shop was closed. He might have known it would be. He *had* known it would be. What he hadn't known was that it would be swarming with Security Police officers, the way cut fruit at a picnic would be swarming with ants.

He tried to amble on by as if he'd never had anything to do with *Rails across Europe* or any of the other games they sold there. One of the men from the Security Police spotted him. "Hey, you!" the officer yelled. "*Sì*, you, kid! C'mere!"

"What do you want?" Gianfranco wasn't so frightened as he might have been. That came from having a father who was a Party official.

"Let's see your identity card and your internal passport," the man said. As in the USSR and most other Communist states, you needed permission to travel inside your own country, not just from one country to another.

"Here you are, Comrade." Gianfranco didn't dream of not handing them over. He had no idea how much trouble you could get in by refusing, and he didn't want to find out.

"So you're Mazzilli's brat, are you?" The officer didn't sound much impressed.

"I'm his son, *sì*, Comrade." Gianfranco made the correction with as much dignity as he could.

It didn't impress the older man. Nothing seemed to impress him—he worked at it. He jerked a thumb toward The Gladiator. "You ever go in there?"

"A couple of times." Gianfranco couldn't have been so casual if he hadn't been thinking about the question since the man called him over. He wanted to say no, but the records they would find inside could prove he was lying if he did. This seemed safer.

When he didn't say anything more, the officer asked, "Well? What did you think?"

"Some of the games looked interesting," Gianfranco answered. "I bought one, but they were pretty expensive, so I didn't get any more."

"What did you think of their ideology?" the man asked, his voice a little too casual.

Whenever anybody asked you about ideology, you were smart to play dumb. When a man from the Security Police asked you, you were *really* smart to play dumb. "I don't know. I leave all that stuff for my father," Gianfranco said. "Besides, how can nineteenth-century trains have an ideology?"

"You'd be amazed, kid. You'd be absolutely amazed," the officer told him. And what was that supposed to mean? Probably that when the Security Police went looking for ideology in a game, they'd find it whether it was there or not.

Gianfranco went right on playing dumb. "Can I go now?" he asked.

"In a minute," the fellow from the Security Police said. "Have you seen any of the people from this shop since we shut it down?"

"No, Comrade," Gianfranco said, almost truthfully.

"If you do, you will report them to us at once." The officer did his best to make that sound like a law of nature.

"Of course, Comrade." Gianfranco did his best to make the man believe he thought it was. As long as you were playing by the rules the government and the security forces set, you could get away with skirting them most of the time.

"You'd better. This is serious business. How could these spies run loose in our country without showing up in our records?" Now the man from the Security Police made it sound as if the people who ran The Gladiator were violating a law of nature.

"Spies? What is there to spy on here?" Gianfranco asked.

"That's not your worry," the officer snapped. Gianfranco knew what that had to mean, too. The man had no clue, and neither did his bosses. He gave Gianfranco one more scowl, then jerked his thumb in an unmistakable gesture. "All right, kid. Get lost."

Gianfranco didn't wait for him to change his mind. Away he went, before the officer could have second thoughts.

He had some thoughts of his own—confused ones. Eduardo and the others at The Gladiator were no more spies than he was. No matter what the Security Police thought, the idea was ridiculous. But how had they kept from landing in the files? That was quite a trick, whatever it was. Gianfranco wished he could have done it himself.

The invisible man. The man who wasn't there. He imagined strolling through Italian society untroubled by the authorities, because officially he didn't exist. The people at The Gladiator and The Conductor's Cap had done it—for a while, anyhow. But once they got noticed, not being in the records must have drawn more attention to them. Bureaucrats and security men were probably climbing the walls trying to figure out how they managed it.

And how had they all vanished at just the right moment? Plainly, the Security Police hadn't caught them. Just as plainly, the Security Police wished they had.

Gianfranco laughed to himself. Anything that made the Security Police unhappy seemed like good news to him.

He spotted a former opponent heading toward The Gladiator. Waving, he called, "*Ciao*, Alfredo. It's no use."

"They're not open?" Alfredo's voice registered despair.

"It's not just that they're not open," Gianfranco said. "The Security Police are crawling all over the place."

"Don't they have more important things to do than pitching fits about people who run a little gaming shop?" Alfredo said. "What are we going to do?"

"They think they're a pack of spies," Gianfranco said. That made Alfredo laugh like a loon. But then Gianfranco explained how the people at The Gladiator weren't in any official records, and Alfredo stopped laughing.

"No way!" he exclaimed.

"Well, if you want to tell the Security Police there's no way, you can go do that," Gianfranco said. "But do you think they'll listen to you?"

"They would have to come from Mars, not to get into the files," Alfred said, and Gianfranco nodded—he'd had the same thought. Alfredo went on, "Or maybe they really are spies. But spies would act like foreigners, and those people are as Milanese as we are."

Again, Gianfranco had had the same idea. "None of this makes any sense," he said.

"I'm sure it does—to somebody," Alfredo said. "But not to

us." He looked unhappy again. "I don't know what I'm going to do. I'm going crazy without the tournaments. Ever been around somebody who just quit smoking? I'm like that."

He hadn't quit. He lit a cigarette, and smoked in quick, nervous puffs. Gianfranco stepped to one side to get away from the smoke, which made him cough.

Alfredo either didn't notice or didn't care. From what Gianfranco had seen, most smokers worried more about keeping their own habit going than about what nonsmokers thought. Lots of people in Italy smoked. For as long as anyone could remember, the government had said it wasn't healthy. That only went to show that even the government had its limits.

"What are we going to do?" Alfredo asked as he crushed the butt under his shoe. "You know what? We all ought to get together and rent a hall where we could play. It wouldn't be that expensive, not if everybody chipped in."

He was a great *Rails across Europe* player. How smart was he away from the game board? Not very, not as far as Gianfranco could see. "Maybe," Gianfranco said, as gently as he could. "But don't you think the Security Police would visit us as soon as we did anything like that?"

"What? Why would they?" No, Alfredo didn't get it.

"Why did they visit The Gladiator?" Gianfranco asked.

"Because they're . . . foolish." Alfredo didn't say everything he might have. He wasn't *too* foolish himself. He wouldn't call the Security Police a pack of idiots—or worse—in front of Gianfranco, whom he didn't know well. But he got the message across. And then, with a mournful nod, he went on his way.

Gianfranco started back toward his apartment building. He wished he hadn't come to the Galleria in the first place. Seeing the Security Police swarming over The Gladiator brought him down—and it was dangerous. He knew that officer could have arrested him.

He went past Hoxha Polytechnic. A chorus was singing the praises of the Communist Party and the illustrious General Secretary. *Rehearsal for May Day*, Gianfranco thought, and then, *What's so great about the Party, if it goes after places like The Gladiator?*

His mind shied away from that like a frightened horse. You couldn't think such thoughts. It was too dangerous—they might show on your face. If he'd been thinking *What's so great about the Party?* while the Security Police officer grilled him, the fellow would have been all over him the way a cat jumped all over a mouse.

He was almost home when somebody called his name: "Gianfranco! Hey, Gianfranco, you've got to help me!"

"Eduardo!" Gianfranco knew the voice—and knew he was in trouble no matter what he did—even before he turned. "What the devil are you doing here?"

"They're after me!" said the clerk from The Gladiator, which Gianfranco already knew. "You've got to help me!"

"Well, I'll try," Gianfranco said, and that told him what kind of trouble he was in.

Six

Annarita hated regular Russian verbs. Irregular Russian verbs drove her crazy. She consoled herself that things could have been worse. Comrade Montefusco said that Polish, a close cousin to Russian, had separate masculine, feminine, and neuter forms for verbs. Annarita tried to imagine little children learning a language that complicated. They evidently could. She wondered how.

When Gianfranco came into the kitchen, she was ready to put the Russian aside for his game. Her mother would cluck, but she didn't care. Then she got a good look at his face. "What's wrong?" she asked, adding, "You look like somebody who just saw a ghost."

"That's not funny," Gianfranco said. "Come out with me for a second, will you?"

"All right." Annarita closed the book and got up. "What's going on? You don't usually act this way."

He didn't try to tell her it was nothing. She would have brained him with the Russian book if he had. It was big and square and heavy—she might have fractured his skull. All he said was, "You'll see."

Out she went. He led her to the stairwell. On the stairs, looking miserable and worried, stood Eduardo. "Ohh," Annarita said, as if someone had punched her in the pit of the stomach.

"He's not a puppy." Gianfranco might have been joking but his tone said he wasn't, "I can't go ask my mother if I can keep him."

"No," Annarita said unhappily. She rounded on Eduardo as if this were his fault. "Why didn't you disappear with your friends?"

That only made the clerk from The Gladiator look even more miserable. "I couldn't," he said. "The Security Police had already raided the shop."

And what was *that* supposed to mean? "Have you got a tunnel in the bottom of it, one that goes through to Australia or the Philippines?" she asked. "Is that how everybody else got away clean?"

Eduardo turned red. Even with the cheap, low-wattage lightbulbs in the stairwell, Annarita could see it plainly. "That's a better guess than you know," he said, and then, to Gianfranco, "We've got a basement after all." The crack didn't make much sense to Annarita, but they both managed rather sickly smiles. Eduardo turned serious again in a hurry. "Shall I disappear from here now, so I don't get you guys in trouble?"

"I'm already in trouble." Gianfranco sounded proud of it, too.

"Not if nobody finds out I was here," Eduardo said.

Part of Annarita wanted to tell him, *Yes, go away!* That was the part she hated, the part that worried about safety ahead of everything else. "Don't go anywhere," she told him. "Just stay here till I get back. It won't be long, one way or another. Gianfranco, you come with me."

"What's going on?" Gianfranco said, but he came. Eduardo

sat down on the stairs and put his head in his hands. He couldn't have seemed more downcast if he were rehearsing in a play. Annarita clicked her tongue between her teeth as the stairwell door closed behind her and Gianfranco. This was a mess, all right, and no two ways about it.

Her father was reading a medical journal in the living room. He looked up in mild surprise when Annarita marched in on him, Gianfranco in her wake. "*Ciao, ragazzi*," he said, and then, "What's up? Something must be—you've got blood in your eye, Annarita."

"You know about The Gladiator, *sì*?" Annarita said.

"The gaming place in the Galleria? I know it's there— that's about all," Papa answered. "And that silly girl was giving you a hard time about it."

"Maria's a lot of things, but silly isn't any of them," Annarita said grimly. "She was giving me a hard time because the Security Police closed the place down. Suspicion of capitalism, I guess you'd say. But all the people who worked there seemed to vanish into thin air."

"Lucky for them," her father remarked. Not for the first time, he reminded her of someone who would smoke a pipe. He didn't, or anything else. But he had that kind of thoughtful air.

"Not for all of them." Annarita nudged Gianfranco.

He jumped. His voice wobbled and broke as he said, "I ran into one of them—a guy named Eduardo. I brought him here. What are we going to do with him, *Dottor* Crosetti? I don't want to give him to the Security Police, not when he really hasn't done anything."

"Hasn't done anything you know of," Annarita's father corrected. He frowned. With a lot of people, it would have been an angry frown. Why not, when Gianfranco and Annarita were involving him in something not only illegal but dangerous? Everybody did illegal things to get by now and then. You almost had to. Most of them couldn't land you in too much trouble. Not letting the Security Police get their hands on a fugitive they wanted? That was a different story.

"They don't want him for anything but working in the shop." Gianfranco sounded more sure of himself now.

"How do you know that?" Dr. Crosetti asked. He didn't *sound* angry.

"Because a Security Police officer was asking me questions outside The Gladiator this afternoon," Gianfranco answered. Annarita hadn't heard that. He went on, "It was all he cared about."

Annarita's father grunted. "I think I'd better talk to this fellow. If he makes me believe he's harmless—well, we'll see. If he doesn't, I'll send him away from here with a flea in his ear. Is that a deal?"

"It sounds wonderful," Gianfranco said.

"It's fine, Father," Annarita agreed.

"Well, then, go get him, and we'll see what's what," Dr. Crosetti said. "And then you can both disappear. I've already talked with you. I want to talk to him."

Gianfranco looked miffed. "It's all right," Annarita told him. "That's how Papa works." He didn't seem convinced. She asked, "Have you got any better ideas?" Reluctantly, he shook his head. "Well, then," she said. "Come on. Let's get Eduardo, before he decides he'd better run away."

Back to the stairwell they went. To Annarita's relief, the clerk from The Gladiator was still there. He looked up at them. "And?" he said.

"Come talk to my father. If anybody can figure out what to do for you, he can," Annarita said.

"I've already talked too much. I don't want to do any more," Eduardo said.

"If you don't want to talk to my father, you can talk to the Security Police instead," she said. Eduardo winced and climbed to his feet. Annarita had thought that would get him moving. He muttered something under his breath. She couldn't make out what it was. Maybe that was just as well.

Down the hall they went. Gianfranco did the introduction: "Dr. Crosetti, this is Eduardo . . . You know what, Eduardo? I don't know your last name."

"Caruso," the clerk said. "Only I can't sing."

That made Annarita's father smile, but only for a moment. "Oh, you'll sing for me, Comrade Caruso. Or else we're both wasting our time." He gestured to Annarita and Gianfranco. "Out, out, out. Give us some room to talk, some room to breath, *per piacere*."

None too willingly, they left the living room. "What's he going to ask him?" Gianfranco whispered. "What's he going to find out that we didn't?"

"I don't know," Annarita answered. "But we can't do this by ourselves, and you didn't seem to want to go to *your* folks."

"I hope not!" Gianfranco exclaimed. "My father would either make speeches at him or hand him to the Security Police. Or both."

That was about what Annarita thought Comrade Mazzilli would do, too. "There you are, then," she said.

Gianfranco nodded. "Here I am, all right, and I wish I were somewhere else."

Algebra homework wasn't what Gianfranco wanted to be doing. Across the kitchen table from him, Annarita went through her schoolwork as if she had not a care in the world. What was her father talking about with Eduardo? How long would it take? Forever? It felt that way.

They got chased away from the table about eight o'clock, so their mothers could set it for supper. Dr. Crosetti came out to eat. Eduardo didn't. What had Annarita's father done with him—done to him? Stuck him in a bookcase? Preserved him in a specimen bottle? Stuffed him under the rug? Whatever it was, he gave no sign. He talked a little about a strange case he'd seen that afternoon, but said not a word about the strange clerk he'd—probably—left in his living room.

As for Gianfranco's father, *he* talked about some bureaucratic silliness even he wouldn't care about day after tomorrow. Nobody else cared now. Even Gianfranco's mother looked bored. The Crosettis didn't, but they weren't family. They worked harder to stay polite.

Supper was good, but Gianfranco paid it less attention than he might have. He wanted to know where Eduardo was and what would happen to him. He couldn't ask, though, not without letting his own folks know what was going on. He was sure he didn't want to do that.

As people were getting up from the table, Annarita said, "Why don't you come over to our place, Gianfranco, and I'll see if I can help you with that algebra."

He hadn't asked her for any help. That had to mean . . . "Sure!" Gianfranco had to work not to sound too eager. Annarita had seemed perfectly casual. He hadn't known she was such a good actress.

Beaming, his father said, "That's good. It's right out of *The Communist Manifesto*—from each according to her abilities, to each according to his needs." Then the smile slipped. "Of course, maybe Gianfranco wouldn't need the help if he worked harder on his own."

"I do work hard," Gianfranco protested. "It just doesn't stick as well as I wish it did."

"What did *you* get in algebra when you were in school?" his mother asked his father. Instead of answering, his father went back to talking about the *Manifesto*. That told Gianfranco everything he needed to know.

He got his algebra book, then followed Annarita into the Crosettis' apartment. "Well?" he said as soon as his own folks couldn't hear him. "Where's Eduardo? What are you going to do with him?"

"What? You don't want to do algebra?" Annarita said, as innocently as if she thought he did.

What he said about algebra wasn't quite suited to polite company, even if, at the last moment, he made it milder than he'd first intended. "Where's Eduardo?" he asked.

"Who?" Annarita said. Gianfranco didn't clobber her and he didn't scream, which only proved he had more self-control than he thought. She took him by the arm. "Come on." She led him into the Crosettis' living room.

Eduardo sat on the sofa there, a glass of wine in front of him. Dr. Crosetti sat in his favorite chair, a glass of wine on the end table next to him. They both looked pleased with themselves. "*Ciao*, Gianfranco," Annarita's father said. "I'd like you to meet my distant cousin, Silvio Pagnozzi." He waved towards Eduardo.

Gianfranco gaped. He started to squawk. Then he realized something was going on. He held out his hand. "*Molto lieto . . .* Silvio."

Eduardo stood up and gravely shook hands with him. "Pleased to meet you, too, Gianfranco," he said, for all the world as if Gianfranco weren't a regular at The Gladiator.

"I hope your papers are in order . . . Silvio," Gianfranco said. "They're liable to be doing a lot of checking for a while. Looking for dangerous criminals like murderers and bank robbers and gaming-store clerks, you know."

"*Sì, sì.*" Eduardo pulled out an identity card and an internal passport. Gianfranco wasn't astonished to see that they had Eduardo's photo, a fingerprint likely to be his, and the name of Silvio Pagnozzi. The internal passport said he was born in Acireale, down on Sicily, but had moved to Milan when he was only two. That made sense—he didn't talk like a Sicilian, so he couldn't have lived in the south for long.

"What happens if the Security Police telephone Acireale to find out if you were really born there?" Gianfranco asked.

Eduardo shrugged. "Acireale's right by Mount Etna. Most of the records there were lost in the earthquake of 2081," he said. "They can't prove anything one way or the other."

"I see." Gianfranco nodded and gave the documents back. "These look good. They look real."

"They're as good as the ones you've got," Eduardo—Silvio?—answered.

"If someone with a different name who looks like you had papers, would his be just as good, too?"

"Well, of course," Eduardo answered, smiling. "You're not a human being at all if you don't have papers that say you are, eh?" He winked.

Gianfranco didn't. "Where do you get papers like that?" he asked. *Are you a spy?* he meant. He hadn't wanted to believe that, but seeing those perfect documents in a false name made him wonder. Or was Silvio Pagnozzi a false name? Gianfranco realized he couldn't be sure.

Eduardo stopped smiling. "I've told Dr. Crosetti where I got them. The fewer people who know, the fewer who can tell."

That wasn't good enough for Gianfranco. "I've earned the right to know. The Security Police can already slice me into carpaccio or chop me up for salami. If I'm putting my neck on the line, I've got a right to know why."

"He's right," Annarita said. "I feel the same way."

Her father looked surprised—mutiny in the family? And Gianfranco *was* surprised, and tried to hide it. So Dr. Crosetti hadn't told Annarita whatever it was, either. Gianfranco would have guessed she'd know. Evidently not.

"What do you think?" Annarita's father asked Eduardo.

"Maybe I'd better tell them," answered the man with the interesting papers.

"They're children," Dr. Crosetti said.

Before Gianfranco could get angry, Eduardo said, "If not for them, I'd be wandering the streets right now—or else the Security Police would have grabbed me. They're acting like grown-ups. Don't you think we ought to treat them that way?"

"Mmrm." Dr. Crosetti made a discontented noise, down deep in his throat. "I wouldn't trust grown-ups with this, either. Who saw you on the stairwell?"

"Nobody who paid any attention to me. I made a point of looking away from the two or three people who came by—you'd better believe I did," Eduardo said.

Annarita's father grunted again. "And you may have looked straight into a surveillance camera, too. Those miserable things are common as cockroaches."

Eduardo smiled again. "They won't have picked me up. I have the power to cloud cameras' minds—or at least to jam their signals."

"How do you do that?" Gianfranco blurted.

"It has to do with where I come from," Eduardo said.

"And where's that?" Annarita asked. "From right around here, by the way you talk."

"I do come from Milan—from Arese, actually," Eduardo said. Gianfranco and Annarita both nodded—that was a suburb northwest of the city. "But I come from Milan in the Italian Republic, not Milan in the Italian People's Republic."

"Huh?" Gianfranco said, at the same time as Annarita asked, "What does that mean?" They both amounted to the same thing, even if Annarita was more polite.

"In my world"—Eduardo brought the phrase out as calmly as if it were something as ordinary as *on my block*— "Communism didn't win the Cold War. Capitalism did."

"Marx says that's impossible." Gianfranco brought out the first objection that popped into his head. Others stood in line behind it, waiting their turn.

"*Sì*," Eduardo said. "What about it? A believer might think the sun goes around the earth because the Bible says the sun stood still. Does that make it true? Do you want to believe something because a book says it's so, or do you want to look at the evidence?"

"What *is* your evidence?" Annarita asked, beating Gianfranco to the punch. "So far, we've heard nothing but talk, and talk is cheap."

"It's also very light," Gianfranco said with a grin. "You can haul boxcars of it with a beat-up old locomotive in *Rails across Europe*."

"The game is part of my evidence," Eduardo said. "Do you think it would be legal—or safe—to make it anywhere in this world?"

Annarita looked very unhappy. "You sound like one of the hardcore people in the Young Socialists' League."

"I wouldn't be surprised. They're not all blind. I wish they were. My life would be easier," Eduardo answered.

"How do we know this isn't some sort of fancy scam?" Gianfranco asked.

Dr. Crosetti beamed at him. "I said the same thing. I didn't think the game was enough, either."

Eduardo sighed. "By rights, I shouldn't show you anything like this. By rights, I shouldn't be here at all. I should be back in the home timeline." He looked even more unhappy than Annarita had. "I should have gone home with everybody else. I should have been in The Gladiator before the Security Police raided it. But they must have planned the raid in a place where we didn't have bugs. I thought we'd done a better job of covering them than we must have."

"You . . . bugged the Security Police?" Gianfranco said slowly. Eduardo nodded. Gianfranco stared at him. "Nobody can do that—except the Russians, I guess. They can do whatever they want."

"They make junk. Everybody here makes junk." Eduardo's flat, take-it-or-leave-it tone was hard to disbelieve. Either he believed himself or he was one devil of an actor. Still gloomily, he went on, "But anyway, I was out shopping when the raid went down. I almost walked into the Security Police when I came back."

"That doesn't do anything toward showing me what I asked for," Gianfranco said.

"I know, The point of it is, though, I've got my mini in my pocket."

"Your mini what?" Gianfranco and Annarita asked the question at the same time.

"My minicomputer, that's what. Against regulations to take it out of the shop, but now I'm kind of glad I did," Eduardo said.

Gianfranco almost decided on the spot that he was lying. Computers were even more carefully regulated than typewriters. The Security Police knew where every single one of them was, and who was authorized to use it. Hoxha Polytechnic had a couple of small ones, but only the most politically reliable kids could get close to them. And they were the size of a small refrigerator. The idea that anybody could carry one around in his pocket was ridiculous.

What Eduardo pulled out of his pocket sure didn't look like any computer Gianfranco had seen or imagined. It was smaller than a pack of cigarettes, and made of white plastic. On one side, something was stamped into it. Eduardo's thumb stayed on the emblem most of the time, but when he moved it Gianfranco saw what looked like an apple with a bite taken out of one side. He wondered what that meant.

Eduardo poked the gadget in a particular way. Then he said, "On," and then he said, "Screen."

It came out of the top of the little plastic box and spread out like a Japanese fan. It seemed about as thick as a butterfly's wing. At first it was white, but then color spread over it. Gianfranco saw that gnawed apple again, but only for a moment.

"Tournament," Eduardo said. "*Rails across Europe* fourteen."

There were the games in the tournament in which Gianfranco had just played, all the way up to his loss to Alfredo. "This isn't a computer!" he exclaimed. "This is magic!"

"No." Eduardo shook his head. "This is technology. Anybody can use it. All you have to do is know how. No hocus-pocus, no abracadabra. You don't have to be a king's son or go to a sorcerers' academy. You just have to walk into a shop, put down a couple of hundred big ones, and it's yours."

"Big ones?" Annarita said.

"What we use for money," Eduardo answered. "A hundred euros make a big one all over Western Europe. In the United States, a hundred dollars make a benjamin."

"What about the Soviet Union?" Annarita beat Gianfranco to the question by a split second.

"Well, Russia uses rubles," Eduardo answered. "Ukraine uses hryvnia, Belarus uses rubels, Armenia has drams, Georgia has lari, Azerbaijan has manats, Moldova uses lei, Estonia uses krooni, Latvia uses—guess what?—lats, Lithuania uses litai—surprise again, right?—and the Central Asian republics all have their own money, too, but I forget what they call it."

Gianfranco needed a moment to take all that in and to realize what it had to mean. "You don't have any Soviet Union?" he blurted. He might have been an antelope on the plain, saying, *You don't have any lions?* to another antelope from some distant grassland.

"Not for more than a hundred years, not in our timeline." Eduardo chuckled. "You might say Communism withered away."

"But that's . . ." Gianfranco's voice withered away before he could bring out *impossible*. He looked at the computer in the palm of Eduardo's hand. Before he saw it, he would have said *it* was impossible. Only the very most important, very most trusted people got to use computers at all. They were just too dangerous, or so the authorities insisted. And no computer looked like a little box that sprouted a screen at an oral command.

Except this one.

"What are you doing here?" Annarita asked.

"Keeping an eye on things, you might say," Eduardo replied.

But that wasn't the whole answer. It couldn't be—Gianfranco saw as much right away. And he saw what some of the real answer had to be. "You *are* counterrevolutionaries!" he said.

Annarita exclaimed softly. Her father blinked. And Eduardo . . . Eduardo turned red. "We're not the kind who assassinate people or blow things up," he said. "We've seen way too much of that back home. We still have too much of it there."

"What other kind could there be?" Annarita sounded bewildered. Gianfranco understood why. Anyone who grew up on the history of the glorious October Revolution and the civil war that followed learned how violence and force drove history forward.

But Eduardo said, "We try to change people's minds. The government and social structure you have now are the thesis. There hasn't been a new antithesis here in a long time, because the powers that be suppress any ideas they don't like. We were doing our best to make one, and to aim for a better synthesis."

He talked in terms of Marx's dialectic. But he and his friends plainly were—had been—aiming to overthrow the ideas that lay behind the Italian People's Republic, if not the republic itself.

"What will you do?" Gianfranco asked. "They're on to you. You won't change any minds in the Security Police."

Instead of answering, Eduardo turned to Dr. Crosetti.

"They're smart," he said. "Between them, they've come up with the same questions you did."

"They've come up with better ones," Annarita's father said. "And I'd like to know what you're going to do, too."

"So would I," Eduardo said bleakly. "If I can be Cousin Silvio for a while, that would sure help. But they'll be watching The Gladiator like a hawk from now on. Same with The Conductor's Cap down in Rome. Those are two of the places where I could get back to my own timeline. I can't do it just anywhere. I don't sprout wings, and it wouldn't help if I did."

"You didn't say those were the only two places." Gianfranco felt like a detective listening for clues. "Where are the others?"

"There's only one more—if it's still open," Eduardo answered. "It's . . . Maybe I'd better not say. I've said way too much already. I'll probably get in trouble for it if I do get home, but I'll worry about that later. I'm in trouble right here. When you're in this kind of mess, you do what you have to do, that's all."

Gianfranco thought about pushing him, then decided that wasn't a good idea. Instead, he grinned at Annarita. "So you've got a new cousin, do you?"

"I guess I do," she said, and nodded at Eduardo. "*Ciao*, Cousin Silvio."

"*Ciao*, Cousin Annarita," Eduardo answered gravely. He didn't look much like her, but cousins didn't have to.

Pointing to him, Gianfranco said, "You're going to have to pay a price for my silence, you know."

"Gianfranco!" Annarita sounded as if she'd just found him in her apple.

"How much?" Eduardo sounded worried, or maybe downright alarmed. "Most of the time, it would be easy, but I can't get my hands on a whole lot of cash right now. Having the Security Police on your tail will do that to you." He managed a wry chuckle that he probably didn't mean.

"What kind of price have you got in mind, Gianfranco?" By the way Dr. Crosetti asked the question, he'd pitch Gianfranco through a wall head first if he didn't like the answer.

But Gianfranco only grinned. "*Rails across Europe.* Lots and lots of *Rails across Europe!*"

Annarita started to giggle. Her father managed a thin smile. Gianfranco got the idea that that was the same as cracking up for most people. Eduardo's laugh was full of relief. "Well, that can probably be arranged. You'll wipe the floor with me, though. I just sell the games. I didn't play them a whole lot."

"I bet you're sandbagging," Gianfranco said. "That way, you can beat me and then look surprised."

"If I beat you, I will look surprised. I promise."

"Can three play?" Annarita asked.

Gianfranco and Eduardo both looked surprised. "Well, yes," Gianfranco said, "but . . ." *Are you sure you really want to?* was what he swallowed this time.

"I was having fun with the game we started," she said. "I'd like to play some more . . . if the two of you don't mind."

"It's all right with me," Eduardo said. "How could I tell my cousin no?" He winked again.

That left it up to Gianfranco—except he didn't really have a choice. If he said no, he'd look like a jerk. And, even though Annarita didn't know what she was doing yet, she was plenty smart. If she wanted to, she could learn. "Why not?" he said. "Three people complicate things all kinds of interesting ways."

Eduardo laughed out loud again. Dr. Crosetti coughed dryly. Annarita looked annoyed. Gianfranco wondered what he'd said that was so funny.

Annarita feared the Security Police would swoop down on her apartment and cart Eduardo off to jail. She also feared they would cart her whole family off with him. They did things like that. Everybody knew it.

When it didn't happen right away, she relaxed—a little. Gianfranco's family took Cousin Silvio for granted. She'd never thought his folks were very bright or very curious. Up till now, that had always seemed a shame to her. All of a sudden, it looked like a blessing in disguise.

Nobody thought anything was strange when Gianfranco dragooned Cousin Silvio into playing his railroad game. Gianfranco would have dragooned the cat into playing if it could roll dice instead of trying to kill them. And if Annarita played too, well, maybe she was just being polite for her cousin's sake.

And maybe she was, at least at first. But *Rails across Europe* was a good game, no two—or three—ways about it. It got harder with three players. Whoever got ahead found the other two ganging up on him . . . or her.

At school, Ludovico backed Maria's motion to change the minority report about The Gladiator to the majority. The motion passed without much comment. Annarita didn't argue against it. How could she, when the Security Police had closed the place down—and when she had a fugitive in her apartment pretending to be her cousin?

Victory made Maria smug. "Nice you finally quit complaining," she said to Annarita after the meeting. "It would have been even better, though, if you'd given some proper self-criticism. Some people will still think you're a capitalist backslider."

"I'll just have to live with it," Annarita said. Maria had no idea how much of a capitalist backslider she really was.

And Maria also had no idea that she had such good reasons for being a backslider. All Maria knew about capitalism was what she'd learned in school. It was dead here, and the people who'd killed it spent all their time afterwards laughing at the corpse. They honestly believed the system they had worked better than the one they'd beaten.

Annarita had believed the same thing. Why not? It was drummed into everybody every day, even before you started school. Every May Day, the whole world celebrated the rise of Communism and scorned the evils of capitalism. Nobody had any standards of comparison.

Nobody except Annarita and her father and mother and Gianfranco. Eduardo talked about a world without the Security Police, a world where people could say what they wanted and do as they pleased without getting in trouble with the government. Well, talk was cheap. But people in Eduardo's world had invented machines that took them across the timelines to this one. No one here even imagined such a thing was possible.

"It isn't possible here," Eduardo said when she mentioned that. "You don't have the technology to go crosstime."

The offhand way he said it made her mad. He might have been telling her that her whole world was nothing but a bunch of South Sea Islanders next to his. "We can do all kinds of things!" she said. "We've been to the moon and back. Why do you say we couldn't build one of your crosstime engines or whatever you call them?"

"Because you can't," he answered, and took his computer

out of his shirt pocket. "See this?" Reluctantly, she nodded. She knew her world had nothing like it. He went on, "Anybody—everybody—back home carries one of these, or a laptop that's a little bigger and stronger. This one's nothing special, but it's got more power than one of your mainframes. Our real computers—the ones you can't carry around—are a lot smarter than this one."

How could she help but believe him? He was there, in her front room, holding that impossible gadget. The more of what it could do he showed her, the more amazed she got. It played movies—movies she'd never seen, never heard of, before, which argued that they didn't come from her world. It created letters and reports. It did complicated math in the blink of an eye. It had a map that showed all of Italy street by street, almost house by house.

That impressed her, both because the map was so interesting and because he was allowed to have it. "A lot of maps here are secret," she said.

"I know," Eduardo answered, and let it go right there. She'd always taken secrecy for granted. You couldn't trust just anybody with information . . . could you? In two words, he asked her, *Why can't you?* She found she couldn't tell him.

One question she did ask was, "Well, why do you bother with us at all if we're so backward?"

"Oh, you're not," he said. "You aren't as far along as we are, but there are plenty of low-tech alternates where the people would think this was heaven on earth. You could be free. We think you ought to be free. We think everybody ought to be free. We were trying to nudge you along a bit, you might say."

"With game shops?" Annarita asked.

"Sure," Eduardo said. "There's an old song in my timeline

about a spoonful of sugar helping medicine go down easier. If we just showed up here and said, 'No, no, you're doing everything all wrong,' what would happen?"

"The Security Police would come after you," Annarita answered. "But they came after you anyway."

"Sì," he said mournfully. "But it took them longer, and we got to spread our ideas more than we would have if we tried to go into politics or something."

"You really are counterrevolutionaries," she said.

"We didn't have the revolution," Eduardo said. "The home timeline's not a perfect place—not even close. I'd be lying if I said it was. But we live better in our Italy than you do in this one. We don't have to share kitchens and bathrooms—and in the poor people's apartments here they crowd two or three families into one flat. We don't do that."

Annarita sighed. "A place all to ourselves *would* be nice."

"Sure it would. And we eat better than you do, too. You're not starving or anything—I will say that for you—but we eat better. Our clothes are more comfortable. I won't talk about style. That's a matter of taste. Our cars are quieter and safer than yours, and they pollute a lot less. We have plenty of things you don't, too—everything from computers for everybody to fasartas."

"What's a fasarta?" Annarita asked.

Eduardo was the one who sighed now. "If I'd gone back in time to 1850 instead of across it and I tried to explain radio, I'd talk about voices and music coming out of the air. People would think I was hearing things. They'd lock me up in an insane asylum and lose the key. Some things you need to experience. Explaining them doesn't make any sense."

"Try," Annarita said. "I know I'm only a primitive girl from a backward, uh, alternate, but maybe I'll understand a little."

She said that, but she didn't mean it. No matter what she said, she thought she was bright and sophisticated. She didn't really believe her alternate was backward, either. They had electricity and clean water and atomic energy. What more did they need?

Then she saw the way Eduardo looked at her. To him, she really *was* a primitive girl from a backward place. She could tell. It embarrassed her and made her angry at the same time.

"Fasartas," he said. "Well, I'll do my best." And he talked for a while, and she got the idea that a fasarta made life more worth living, but she couldn't have said exactly how. He saw he wasn't getting through. "For me, a fasarta is like water to a fish. For you, it's more like water to a hedgehog, isn't it?"

"I'm not prickly!" she said, sounding . . . prickly.

"Sure," Eduardo said, sounding all the more smooth and soothing next to her. She'd never heard disagreeing by agreeing done better.

And so she got mad at Eduardo. She got mad at the place he came from—the home timeline, he called it—for having things her Italy didn't . . . freedom, for instance. She was already mad at Maria Tenace for being Maria. She was mad at the Young Socialists' League for paying attention to Maria, even if (no, especially because) Maria turned out to be right. *A stopped clock is right twice a day*, her father sometimes said. She'd thrown that in Maria's face once. And she was mad at Italy— her Italy, the Italy she'd always taken for granted and loved at the same time—for being less perfect, less a workers' paradise, than she'd thought it was.

And she was mad because she couldn't do anything about anything she was mad at. She had to keep her mouth shut, or somebody would knock on the door in the middle of the night. Then she would learn some things about the workers' paradise that everybody already knew, but no one wanted to discover at first hand. She felt as if she wanted to explode. She knew she couldn't, of course. Maybe that made her maddest of all.

Seven

In the Mazzillis' apartment, Gianfranco's father looked up from the report on the latest Communist Party Congress and said, "That cousin the Crosettis have staying with them seems like a nice young fellow."

"I think so, too." Gianfranco was glad to get away from his literature project, even if it meant talking with his father. The assignment was, *Write a canto in the style of Dante's* Inferno. *Which feudal lords, capitalists, and Fascists would you assign to which circles of hell? Why?*

How was he supposed to do anything like that? To begin with, he was no poet. Then, Dante's language was almost nine hundred years old now. It lay at the core of modern Italian, but nobody had a style like Dante's any more. Would anybody be crazy enough to ask a modern English-speaker to try to write like Chaucer, or even Shakespeare? Gianfranco hoped not, anyhow.

"Yes, that Silvio seems very friendly," his father went on. "You talk with him like you've known him a long time."

Oops, Gianfranco thought. He had known Eduardo for a while, of course. But it wasn't supposed to show. "He has interesting things to say," Gianfranco answered.

"Good. And it's nice that he plays that game you were

teaching Annarita." His father paused, looking for a way to say what he wanted. "If he didn't already know about it, you might have wanted to think before you showed it to him. Annarita's all right, but some people might wonder if you were politically reliable for having it around."

This was the first time he'd said anything about The Gladiator, even in passing. Gianfranco had wondered if he even knew the gaming shop got closed down. There were times when Gianfranco wondered just how connected to the real world his father was. Maybe more than he'd figured. That meant he had to be even more careful than he'd thought.

"It's only a game, Father," he said, as if no other possibility had ever crossed his mind.

"Nothing is *only* anything." His father sounded very sure of that. Gianfranco wondered what it meant, or if it meant anything. He started to ask. Then he noticed his father was deep in the Party Congress report again.

That meant he had to get back to imitating Dante himself. *Rails across Europe* had taught him something about dealing with big, complicated projects. If you could break them down into smaller, simpler pieces and tackle those pieces one at a time, you had a better chance than if you tried to tackle everything at once.

So . . If he were traveling through the circles of hell, whom would he see? He needed to figure that out first. Then he could decide why they were there. And after that . . . Well, after that he could try to sound like Dante. He didn't think he would have much luck, but he didn't think anyone else in the class would, either.

Feudal lords, capitalists, and Fascists. The assignment made it plain he needed at least one of each. The Fascist would be Hitler. He'd already decided that. And he'd put Hitler as close to Satan as he could, because Hitler attacked Stalin and the Soviet Union. Probably more than half the class would pick Hitler, but Gianfranco couldn't help that. Mussolini was the other choice, and he didn't do as much.

"Capitalist," Gianfranco muttered, not loud enough for his father to hear him. When you thought of a capitalist, you thought of . . .

When Gianfranco thought of a capitalist, he thought of Henry Ford. And Ford would definitely do. He made millions of dollars and exploited his workers doing it. Gianfranco had to check a map of Dante's hell to decide which circle to put him in.

The fifth, he decided: the circle of hoarders and spend-thrifts. Didn't that say what capitalists were all about?

Now he needed a feudal lord, and one Dante hadn't used. He smiled when Francesco Sforza came to mind. Sforza had ruled here in Milan. The big castle near the heart of town was his creation. Since he'd taken the city by force in 1450, he probably belonged in the sixth circle of hell, that of the wrath-ful. And Dante had never heard of Francesco Sforza, because the poet was long dead when the soldier of fortune came to power.

I have my people, Gianfranco thought. *Now all I've got to do is sound like Dante.* That would have been funny if it weren't so ridiculous. He could think of all kinds of people he might be when he grew up. He could imagine himself as a game designer if everything went just right. He could imagine himself as a gray functionary like his father if everything went wrong. But a poet? A poet wasn't in the cards.

Still, he had to try. He could steal some lines from Dante and change names. He could adapt some others. But he still had to write some of his own. He had to think about that old-fashioned Italian, and about the rhythm, and about the right number of syllables in every line, *and* about what he was trying to say. It was harder than patting his head and rubbing his stomach at the same time.

Finally, though, he wasn't too unhappy with what he had. "Do you want to listen to my verses, Father?" he asked.

His father looked at the report on the Party Congress. Gianfranco thought he would say no, but he nodded. "Well, why not?" he answered. "They've got to be more interesting than this thing. Doctors could bore patients to sleep with this, and save the cost of ether."

That didn't mean he was eager to listen to Gianfranco, but he'd said he would. Listening was all that really mattered. Gianfranco did his best imitation of Dante. He'd just started Hitler, whom he'd saved for last, when his father broke out laughing. Gianfranco broke off, insulted. "It's not *that* bad," he said.

"*Scusi. Scusi,*" his father said, laughing still. "I wasn't laughing at the poetry."

"No? What, then?" Gianfranco knew he sounded suspicious—he was.

"When I was in high school, oh, a thousand years ago, we had this same assignment," his father said. "I haven't thought about it from then till now, but we did. And do you know the people I picked?"

A light went on in Gianfranco's head. "Ford and Sforza and Hitler?"

His father nodded. "*Sì.* Ford and Sforza and Hitler. So *that's* why I was laughing. Some of what you wrote even sounds familiar, but I can't prove that—it's been too long. Any which way, though, you're a chip off the old block. Now you can finish."

Gianfranco did. He wasn't sure he liked thinking like his father. Like it or not, he didn't know what he could do about it. Probably nothing. "Well, what do you think?" he asked.

"It's not exactly Dante." His father held up a hasty hand. "Neither was mine, believe me. The only one who was Dante . . . was Dante. But it does what it's supposed to do, and I think it's good enough to get you a pretty high grade. All right?"

"I guess so." Gianfranco didn't want to admit too much.

His father eyed him. "You've been doing better in school lately, haven't you?"

"Some, maybe." Gianfranco wondered where that was going. Would his father ask him why he hadn't done so well before? That would be good for a row.

But it didn't go anywhere much. His father just said, "Well, I'm glad," and went back to the Party Congress report. Gianfranco'd been ready to argue. Now he didn't have anything to argue about. He felt vaguely deflated as tension leaked out of him.

He'd got rid of the assignment, anyway. He stuck it in his notebook and looked to see what he had to do for history.

"Why can't you telephone your friends—wherever they are— and find out if they're all right?" Annarita asked Eduardo. *Silvio*, she told herself. *He has to be Silvio.*

"Well, I will if I have to, but I don't much want to," Eduardo answered. "Even if nobody's dropped on them, the Security Police are bound to be tapping their telephone lines. I don't want to do anything to hurt them, or to give myself away, either."

"Ah." Annarita nodded. "I thought you might have ways to get around the bugs."

"I don't, not with me. They do," Eduardo said. "But they don't use them all the time—what would the point be? So chances are I'd give myself away before they realized who I was. We don't work miracles. I wish we did."

"You have that little computer in your pocket, and you tell me you don't?" Annarita worked an eyebrow. If that gadget wasn't a miracle, she'd never seen one.

But Eduardo shook his head. "The computer can work by itself. If I use the telephone or write a letter, it has to go through the government phone lines or the postal system."

"You don't have your own phones?" Annarita was disappointed.

"Sure we do. There's one in the computer, in fact. It works great in the home timeline, but not here," Eduardo said. "A phone isn't just a phone—it's part of a network. The only network it can be part of here is the one you've already got. We don't have our own satellites—people would notice if we launched one. They'd notice if we built our own relay towers, too, even if we did disguise them as trees or something."

Annarita laughed. He was right, no doubt about it. He and the other people from his home timeline had been thinking about this stuff longer than she had. They had more of the answers worked out than she did.

But one other thing occurred to her. "If you can use your computer like a phone, can you use it like a radio, too?"

"Not . . . as far off as my friends are, if they're still here," Eduardo said. "And even if I could, the Security Police would be listening. Best thing I can do right now is sit tight and wait for the hullabaloo to die down. Maybe the goons will decide everybody got away and stop being interested in me."

"Maybe." Annarita didn't believe it. "From what Gianfranco said, the Security Police knew you weren't with the others."

Eduardo sighed. "You're right, of course, no matter how much I wish you were wrong. I don't dare take anything for granted."

"Do you want to hear something funny?" Annarita asked.

"Right now, I'd *love* to hear something funny," Eduardo answered. "What is it?"

"Talking about Gianfranco put it into my head," Annarita said. "I think he's jealous of you." She laughed to show how silly that was.

By the look on Eduardo's face, he didn't think it was even a little silly. He seemed ready to jump up from the sofa and run. "How jealous? Jealous why?" he demanded. "That could be very bad. He's a Party official's kid. If he goes to the Security Police, they'll listen to him, sure as the devil."

"He wouldn't do that!" Annarita could imagine Gianfranco doing a lot of things, but turning informer? She didn't believe it.

"Hmm." Eduardo didn't sound convinced. He didn't know Gianfranco the way she did. But her neck wasn't on the line— at least not directly—and Eduardo's was. He went on, "You didn't answer my question. What's he jealous about?"

"Well, he kind of likes me," Annarita said. "And here you are, staying in the same apartment with me. And you're already grown up and everything, and he's . . . not finished, if you know what I mean."

"*Diavolo!*" Eduardo clapped a hand to his forehead. "Will you please tell him nothing's going on? Nothing will be going on, either. Or maybe I should talk to him myself. *Sì*, that'd be better. I'll do it."

"*Grazie*," Annarita said. "The whole idea is silly, anyway."

"Well . . . Not as silly as you think, maybe," Eduardo said slowly. "If you were twenty-one, say, instead of seventeen . . . If I weren't in a jam . . ." He kept starting sentences he didn't finish. "But you aren't, and I am," he went on, confusing Annarita till she figured out what he meant. "And so, the way things are, nothing's going on, and nothing's going to go on. Right?"

"Uh, right," Annarita said. She wasn't just confused now—she was flustered. She realized Eduardo had paid her a compliment, and not a small one, either. She'd probably never had one, though, that she felt less ready to deal with. If Gianfranco liked her, that was one thing. She knew what she needed to do about it—not much. If Eduardo liked her, or could like her . . .

Now she was starting sentences and not finishing them. And maybe that was just as well, too.

Gianfranco rolled the dice and moved his locomotive from Berlin toward Vienna. When he got there, he was going to unload beer and fill his train with chocolate for the return trip.

Annarita yawned. "What time is it?" she asked.

"Getting on towards one in the morning," Eduardo said after looking at his watch.

She yawned again. "I'm going to bed. I don't care if tomorrow—I mean, today—is Sunday. I'm too sleepy to play anymore. Good night." She slipped away before Gianfranco could even try to talk her into going on a little longer.

He sighed and shrugged. "We'll just mark everything and pick it up again later on."

"Right." Eduardo took care of that and put the game back in the box. Then he said, "It ought to be pretty quiet out on the street, right? Come on out, why don't you? I've got some stuff I want to talk to you about."

"What kind of stuff?" Gianfranco asked.

"Stuff, that's what." Eduardo got up. "You coming or not?"

"I'm coming," Gianfranco said. "What do you want to say out there that you don't want to say in here?"

Eduardo didn't answer. Whatever it was, he *didn't* want to say it in here. They went down the stairs together. Somebody from the floor above Gianfranco's was coming up. He'd had a good bit to drink. "*Ciao*," he said thickly. He reeled on the stairs. Gianfranco hoped he wouldn't trip and break his neck.

It was cool and dark and quiet outside. Well, not too quiet—Milan was a big city. In the distance, car horns blared. Dogs were barking. Somebody yelled at somebody else. But none of that was close. Gianfranco and Eduardo could stand on the sidewalk and not worry about it.

Gianfranco looked up into the sky. Even at one in the morning, city lights washed out all but the brighter stars. But he hadn't come out here to find the Big Dipper. "So what's going on?" he asked Eduardo.

"I'm not trying to take your girl away," the older man said bluntly. "I'm not—all right?"

"Annarita's not my girl," Gianfranco said with a sour laugh. "Ask her if you don't believe me."

"She's more your girl than she is mine," Eduardo said. "That's how it'll stay, too. She's too young for me, for one thing. And I don't belong here. This isn't my world. What I want most is to get back to the home timeline."

He'd said that before, but never so strongly. "You have somebody back there waiting for you?" Gianfranco asked.

"Not . . . like that, no," Eduardo admitted. "But it's my

home. It's where I belong. So I'm not trying to muscle in on you, *capisce?*"

"I never said you were," Gianfranco answered. True—he hadn't. But that didn't mean it wasn't on his mind.

"All right. But I wanted you to know. You don't have anything to worry about there, anyhow," Eduardo said.

"Thanks." Gianfranco said it even if he wasn't sure he meant it. *If Annarita decides she likes Eduardo, what can I do about it?* he wondered. But he knew the answer to that—he couldn't do anything. And she might. Eduardo was an older man, he wasn't bad-looking, and he had a genuine mystery hanging over him. What could be more intriguing? And even if she didn't, Gianfranco knew he had other things to worry about. The Security Police, for instance. He shivered, though it wasn't very cold. "Let's go back inside."

"Sure," Eduardo said. "But I wanted you to hear that, and I wanted to make sure nobody else did."

They both turned to walk back up the steps. A police car came around the corner as they did. A spotlight blinded Gianfranco. "Stay right there!" one of the *carabinieri* called. "Let's see your papers! What are you doing out on the street in the middle of the night?"

Gianfranco's teeth started to chatter. He had his identity card and his internal passport with him. He would no more go outside without them than without his pants. Nobody would, not in the Italian People's Republic, not anywhere. He assumed Eduardo had his papers, too. But would they pass muster?

Both policemen got out of the car. One covered Eduardo and Gianfranco with a submachine gun while the other came up and held out his hand. He looked at Gianfranco's documents first. Nodding, he gave them back. "I know who your father is. But who's this guy?"

"I'm Dr. Crosetti's cousin," Eduardo said, giving the policeman his papers. "I'm staying in their apartment till I find something for myself here."

"He is," Gianfranco said.

"How do you know, kid?" the policeman asked.

"I ought to. We share a kitchen and bathroom with the Crosettis," Gianfranco answered.

The policeman only grunted. He shone his flashlight on Eduardo's papers. "Is he all right?" the other policeman asked. "Shall I radio headquarters?"

No! Gianfranco all but screamed it. That wouldn't do anybody any good. He bit down on the inside of his lower lip. "I don't *think* so," said the *carabiniere* with Eduardo's papers. Instead of returning them, he asked, "What *are* you doing out here at this time of night?"

"Talking about girls," Eduardo answered, and it wasn't even a lie.

The policeman thought it over. After a moment, he decided it was funny and laughed. Even better, he handed back the identity card and internal passport. "Well, Pagnozzi, that's a nice way to pass the time, but do it somewhere else from now on, you hear?"

"We'll do that." Eduardo stuck them in his pockets. "Thanks."

With another grunt, the *carabiniere* turned to his partner. "They're clean. And we got that drunk an hour ago, so we're on quota. Let's go."

They drove off. Gianfranco noticed his knees were knocking. He tried to make them stop, but they didn't want to. If the policemen hadn't picked up the drunk, would they have hauled him and Eduardo to the station instead? It sure sounded that way.

Eduardo wore a small, tight smile. "Boy, that was fun, wasn't it?" he said.

"As a matter of fact, no." Gianfranco could play the game of understatement, too. Without another word, he went back into the apartment building.

"You did real well," Eduardo told him as they trudged up the stairs. Would the elevator ever get fixed? Gianfranco wasn't holding his breath.

"Maybe I did," he said after a few steps. "I didn't like it."

"Well, who would?" Eduardo said. "Police shouldn't be able to bother you whenever they want to. In a free country, they can't."

As far as Gianfranco was concerned, he might as well have started speaking Korean. "What would stop them? What *could* stop them?" Gianfranco asked, certain Eduardo had no answer.

But Eduardo did. "The laws would," he said. "If the police do something wrong or bother people they've got no business bothering, they get in trouble."

"How?" Gianfranco still had trouble seeing it. "The police are . . . the police. They're part of the government. The government can't get in trouble." He might have been saying, *The sun will come up tomorrow.*

"Sure it can. Why shouldn't it, if it does something wrong? In a free country, you can sue the government. You can sue the police if they beat you up for no reason. And if a court decides they're guilty, they have to pay." Eduardo spoke with a certain somber relish. "It happens now and again. And because it can happen, the government is more careful about what it does."

"People . . . sue the government?" Gianfranco missed a step. Eduardo grabbed him by the arm and kept him from falling on his face. The idea was so strange, he might have been saying, *The sun will come up tomorrow . . . in the west.*

"Why not?" Eduardo seemed to enjoy provoking him. "You live in the Italian People's Republic, don't you?"

"Yes, but . . ." Gianfranco tried to imagine what would happen if someone tried to sue the government. He didn't need much imagination to figure it out. The Security Police would land on the poor crackbrained fool like a ton of bricks, and that would be that. "What about the Security Police?" he demanded.

"We don't have any, not like that, not to keep track of people who haven't done anything wrong," Eduardo said, and Gianfranco's jaw dropped. Eduardo went on, "We have *carabinieri* to go after criminals, but that's different. Some people *will* try to cheat no matter what kind of society they live in."

"I suppose." Gianfranco wasn't sure he would have walked past his floor if Eduardo didn't hold the door open, but he wasn't sure he wouldn't have, either. Eduardo had hit him with too many new ideas, too hard, too fast. He needed some time to get used to them.

"We wanted things to be like that here, too," Eduardo said as they walked down the hall to the Mazzillis' apartment and the Crosettis'. "That's what we were working toward." He shrugged. "Things don't always turn out the way you wish they would. We'll have to come up with something else and try again, that's all."

He paused at his doorway, Gianfranco at his. They nodded to each other and went inside. Gianfranco undressed and got ready for bed—quietly, so he wouldn't bother his folks. He lay down, but sleep was a long time coming. Some of the things Eduardo had said . . .

A country without Security Police? A country where the people actually had power instead of just giving the state their name? A country where, if people didn't like what the government was up to, they could do something about it? What would that kind of country be like? What would living in that kind of country be like?

Gianfranco didn't know. How could he, when it was so different from everything he'd grown up with? But he knew one thing: he wished he could find out.

After a moment, he realized something else. Without intending to, he'd just turned into a counterrevolutionary. Then he *really* had a hard time going to sleep.

Walking to school Monday morning, Annarita thought Gianfranco seemed quieter than usual. Had Eduardo talked to him? If he had, what had he said? Annarita didn't want to come straight out and ask. She tried a different question, a safer question, instead: "You all right, Gianfranco?"

He blinked. He thought it over. She watched him doing it. "Well, I'm not sure," he said at last, quite seriously.

She eyed him, exasperated and curious at the same time. "What's that supposed to mean?"

He looked around to make sure nobody was paying any special attention to him. In the Italian People's Republic, that kind of glance was automatic for anyone older than seven or so. Annarita suspected it worked the same way all over the world. Gianfranco said, "Wouldn't it be nice if there were no Security Police?"

"Sure it would," Annarita answered. "And it would be nice if everybody were rich and everybody were beautiful, too. Don't sit up nights waiting, that's all."

He said something rude—rude enough to startle her. Then he turned red and said, "*Scusi.* But I'm serious. I really am."

"That's nice," Annarita said. "No matter how serious you are, though, what can you do about it?"

"By myself? Nothing," Gianfranco said. "But if all the people united . . ."

"The Security Police would throw everybody into camps." Annarita finished the sentence when Gianfranco's voice trailed away.

He shook his head. "They couldn't do it to everybody, not all at once. There aren't enough camps for that. Not enough Security Policemen, either."

"Well, in that case the Russians would say we're trying to overthrow Socialism, and they'd invade," Annarita said. "Either they'd build more camps or they'd kill enough people so the ones who are left would fit into the camps they've got."

"But what if the *Russian* people united, too?" Gianfranco said.

Annarita stared at him. "You weren't drinking wine at breakfast. I saw what you had: cappuccino, just like me." Like most Italian kids their age, they did drink wine with dinner. Nobody here fussed about it, though people from northern Europe and America sometimes squawked.

"I was thinking about . . . freedom," Gianfranco said. "That gets you drunk like too much *vino*, but you don't come down again afterwards."

"I guess not, to look at you," Annarita said. "Be careful you don't get in trouble once you're in school."

"I'll try," Gianfranco said.

A car went two wheels up on the sidewalk in front of them to let somebody off. It still blocked traffic. All the drivers behind the offender leaned on their horns. Some of them yelled at him, too. He ignored them. Annarita wasn't much impressed. She saw things like that almost every day. Keeping Gianfranco out of trouble was more important—and more interesting. Now she could say what she needed to say: "All this talk about freedom. You must have been listening to Cousin Silvio." In public, she wouldn't call him Eduardo.

"Well, what if I was?" Gianfranco said. "He likes to talk, you know."

He does not! But the hot retort never came out. If Annarita said something like that, Gianfranco would be sure she was sweet on Eduardo. And she wasn't, not really. So all she did say was, "What else were you talking about?"

"Oh, stuff," Gianfranco answered vaguely. Annarita wanted to clout him. She kept quiet and waited instead. It wasn't easy, but she did it. When Gianfranco spoke again, a few steps later, he sounded almost like a gruff old man: "He said he wasn't going to run off to Sicily with you."

"I should hope not!" Annarita exclaimed. "It's too hot down there in the summertime, and I wouldn't want to have to try to understand that funny dialect." She paused, too. "I suppose they think we talk funny, too."

"Wouldn't be surprised." Gianfranco took a deep breath. He seemed to look every which way but right at her. "Maybe we could go to a movie or something one of these days before too long."

"Maybe we could," Annarita said. Nothing wrong with a movie. "It might be fun."

Gianfranco lit up like a neon sign. He hopped in the air. He seemed so happy, Annarita wondered if he would come down. He did, of course. "Wonderful!" he said. "How about Friday night?"

"All right," Annarita answered, and he lit up all over again. He didn't seem so worried about freedom and overthrowing the Italian People's Republic any more. He didn't seem so worried about Eduardo, either, which was also good.

Would he have blamed Eduardo if Annarita told him she didn't want to go out with him? She hoped she hadn't said yes to keep him from blaming Eduardo. That was no reason to go to a movie with somebody.

What would I have done if Eduardo asked me? she wondered. After a moment, she shrugged. She didn't know, and she didn't seem likely to find out, either. Eduardo made a point—even stretched a point—of being a gentleman. And he was playing the role of her cousin.

Was that just as well, or was it a shame?

Before she could come close to finding an answer, they got to Hoxha Polytechnic. Then she had to worry about Russian prepositions instead. At least with Russian prepositions, you knew when you were right and when you were wrong. This other stuff? It wasn't nearly so obvious.

Gianfranco wanted to use the bathroom mirror to comb his hair. He'd already used it twice, but that didn't matter to him. He wanted to look perfect, or as close to perfect as he could. He was unhappily aware of the distance between the one and the other.

He couldn't use the bathroom right now because Annarita

was in it. His mother saw his glance toward the door and smiled at him. "She'll be out soon," she said. "She wants to look nice for you. That's good."

"Is it? I guess so." To Gianfranco, Annarita already looked nice. Why did she need to do anything more?

But when she came out, she looked nicer. Gianfranco couldn't have said how, but she did. He ducked in there, ran the comb through his hair again, and wished he wouldn't have picked this exact moment to get a zit on his chin. He couldn't do much about that, though.

He stuck the comb in his pocket and went out again. "Shall we go?" he said, trying to sound like someone who did this all the time.

"Sure." Annarita seemed to take it for granted. Maybe that would help him do the same. He could hope so, anyway.

"Have fun, you two." Eduardo sounded as if he meant it. Gianfranco hoped he did.

"*Grazie*, Cousin Silvio," Annarita said.

She and Gianfranco walked down the stairs together. He wondered if his feet were touching the ground. When they got to the bottom, Annarita said, "It would be nice if the elevator worked. Coming down is easy, but going back up, especially when you're tired. . . ." She shook her head.

"If somebody could make a nice profit fixing elevators, it would have been fixed a long time ago," Gianfranco said.

She looked at him as if he'd just told a dirty joke. His ears got hot. Profit was evil—everybody learned that in school. But then she sighed. She looked around to make sure no one could overhear, then said, "Cousin Silvio tells me the same thing. It still feels wrong, though—know what I mean?"

"*Sì*," he answered. "But what we've got doesn't work the

way it's supposed to. If it did, the elevator would run. So shouldn't we think differently?"

"I don't know if we should think that different," Annarita said.

"Why not?" he asked.

She gave a perfectly practical answer: "Because we'll get in trouble with the Security Police if we make too much noise about profit. Look what happened to The Gladiator."

"Somebody ought to do something about the Security Police," Gianfranco said. "They just hold us back."

Annarita stopped, right there outside the apartment building. "If you keep talking like that, I'm going back upstairs. It's not safe to be around you. It's not safe to be anywhere near you. Cut it out, all right?"

He wished he could tell her she was worrying too much. He wished he could, but he knew he couldn't. "All right," he said meekly. "Let's go watch the movie."

"That's more like it," Annarita said. "This other stuff . . . Do you *want* to end up a zek in a camp?"

There shouldn't be zeks. There shouldn't be camps. If Gianfranco said that, he'd just get in more trouble with Annarita, no matter how true it was. But people who couldn't learn to keep their mouths shut were the kind who did end up in camps. So all he said was, "No," which was also true. Annarita nodded. Not only was it true, it was the right answer—not always the same thing.

The theater was about three blocks from their apartment building. It was showing a remake of the great early Soviet film, *Battleship Potemkin*. Gianfranco had seen the black-and-white original—with Italian subtitles—in his history class. So had almost everybody. He knew Annarita had. Even though it was more than 150 years old, with acting ridiculously over the top, it still had the power of a punch in the face.

He bought tickets, then sodas and roasted chestnuts when he went inside. When he and Annarita sat down, other people nearby were already crunching away. "Do you think it will be as good as the first one?" he asked her—that was a safe question.

"Remakes hardly ever are," she said. "People who do something the first time really mean it. The ones who do remakes are just copycats."

Gianfranco thought about that for a little while, then nodded. "You say interesting things, you know?" he said.

She shrugged. The house lights dimmed. The newsreel came on. Halfway through a story about a dam going up in South America (and how many of the laborers building it were zeks?), something went wrong with the projector. The house lights came up again. "One moment, please!" someone called from the projectionist's booth.

That moment stretched and stretched. People got restless. "Fix it, you bums!" a man with a deep voice yelled.

"Don't you know how to fix it?" somebody else said. No one from up in the booth answered. Gianfranco feared that meant nobody up there did know.

After a few minutes where nothing happened, a wit sang out: "You must be the jerks who worked on my car!" He won a laugh.

The house lights went down again. Sarcastic cheers rose. The newsreel started once more—upside down. Billions of liters of water seemed ready to spill out from behind the dam. The audience booed and jeered. The newsreel stopped. The lights brightened. "Sorry about that!" a man called from the booth. People went on booing.

At last, after half an hour or so, they got it right and fin-

ished the newsreel. It probably got more applause at that theater than anywhere else in Italy. The remake of *Battleship
Potemkin* started. It was a Russian film dubbed into Italian. All
the effects were bigger and fancier than the ones in the original.
It was in color. The actors didn't ham it up. It should have been
better than Eisenstein's version, but Gianfranco found himself
yawning, not getting excited.

"You're right," he whispered to Annarita. "It's no big deal."

"Well, so what?" she whispered back. "We got to watch an
upside-down newsreel instead. That's more interesting than the
movie would have been even if it were good."

She was right again. Gianfranco wouldn't have thought of it
like that, but he knew the truth when he heard it. He stopped
being so disappointed in *Battleship Potemkin* and settled down
to watch it—and to listen to it. All the boring speeches about
the glorious Soviet Revolution, all the propaganda about the
wicked Russian landowners and capitalists . . . Everything
seemed different to him now that he knew Eduardo.

He wasn't the only one yawning. People had a lot of practice tuning out propaganda. But being bored didn't seem
enough. What would happen if he yelled, *We'd be better off if
the Revolution failed!*?

That was a dumb question. He knew what would happen.
They'd grab him and haul him off to a camp. His father would
get in trouble, too, for raising a subversive son. However much
he wanted to come out and tell the truth, the price would be too
high to pay.

Can we ever change things, then? he wondered. If they were
ever going to, *somebody* would have to stand up and tell the
government it was wrong. Somebody, yes, but who? Who would
be that brave? Gianfranco wished he knew.

Eight

"Did you have a good time at the movie?" Eduardo asked after Annarita came back to her apartment.

"Well, the remake wasn't anything much, but we had fun anyway." She told him about the foul-up with the newsreel.

"That's pretty good," he said, smiling. "Or pretty bad, depending on how you look at things. They make movies over again in the home timeline, too, and most of the time you wish they didn't."

"Why do they, then?" Annarita said. "If you're so free, why don't you make new things all the time?"

"Because doing old, familiar ones over again makes the studios money," Eduardo answered.

Annarita's mouth twisted. "Profit doesn't sound so wonderful, then."

"It's not perfect. Nothing's perfect, far as I can see," Eduardo said. "But it works better than this—most of the time, anyhow."

"Have they remade *Battleship Potemkin* in the, uh, home timeline?" Annarita asked. Then another question occurred to her: "Do you even have *Battleship Potemkin* there?"

"We've got the original, *sì*," Eduardo replied. "It dates from before the breakpoint. Up till then, everything's the same in both alternates. But here, the Soviet Union won the Cold War. There, the United States did. The United States is still the strongest country in the home timeline. It throws its weight around sometimes, but it doesn't sit on everybody else all the time the way the USSR does here."

Annarita tried to imagine a world that had branched off from hers somewhere in the middle of the twentieth century. Why did the two alternates separate? Somebody decided something one way here, a different way over there. And this alternate turned out ordinary, and in that one. . . . In that one, they had computers that fit in your pocket. They had a way to travel between alternates.

They had freedom, too. Annarita had hardly known she missed it till Eduardo's arrival made her think about it. She didn't want to run up barricades and start an uprising the way Gianfranco seemed to, but she could tell what wasn't there and should have been.

"And yes, they did make *Potemkin* again in the home timeline," Eduardo said. "This was before I was born, you understand. The remake sank like a rock. When people watch now, they watch the original."

"In theaters, you mean," Annarita said.

"Well, there, too," Eduardo said. "But we can get recorded disks with movies on them and watch on our TVs. Or we can pay a little and download the films from the Net and watch them on our computers."

"You showed me that before," Annarita said. "I still don't see how you can put a whole movie, let alone lots of movies, on a little thing like the one in your pocket."

He grinned at her. "Easy as pie. You could do it here, too—

not as well, but you could. You know enough. Your governments won't let you, though. Anything that spreads information around so easily is dangerous to them."

Annarita found herself nodding. In a country that registered typewriters like guns and kept computers under lock and key for the trusted elite, the idea that everybody could own a computer and use it all kinds of ways had to seem like anarchy loosed upon the world. But that wasn't the main thing on her mind. "You've just let me see little bits of the movies from your home timeline, to show that they weren't from here," she said. "Could I watch a whole one?"

"I'm supposed to tell you no," he answered. "You're not supposed to know what things are like there. But sometimes you've got to bend the rules. And so . . ." He pulled the little box from his pocket and told it to display its screen. Annarita had to lean forward to see well. It wasn't like watching a movie in the theater, or even on TV.

The movie was called *The Incredibles*. It wasn't like anything Annarita had ever seen before, or even imagined. It wasn't live action, but it wasn't exactly a cartoon, either. "How do they do that?" she asked partway through.

"More computers," Eduardo said. "This one's ninety years old. It's a classic, sure, but they can do a lot more now."

She wasn't fussy. *The Incredibles* might seem old-fashioned to him, but it was thousands of kilometers ahead of anything people here were doing. And it was a good movie, no matter how they did it. It was funny, and the plot made sense. The writers didn't lose track of details, the way they did too often here.

When Annarita remarked on that, Eduardo nodded. "It

happens in the home timeline, too. Some people are stupid. Some people are lazy. Some are greedy, and out for quick money. But I bet it happens more here, because there's less competition. Bad movies here don't bomb. They just bore people over and over again."

"Well, you're right." Annarita remembered how many times she'd seen some movies. The authorities put them out there, and they didn't put anything else out there opposite them. If you wanted to go to a movie, you went to one of them. "They call them classics."

"That would be fine if they really were," Eduardo said. "The original *Battleship Potemkin* is—no arguments. But a lot of them are just turkeys from the Propaganda Ministry."

"Turkeys?" Annarita needed a second to figure that out. Maybe it was slang in his home timeline, but it wasn't here. When she got it, she laughed. "You know what else was amazing in *The Incredibles?*"

"No, but you're going to tell me, so that's all right." Eduardo could tease without making it sting. From everything Annarita had seen, that was a rare talent.

"I *am* going to tell you," she agreed. "All those houses. Rows and rows of houses, with lots of middle-class people— well, middle-class cartoon people—living in them. Even though the movie is animated, it's based on something real, isn't it?"

"*Sì,*" Eduardo said. "But it's based on the United States, where they have more room than they do here. And the United States had more room at the start of the twenty-first century than it does now. But Italy was mostly apartments even then— only rich people had houses."

"Rich people." Annarita said the words as if they were almost obscene. And, in the Italian People's Republic, they were. "We don't have rich people here." She spoke with more than a little pride.

Eduardo wasn't impressed. "You ought to have rich people. Rich people aren't what's wrong. Poor people are. Compared to the way people live in the home timeline, everybody here is poor."

"You can say that," Annarita sniffed. Yes, she took pride in her country the way it was. Who wouldn't? It was *hers*. Inside, though, she feared Eduardo was right. If everybody in his world had a pocket computer, who could guess what else people there had? He'd talked about fasartas, and she didn't even know just what they did.

Instead of reminding her of that, he took a different tack: "You know what you have instead of rich people?"

"What?" she asked suspiciously.

"Apparatchiks," he said.

Apparatchiks weren't all bad. They made the wheels of government turn . . . when the wheels did turn. Gianfranco's father was an apparatchik, though he would have got mad if you said so. Apparatchiks always thought other people were apparatchiks. What they did themselves was important. If you didn't believe it, you could just ask them.

And Eduardo had hit that nail right on the head. Apparatchiks might not have a lot of money in the bank. But they got the best apartments, the best summer houses, the best cars, and doctors. Annarita's father had this flat because a lot of his patients were apparatchiks.

Apparatchiks also got to travel more than ordinary people

did. Their children got into good universities whether they deserved to or not. If you quarreled with an apparatchik and you were just somebody ordinary, you were in trouble if he took you to court. They might not have money, no, but they sure had privileges.

"What can we do about that?" Annarita asked.

"Make those people really work for a living," Eduardo answered. "If they don't do anything useful, throw the bums out."

"Easy to say. Not so easy to do," Annarita pointed out.

She wondered if he would deny that and try to make a counterrevolution sound simple. She gave him credit when he didn't. "Well, you're right," he said. "That's why we were trying to come at it sideways. We thought we could get new ideas in with the games."

"It didn't work," Annarita said.

"Tell me about it!" Eduardo exclaimed. "We were hoping your government was fatter and lazier than it turned out to be. I'm sure we won't give up, but I'm not sure what we can do right now. I hope like anything I'm not stuck here."

"What about your friends, wherever they are?" she asked.

"If they don't find me, I'll have to try to get hold of them sooner or later," he said. "I hope they didn't have to pull out, too. If they did . . . If they did, I'm in trouble. Sooner or later, the Security Police will start getting closer to me, too." He smiled a crooked smile. "Isn't life grand?"

He had his wonderful computer. He had the memories of all the things his people could do that no one here knew anything about. And all of that did him not one bit of good. Had anyone in the history of the world—in the history of many worlds—ever been so alone?

Comrade Donofrio gave Gianfranco his report card. The algebra teacher actually smiled when he did. "You've improved, Mazzilli," he said.

"*Grazie*, Comrade," Gianfranco answered.

He looked at his grade. A B! He hadn't got a B in math since . . . He couldn't remember the last time he got a B. His grades in his other subjects were up, too. He wouldn't get first honors, but he might get second.

He knew Annarita *would* get first honors. She always did. He knew he would hear about it from his parents, too. *If she does it, why don't you?* How many times had he heard that? More than he wanted to, anyhow. But if he came home with some kind of honors for a change, maybe they wouldn't rag on him so much.

And he did. He got a B+ in history to put him over the top. That was another bolt out of the blue. If *Rails across Europe* hadn't got him interested in the subject, he never could have done it. But the game had, and he did.

He missed The Gladiator. Even with Eduardo next door, he missed the camaraderie and the arguments and the games with different people. He missed having somewhere besides home to go when school let out. He missed the models and the books.

Those books! No wonder you couldn't find them anywhere else! A lot of them came from what Eduardo called the home timeline. Nobody there thought they were subversive. They were just . . . books. And that, or so it seemed to Gianfranco, was how things were supposed to be.

He even got a B– in literature, though he didn't think he had much of a future as a poet. Italian would just have to go on making do with Dante. Gianfranco Mazzilli had other things on his plate.

First among those other things was taking his report card

home and showing it off. He walked back with Annarita and showed it to her. "Good for you, Gianfranco," she said, really sounding pleased. "You mother and father will be happy for you."

"I know you've got a better one," he said.

"So what?" she answered. "You haven't even been interested till now. It's hard to do good work if you don't care."

"*Sì*," he said, and left it right there. Had he said anything more, he might have started babbling out thanks. Annarita understood! He hadn't thought anybody in the world did. In that glowing moment, he wasn't far from being in love.

And what would she do if he said something like *that*? She wouldn't laugh in his face—she was too nice. But she wouldn't take him seriously, either. He didn't feel like listening to jokes, even from Annarita, so he kept his mouth shut.

When he got up to the apartment, his mother was out shopping and his father hadn't come home yet. That left him all dressed up with no place to go. *Like an atheist at his own funeral*, he thought. Even with a good report card, he didn't feel like starting in on his homework right away.

He turned on the TV. He'd always taken it for granted before. Now he saw that the picture wasn't nearly so sharp as the one on the screen of Eduardo's impossible handheld computer. The colors weren't so bright and vivid, either. Gianfranco wanted a machine like that. He wanted a world where everybody used a machine like that.

He had . . . this. Four channels showed different flavors of propaganda. The news told him how the goals for the twenty-third Five-Year Plan were being exceeded. The goals for the other Five-Year Plans had all been exceeded, too. So why weren't things better?

On another channel, a Russian and an Italian were hunting

down an American spy. If a villain wasn't a Nazi, he was bound
to be an American. Sometimes he was an American who
wanted to bring back the Nazis. These days, the USA was
harmless. It did what the USSR told it to do. If it didn't, it suffered. Sometimes it suffered anyway, just because it had been
the Soviet Union's most dangerous rival before the Russians
won the Cold War.

Eduardo said the USA was top dog where he came from.
Gianfranco wondered what that was like. Were all the villains
on American TV Russians? The ones who weren't Nazis, anyhow? He wouldn't have been surprised.

But Eduardo also said the USA was where the idea for computers came from. He said some of the games The Gladiator
sold—had sold—came from there. That made Gianfranco think
better of it than he would have otherwise.

The door opened. In came his father, with a heavy brief-
case. "*Buon giorno*, Father," Gianfranco said. "How are you?"

"Tired," his father answered. "Some of the people in the
provincial planning administration are donkeys. Real donkeys.
They should have reins and harness, so they could haul bread
carts around. We'd get some use out of them that way." He sank
into a chair with a martyred sigh.

He came home complaining about the people he worked
with maybe one day in three. "Guess what?" he said.

"I don't know," his father said. "Will you fetch me a bottle
of beer?"

"Sure." Gianfranco brought him one from the refrigerator.
Then he said, "Guess what?" again.

His father drank half the bottle at one long, blissful pull.
"Ah!" he said. "That's good. Takes the edge off the day—know
what I mean?"

"I suppose." Gianfranco liked wine much better than beer. He tried once more: "Guess what?"

His father paused with the beer bottle halfway to his mouth. "What?" he said at last, and the bottle finished the journey.

"I got second honors," Gianfranco said.

"No kidding?" That made his father stop without emptying the beer. "Not bad, kid, not bad." Then he said what Gianfranco knew what he would say: "I bet Annarita made first."

"She did." Gianfranco couldn't very well deny it, not when it was true. "She always does. Some people are like that."

"Greasy grinds." But his father caught himself. "Can't say Annarita's one of those. She's smart, but she's not stuck-up about it." He did kill the beer then, and set the bottle on the little table next to his chair. "But you got second, eh? How about that? Your first time. Way to go."

"*Grazie*," Gianfranco said.

The way his father looked at the beer bottle, he was thinking about having another one. But he didn't get up, and he didn't send Gianfranco after it, either. "What took you so long?" he asked. "I didn't think you'd ever do it. I didn't think you cared enough."

"Up till this semester, I didn't," Gianfranco said. "Things seemed to get more interesting, though, so I guess I worked harder."

"Well, a little hard work never hurt anybody much," his father said.

Maybe that was a joke. Then again, maybe it wasn't. That joke about pretending to work and pretending to get paid ran through Gianfranco's mind. Workers got money, but a lot of the time money couldn't buy what they wanted. When the wait for things like TVs and cars and apartments was so long, getting excited about money wasn't easy. Getting excited about work wasn't easy, either.

His father proved as much, saying, "Sometimes I don't know why I bother getting upset with those *asini*. How much will it matter ten years from now? How much will it matter ten days from now?"

Before Gianfranco could answer, his mother walked in. "They had the outfit I wanted in the window at three different shops," she said unhappily. "But when I went in, two were sold out and it was a two months' wait at the third one. Sometimes I think you can only buy things with a prescription."

"If that were so, the Crosettis would have more, and they don't," his father said. "Guess what, though?"

"What?" his mother asked. Only one try—Gianfranco was jealous.

His father pointed at him. "Second honors."

"Gianfranco?" His mother's eyes went big and round. She couldn't have been more surprised had his father said he'd been kidnapped by green men from outer space. "How about that?"

"Not bad, eh?" his father said. "I don't think he takes after either one of us. Must be the milkman."

"Oh, stop that, you—man, you," his mother said. "Besides, when did this building ever have a milkman? Not since before we lived here, that's for sure."

"All right. The plumber, then," his father said.

His mother made as if to throw her purse at his father. She seemed satisfied when he ducked. Then she turned back to Gianfranco. "So why didn't you do this a long time ago? The Crosetti girl always does, regular as clockwork."

There it was again, thrown in his face in a different way. It would have made him angrier if he hadn't known ahead of time it was coming. He shrugged. "I don't know. Things seem more interesting now."

"Annarita's smart. Maybe he thinks he has to be smart, too, if he wants to keep taking her out." His mother talked about him as if he weren't there. That did make him mad.

"Whatever works," his father said. Then he did the same thing: "That can't be all of it, though. The grades are for more time than when he started going out with her."

"Is there anything else you want to say about me?" Gianfranco asked. "Do you want to talk about my shoes, maybe? Or this cut I got shaving my chin?"

"No, I don't think we need to worry about those." His father didn't even notice the sarcasm, which only ticked him off worse. "And your beard isn't as heavy as mine, I don't think, so you won't cut yourself very often."

"My father and my brother—your Uncle Luigi, Gianfranco—only have to shave maybe once every other day," his mother said, so she didn't get it, either. Gianfranco wondered how he'd ended up stuck with such totally normal parents. It didn't seem fair, not when he prided himself on being strange.

"You'll have to tell that Silvio. He'll be happy for you," his father said. "He looks like the kind who got high marks in school."

"Much good it did him," his mother said. "Here he is, scrounging off of family instead of going out and finding work for himself."

"*Sì.*" His father nodded. "He doesn't go anywhere, does he? He couldn't stick any closer to the Crosettis' flat if the Security Police were waiting for him outside."

He was joking. Gianfranco understood that, but only after a

split second of something worse than alarm. He felt as if someone dropped a big icicle down the back of his shirt. The laugh he managed sounded hollow in his own ears, and his smile must have looked pasted on. But his parents didn't notice anything wrong. Most of the time, they just saw what they expected to see.

He often got angry at them for not paying more attention to him. Every once in a while, though, that was nothing but good luck.

He did mention his second honors at dinner, but only after his mother poked him in the ribs three different times. "Yes, Annarita already told us," her father said. "Good for you. Sooner or later, studying usually pays off. Sometimes it's so much later that it hardly seems worth it at the time, though. I can't say anything different."

A lot of families would have thrown Annarita's first honors back in the Mazzillis' faces like a grenade. None of the Crosettis said a word. To listen to them, she might have earned ordinary marks, not outstanding ones. In their own quiet way, they had style.

"*Bravo*, Gianfranco!" Eduardo—"Cousin Silvio"—said. "Good grades impress people—more than they should sometimes, but they do."

Is that true in his home timeline, too? Gianfranco wondered. *Too bad if it is.* Because the home timeline was the source of the games and books and ideas he liked so much, he thought everything about it should be perfect.

He got a chance to talk with Eduardo about that a couple of days later. "No, no, no." Eduardo shook his head. "Don't idealize us. If you think you've found paradise anywhere, you're bound to be wrong. That's one of the things that's wrong with

Marxism-Leninism-Stalinism. The proletariat isn't made up of nothing but saints, and capitalists aren't all devils."

Gianfranco felt a delicious thrill at hearing him say anything was wrong with the world's leading—the world's only legal—ideology. He supposed a priest hearing clever talk of heresy might have felt the same way. Like any Communist state, the Italian People's Republic glorified the workers. It said so, loudly, whenever it got the chance—especially on May Day every year. But the apartments the proletariat lived in made Gianfranco's seem a palace by comparison.

He knew hypocrisy when he saw and heard it. Some things, though, he didn't know. Shyly, he asked, "What are capitalists like? Do they really think of nothing but money? Do they really want to exploit their workers as much as they can?"

"Some of them do think about nothing but money," Eduardo answered, which disappointed him. "You need to think about money. And some of them would exploit workers as much as they could. That's why you have taxes, so some of the money capitalists make helps everybody. And that's why you have labor unions and you have laws regulating what corporations can do. The idea isn't to kill the goose that lays the golden eggs. It's to keep the goose healthy and get some of the gold."

"How do we get capitalists here, then?" Gianfranco found something else to ask: "How do we do it without making the government crack down, the way it did on you?"

"Good question. If there are no other good questions, class is dismissed," Eduardo said.

"Come on!" Gianfranco yelped.

"I don't know how you do that. Nobody in the home timeline knows. That's why we were trying the shops. They didn't work—or maybe they worked too well," Eduardo said. "However you do it, it'll have to be by stealth. That seems plain."

"Stealth? What do you mean?"

"People will have to start buying and selling and investing without realizing it's capitalism. You'd have to call it something else, something that sounds properly Communist. Stakhanovite economic effort, maybe. The idea of working harder than other people doesn't go away—it just gets changed around."

"It sure does," Gianfranco said. "Stakhanovites aren't supposed to work for themselves, though. They work for the state."

"But they can get rewarded for it," Eduardo said. "That's the point. If the state thinks your work toward getting rich will help it, it won't get in the way— except states always get in the way some, because they're like that."

"Hang on." Gianfranco raised a warning hand. "A minute ago, you said states needed laws to keep capitalists from exploiting workers. Now you say states get in the way. You can't have it both ways."

"Sure you can—why not?" Eduardo answered. "You need some laws, and ways to enforce them. That's why there are states in the first place. Otherwise, the strong and the rich would oppress the weak and the poor. But if you have too many laws and too many taxes, who's strong and rich then? The state is. And it oppresses everybody. Does that sound familiar?"

"Oh, maybe a little," Gianfranco allowed.

Eduardo laughed. "I thought it might. The question is, what kind of laws do you really need? Drawing the line is what politics ought to be all about, if you ask me."

Gianfranco had been asking him. His own political ideas were murky before he started going to The Gladiator. He largely accepted the system he was born into. Why not? It was all he knew, and his father had done well under it.

But now he saw some reasons why not. He hadn't missed freedom because he hadn't known there was anything to miss. Talking with Eduardo was like looking at another world. *Just like that*, he thought. And, no matter how Eduardo downplayed it, Gianfranco was convinced it was a better world.

How could it be anything else? People from Eduardo's home timeline knew how to come here. The cleverest scientists in this whole world had no idea any others lay off to the side, as it were. That right there said everything that needed saying about who knew more.

And Eduardo's computer put all the electronics in this whole world to shame. People here wouldn't be able to make anything so small yet powerful for a hundred years—if they ever figured out how. And even if they did, chances were the government wouldn't let them build the machine.

If everybody had a computer like that, what would stop people from hooking all their computers together? They'd be able to figure out in an instant if somebody in the government was lying. And people in the government lied all the time. All those Five-Year Plans got overfulfilled again and again, yet somehow life never looked any better. The state didn't wither away—it got stronger. And anyone who said out loud that the Emperor had no clothes discovered that, while the Emperor might be naked, he did have the Security Police.

If you kick up a fuss, they'll get you, too, Gianfranco thought. But if he didn't kick up a fuss, he'd never be free. He was damned if he didn't, doomed if he did. He saw no way out.

Final exams were coming. Everybody at Hoxha Polytechnic started going crazy. Seniors got especially jumpy. How they did would tell the story of who got into the good universities and who didn't. Anyhow, it would if they didn't have the right connections. You could tell the people who did. They were the ones who could afford to smile and take it easy. Everybody else hated them.

Annarita was only a junior, so she wasn't quite so frantic. She still wanted to do well. She had her own stubborn pride, and she knew her parents expected good marks from her. And, in spite of all the talking she'd done with Eduardo, she still took "from each according to his abilities" seriously. If she was able—and she was—she was supposed to do as well as she could.

She knew Gianfranco was also studying hard. He'd even turned down a couple of chances to play *Rails across Europe*. She hadn't thought a new outbreak of the Black Death could make him do that.

Neither had Eduardo. When he wasn't playing the railroad game with Gianfranco and her, he played chess with her father. He lost more often than he won, but he won often enough to keep him interested and playing. He fit in well with the Crosettis—he might almost have been a real cousin. If the Security Police weren't after him, everything would have been fine.

When Annarita said as much one evening, her father looked up from his book. "That's a big if, sweetheart."

"Well, yes, but—" Annarita stopped, not sure how to go on.

"But they haven't knocked on the door yet. That's what you mean, isn't it?" her father said.

"I guess it is," she admitted sheepishly.

"That's not a reason to relax," he said. "If it's anything, it's a reason to be more careful. You and Gianfranco have done very well—and the proof is, nobody's arrested us yet. You have to keep doing it, though, both of you."

"We know," Annarita said.

"I hope so," her father said. "Do you really understand everything that's at stake? We don't have everything you wish we did. We aren't as free as you wish we were. But we do have enough—more than enough, really. And nobody would come down on us as long as we didn't stick our necks out. Now we've done it. If the Security Police do get us, we lose everything we've got. And you lose your future. That's worst of all."

It didn't seem real to Annarita. Nothing after exams seemed real to her. That must have shown on her face, because her father laughed the saddest laugh she'd ever heard. "What is it?" she asked.

"I remember what it's like not to think past day after tomorrow—next week at the latest," he answered. "You think I don't? I was like that once upon a time. Everybody is. You get older, though, you change. You'd better. If you don't, you make a foolish grown-up—that's for sure. You have to start looking further down the road."

"How do you do that?" Annarita didn't really believe she could do it if he told her how. She didn't believe it, but she hoped.

"Experience," her father said.

That made her angry. "Experience is what grown-ups say when they mean, 'Go away, kid. Get lost.'"

Her father laughed again, this time with something closer to real amusement. "Well, sweetheart, you've got something there. Ten years ago, you were a little girl. Ten years ago, I was pretty much the same as I am now. I have a wider platform than you do. Only time can give you one like it."

"Your hair had less gray in it," Annarita said. "Pictures show that, anyway—you look about the same to me."

"I had a little more hair, too." Her father touched his temples, where it had receded. "You hadn't given me so much gray then. These past few weeks, I'm surprised my hair hasn't turned white."

"Is it as bad as that?"

He shook his head. "It's worse. If we get caught, all this is kaput. Kaput, you hear? Gone. Lost. Forever. You always get the dirty end of the stick after they let you out of camp. You're just a zek after that, not a person any more. *If* they let you out. For something like this, they might not."

"They don't keep people forever." Like anyone else, Annarita had a good notion of what happened after you vanished into the netherworld of the camps.

"No, they don't." Her father nodded, but he looked grim. "But they don't always let them out, either. Sometimes people die in there. *Heart failure*, the death certificates say, or, *Brain hemorrhage*. A 9mm bullet can cause either one."

Annarita bit her lip. Again like anyone else, she knew those things could happen. But she didn't like to think about them. She especially didn't like to think about them happening to her.

When she said so, her father's mouth tightened. He didn't get angry at her very often, but he did now. She'd disappointed him. "Anything that can happen can happen to you. If you don't know that here *and* here" —he tapped his forehead, then his belly—"you don't know anything."

He was right, which didn't make Annarita any happier.

"What are we going to do?" she wondered out loud.

"You should have asked that when you brought your stray puppy home and asked if we could keep it," her father said.

"Edu—Silvio's no puppy!"

"No. He's more dangerous than a puppy ever could be."

"Why didn't you send him away, then?"

"I probably should have." Her father sighed. "But he made me too curious. He persuaded me he really isn't from here, from this world, at all. I never imagined anyone could do that. It's one reason I let him stay. And the other one is even simpler—it was already too late to kick him out."

"Why?" Annarita said. "He carries a computer in his pocket, not a gun like a gangster. What could he do?"

"He could get caught by the Security Police, that's what," her father answered. "And after that, he could tell them he was here."

"He wouldn't do that!" she exclaimed.

"He wouldn't want to, I'm sure. When they start squeezing, what you want has nothing to do with anything." Her father looked and sounded very unhappy. "So they would find out he was here, and we didn't turn him in. And not turning him in is as bad to them as sheltering him. So if I'm going to be hung, I might as well be hung for a sheep as for a lamb."

Annarita eyed him. "All his talk about freedom has you going just like Gianfranco, doesn't it?"

"I don't want to admit that. I'm supposed to be too old and cynical to care about such things," her father said. "But yes, I'm afraid it does. And I *am* afraid, because I can't see how this is likely to end up well for anybody."

"If he gets away, if he goes back to the home timeline, then it's as if he were never really here," Annarita said.

"If pigs had wings, we'd all carry umbrellas," her father said.

That made her blink. He wasn't usually so blunt. "Everything will be fine," she said.

He got up from his chair, walked over, and kissed her on top of the head. "I wish I were seventeen again. Then I could close my eyes and all my problems would disappear just like *that*." He snapped his fingers.

"I'm not an ostrich. I don't stick my head in the sand," Annarita said. "And if you think I do, you ought to listen to Gianfranco."

"Boys are born radicals at that age. They want Causes." The way her father said it, she could hear the capital letter. He went on, "It makes them good soldiers, too. The captain says, 'Take that hill for the country,' and they go, 'Yes, sir!' instead of, 'What? Are you nuts? I'll get shot!'"

"Freedom is a good cause, *sì*?" Annarita said.

"One of the best," her father answered. "But it's also one of the ones most likely to get somebody shot."

Nine

"Time!" the teacher said loudly. "Put your pencils down *now*. Do not mark any more answers on your tests. Pass your papers forward *immediately*."

Gianfranco let out a long, loud, weary sigh. Most of the time, such an uncouth noise would have landed him in trouble. Now it was just one of a chorus. He waggled his wrist back and forth, trying to work out writer's cramp. Something inside the wrist cracked as if it were a knuckle. He stared at it in dismay. It wasn't supposed to do that . . . was it?

The last final. Everything was over for the year. Well, almost over. Everybody had to come back Monday to get report cards marked. Teachers would spend the weekend figuring out what everybody's grades were. That was a lot of work, but Gianfranco didn't worry about it. The only thing he worried about was what marks he'd end up with.

A year earlier, he wouldn't have cared much about that. But when you started doing well, you wanted to do better. He wouldn't have believed that before, but it turned out to be true.

After counting the exams, the teacher nodded. "I have all your papers," he said formally. "You are dismissed."

Again, there was more noise than usual as the students got

up. Something in Gianfranco's back popped, too. *I'm wearing out,* he thought. *I need oiling or something.*

As he walked toward the entrance to wait for Annarita, another thought crossed his mind. *I'll be a junior next year. Where did the time go?* Hadn't he been in primary school just a little while ago? No matter what he felt like, the answer was no.

Annarita got there less than a minute after he did. "How'd it go?" she asked.

He shrugged. "I'll know for sure on Monday. It didn't seem too bad, though." He made as if to knock on wood. "How about you?" he said.

"I'm glad it's over," Annarita said. "I hope it turned out all right." She always talked that way. Anybody who didn't know her would think she was worried. Gianfranco knew better. She always came through

"Want to go to a movie to celebrate finishing?" Gianfranco asked.

"We can do that," Annarita answered. Gianfranco hoped that meant she wasn't saying yes to be nice. *Better than saying no,* he thought. She went on, "What I want to do right now is go home and catch up on my sleep. That would be wonderful."

"Sure, but do you have five years to do it in?" he said. She laughed, for all the world as if he were kidding. He knew how hard she worked.

They left Hoxha Polytechnic behind for another school year. She would be a senior when they came back in six weeks. She would have to worry about the university and the rest of her life. Gianfranco wasn't ready for that yet. He wondered whether Annarita was.

Maria Tenace came up to Annarita and wagged a finger in

her face. "You'll never be president of the Young Socialists' League!" she said. "Never!"

"I wasn't really worried about it," Annarita said.

"You were wrong about The Gladiator," Maria continued, as if she hadn't spoken. "Wrong! Wrong! Wrong!" She lovingly sang the word. "And you're going to pay for it. Pay! Pay! Pay!" Then she waltzed off without giving Annarita a chance to answer.

"You sure know some nice people," Gianfranco remarked.

"*Sì*. And I know Maria, too," Annarita said.

That was funny and sad and true, all at the same time. "I hope she can't do anything worse than keep you from being president," Gianfranco said.

"I'm not even sure she can do that," Annarita answered. "She probably means she'll run against me, and everybody will be afraid to vote for me because I was wrong. Maybe yes, maybe no." She waggled her hand. "She doesn't realize she scares people to death herself. Fanatics never think they're fanatics, but they are anyway."

"If we could all see ourselves the way other people do . . ." Gianfranco said.

"There's a poem about that in English." Annarita frowned. "I read it for European lit. They translated it into a funny mountain dialect—the notes said the English was in dialect, too."

He stared. "How do you remember stuff like that?"

"I don't know. I just do." Annarita stared, too, imitating his expression. He laughed. He must have looked pretty silly. "How come you don't?" she asked.

Gianfranco hadn't thought about it like that. "Most people don't, I bet," he said.

"That doesn't make it wrong if you do," Annarita said,

which struck Gianfranco as being true and not true at the same time. If you got too far out of step with what most people did and thought, you'd probably end up in trouble.

When he said so, Annarita frowned. "You shouldn't, unless you hurt somebody or something."

"I didn't say anything about what should happen," he answered. "I just said what *would*."

She looked at him as if he'd grown another head. "You know what?" she said. "You sound like my father. I never expected that."

"Neither did I!" Gianfranco exclaimed. Not only did he not expect it, he didn't much like it.

That must have shown on his face, because Annarita said, "Don't worry. It probably won't happen again soon."

"I hope not!" Gianfranco said. "I mean, I like your father and everything, but I want to sound like me, not like him."

To his relief, Annarita said, "Well, that's probably good."

He didn't have to cram any more. Neither did Annarita. They celebrated by going to see a remake of *The Grapes of Wrath*. It might as well have used a sledgehammer to drive home how wicked and corrupt American capitalism had been. Bang, bang, bang—each point thudded home, subtle as an earthquake.

"The book was better," Annarita said when they came out.

"I wonder if there's ever been a movie that was better than the book," Gianfranco said.

Annarita thought for a moment. "I wouldn't bet on it."

"Neither would I," Gianfranco said.

They stopped and had gelato to get the taste of *The Grapes of Wrath* out of their mouths. Then they went back to their building and trudged up the stairs to their apartments. "I do wish somebody would fix the elevator," Annarita sighed.

"If somebody made money doing it—" But this time Gianfranco stopped before he really got going. He couldn't make himself believe anything like that would happen here, not any time soon.

"Well, it was nice even if the movie wasn't everything it might have been," Annarita said as they paused in front of her front door.

Did she expect him to kiss her? The only way to find out was to try. When he put his arms around her, she didn't try to push him away. And when he kissed her, she kissed him back. That was all good. That was all wonderful, in fact.

"Good night," he said after reluctantly ending the kiss. "We'll have to do this again soon." Did he mean go out again or kiss some more? All of the above, probably.

"Sure. Why not?" Annarita said, and went inside.

Gianfranco didn't think his feet touched the floor once as he walked the handful of steps to his own apartment.

Monday after finals. Judgment Day, people called it, even if the Italian People's Republic officially looked down its nose at religion. A year's work, there in black and white. If you did well, you were glad to see it proved. If you didn't . . .

Annarita knew she'd worked hard. She hoped it would pay off. Even so, she worried. She couldn't help it. Some people had a *Chè serà, serà* attitude—whatever will be, will be. She wished she could feel that way, but didn't expect she ever would.

Into Russian she went. Because it was her first class, she got her report card there. Then she had to turn it in again so Comrade Montefusco could write her mark on it. Giving it to her with the grade already written in would have been more efficient. Teachers didn't do it that way. Why not? Because they didn't, as far as she could tell. Maybe there was some obscure rule against it. Maybe nobody in the bureaucracy cared about being efficient. She figured it was about fifty-fifty either way.

Back came the report card, this time with a grade. An A— she breathed a sigh of relief. She hadn't messed up the final, then. A few other people looked happy. A few looked disappointed or angry. Most seemed to have got about what they'd expected.

"Comrade!" A boy raised his hand.

"*Sì*, Abbaticchio?" The teacher was always polite.

"Why did you give me a C? I need at least a B+ if I'm going to get into the university I want to go to."

"Well, Abbaticchio, maybe you should have thought more about that during the year, not when all the work is done and it's too late to change anything."

"But I need a B+!" The way Abbaticchio said it, someone—maybe God, maybe the General Secretary of the Italian Communist Party—had promised him the grade.

Comrade Montefusco shrugged. "I'm sorry. That's not what you earned."

"You mean you won't change it?" The boy sounded as if he couldn't believe his ears.

"I'm afraid so," the teacher answered.

Abbaticchio turned red. "You think you're sorry now? Wait till my father gets through with you! I'm not going to let some miserable flunky of a teacher mess with my life."

"I have had terrorist threats made against me before," Comrade Montefusco said calmly. "I am still here. I expect to be back after the summer break, too."

"You don't know who my father is," Abbaticchio warned. "He took down The Gladiator, so he can sure take you out."

"What on earth is The Gladiator?" the Russian teacher said. "There haven't been any gladiators in Milan for almost two thousand years."

The angry student rolled his eyes. Several others in the classroom whispered behind their hands. Annarita didn't, but her heart beat faster. So Abbaticchio's father was a big shot in the Security Police, was he? If he found out about Eduardo . . . *Cousin Silvio*, she told herself fiercely. *He's Cousin Silvio.*

No matter how Abbaticchio blustered, Comrade Montefusco wouldn't change his grade. When the bell rang at the end of the shortened period, Abbaticchio stormed out of the classroom. Some of the things he said would have got him suspended, or maybe expelled, any other time. Students had some license on Judgment Day. The authorities knew the kind of pressure they were under. Did they have *that* much license? Annarita wouldn't have thought so, but the teacher didn't call Abbaticchio on it.

Now all I need is for him to get together with Maria Tenace, Annarita thought. *That would really make a mess of things, wouldn't it?* She had no idea if they knew each other. She didn't keep track of who their friends were. She wouldn't have guessed either one of them had any friends.

She sighed. All she could do was try not to draw attention to herself. Usually, that was easy for her. Now, when she needed it to be easy, it wasn't. How unfair was that?

She didn't quite get straight A's. Her dialectics teacher didn't believe in giving them. People said Karl Marx himself couldn't get an A in that class. People also said the teacher had given an A once, and the girl who got it fainted and fell over and split her forehead open. Annarita didn't believe that. As far as she could tell, the teacher had always been the way he was. She wasn't so sure about Marx.

Other than the dialectics class, she made a clean sweep. Even with a B+ there, her grades were plenty good enough for first honors again. She wondered how Gianfranco was doing. She hoped he'd held on to second honors. His folks would be on him something fierce if he didn't. She would be disappointed herself if he didn't, too. One corner of her mouth quirked up. That probably mattered more to him than all the yelling in the world from his parents would.

And what he thought about the things she did mattered to her, too. A year earlier, it wouldn't have. They'd just been a couple of people kind of stuck with each other because of their living arrangements. *I didn't think I'd have a boyfriend a year younger than I am* went through her mind.

She wondered how long he would stay her boyfriend. Till they stopped getting along, she supposed. Right now, everything seemed fine. Why borrow trouble?

Here he came. He was grinning, which was a good sign. Annarita thought it was safe to ask, "Did you?"

"You'd better believe it!" he answered, and waved his report card like a flag. "I should have started busting my hump sooner. I might have got firsts like you. . . . You did, right?"

"*Sì.*" She felt better about admitting it than she would have if he hadn't made seconds. It was easy this way. "Maybe you *will* be up there too next year."

"Hope so," Gianfranco said. "I think I *can* do it. Now the question is whether I'll kick myself in the rear and make myself do it."

"You did it over the last couple of grading periods this

time," Annarita said. "You'll start fresh next year, so if you push hard right from the start. . . ."

"If," he agreed. "Well, I'll give it my best shot and see what happens, that's all." He waved the report card again, and almost hit somebody in the face with it. "Now I want to go home and show this off."

"I don't blame you." Annarita was proud of him, but she didn't want to come right out and say so. It would make him feel he was listening to his mother.

When they got back to the apartment building, a truck was parked in front of it, two wheels on the street, the other two on the sidewalk. That was illegal, of course, but people did it all the time. What was more surprising was the word painted in big green letters on the truck's door: REPAIRS.

Annarita and Gianfranco looked at each other. "You don't suppose—?" Gianfranco sounded like someone in whom hope had just flowered against all odds.

"Let's go look!" Annarita said. They hurried into the lobby together.

Sure enough, the elevator door was open. Annarita couldn't remember the last time she'd seen that. A man in coveralls and a cap and wearing a fat belt full of tools came out of the elevator car. Another man in the same getup stayed in there working.

"Are you really going to fix it?" Gianfranco might have been an acolyte in church witnessing a miracle.

"Better believe it, kid." The man who'd come out of the elevator paused to light a cigar and puff smoke towards Annarita and Gianfranco. She coughed—the cigar was vile. The repairman went on, "Nothing real big wrong with it. Somebody could've got it working a long time ago."

"How come nobody did, then?" Annarita asked.

He shrugged. "Beats me. Probably on account of nobody bothered to look and see how hard it'd be. Probably on account of nobody figured he'd make any money fixing it."

"But you will?" Annarita said.

"I . . . sure will." Plainly, the repairman almost said something more pungent. "I wouldn't be here if there wasn't some loot in it for me and Giulio. Isn't that right, Giulio?" This time, he blew a noxious cloud toward the other workman.

"Isn't what right?" Giulio asked, looking up from whatever he was doing inside the elevator car.

"We wouldn't be doing this if they weren't paying us good money."

"What? You think I'm dumb or something? Of course not," Giulio said.

"You guys sound like capitalists," Gianfranco said.

He meant it as a compliment. Annarita knew that. She wasn't sure the repairman would. The cigar twitched in the man's mouth. But all he said was, "Never yet been anybody born who was allergic to cash." He turned again. "Isn't *that* right, Giulio?"

"I dunno, Rocco," Giulio said. "I know I'm not."

"I wouldn't be allergic to riding the elevator instead of climbing stairs every time I need to go to the apartment," Annarita said.

"Won't be long," said the man with the cigar—Rocco.

She and Gianfranco still had to climb the stairs now. The trudge seemed twice as long as usual because soon she wouldn't have to make it any more. Halfway up, Gianfranco said, "They really did sound like capitalists. They only seemed to care about making a profit for their work."

"Even if that is all they care about, you don't expect them to come right out and admit it, do you?" Annarita was surprised they'd come so close. "It would be like admitting you eat with your fingers or pick your nose or something."

"I suppose." Gianfranco climbed a few more steps. Then he turned to her and said, "It shouldn't be like that, you know? It's not like that in the game. You want to make as much money as you can there."

"That's a game," Annarita said gently. "This is life. It's not the same thing, and you'll get in trouble—you'll get everybody in trouble—if you think it is." The game could suck you in. Even she knew that, and she played much more casually than Gianfranco did. But he had to remember what was real and what wasn't.

With an impatient gesture, he showed he did. "I know, I know. Those guys down there didn't exactly deny they were doing it for the money."

"No, they didn't." Annarita didn't say that showed what a crude pair they were. To her, it was obvious. It should have been obvious to Gianfranco, too. No doubt it would have been if the game didn't make it hard for him to think straight.

The game. The game from another world. The game from a world where capitalism worked—by the things Eduardo said and by the things he had, it worked better than Communism did. The game from a world where Communism lay on—what was Marx's phrase?—the ash-heap of history, that was it. The game from a world with no Security Police. No wonder it made Gianfranco think dangerous thoughts. No wonder it made him think political thoughts, economic thoughts.

Annarita laughed at herself. As if political and economic thoughts weren't dangerous by definition!

"What's funny?" Gianfranco asked, so she must have snorted out loud. She told him. He thought about it for two or three steps. Then he said, "Ideas like that shouldn't be dangerous. That's the point, right?—to make it so they aren't dangerous any more."

"*Sì*, that's the point," Annarita said. "The other point is, it hasn't happened yet, and it won't happen any time soon."

"I know," he said again, and gave her a crooked grin. "I won't slip up, Annarita. Honest, I won't."

"I didn't think you would," Annarita answered, which was . . . close enough to true that she didn't feel too much like a liar saying it.

Mechanical noises came from the elevator shaft when she and Gianfranco walked past it. They looked at it. Annarita saw something close to awe on Gianfranco's face. Her own probably held the same expression. "Wow!" he said, "They really are fixing it."

"I don't remember the last time it worked," Annarita said. "Do you?"

He shook his head. "Not really. I was a lot smaller than I am now—I know that. I remember how hard climbing all those stairs seemed then. Now I'm used to it. But I could get used to riding the elevator real quick, I bet."

"Me, too." Annarita stopped at the door to her apartment. "See you at dinner. And congratulations again!"

"*Grazie!*" Gianfranco grinned at her. "I only get second-class congratulations. You get first."

"Next year," she said. She'd got first honors plenty of times before, too. They didn't seem such a big deal to her. For Gianfranco to earn second honors—especially on year-end grades—was further out of the ordinary.

Eduardo was reading the newspaper when she came in. "*Ciao*," he said. "How did you do?"

"Pretty well," she answered. "I didn't get the grade in dialectics, though. I don't know what kind of hoop I was supposed to jump through. Whatever it was, I didn't."

"Too bad." He shook his head in sympathy. "There's always somebody like that."

"Even in your perfect home timeline?" Annarita teased.

"It's not perfect. All kinds of things wrong there. Our troubles are different from yours, but we've still got 'em. Some of them, I guess you say, are the troubles that go with too much freedom," Eduardo answered.

"How can you have too much freedom?" Annarita asked. "Don't you just do whatever you want then?"

"Sure. I mean, that's what you do, *sì*, but it's not always so simple. If what I'm doing makes me happy but bothers other people, where do you draw the line? How much should the state do to take care of poor people and people who don't want to work? Countries all find different answers."

"Different how?"

"Well, in Italy—in most of Europe—people pay more taxes, and the countries do more for their people who don't have so much. In America, taxes are lower, but the state does less to take care of you. If you make it in America, you can make it bigger than you can on this side of the Atlantic. If you don't, you'll have a harder time than you would here."

"Which is better?" Annarita asked.

"Depends on who's answering," Eduardo said, which struck her as an honest reply. "Me, I'm an Italian, and I think our way works pretty well. But the Americans like what they do, too. If they didn't, they'd change it."

"Don't they make everybody do things the.. Russians here?"

He shook his head. "They do throw their weight arou.. but not like that. Most of the time, anyway."

She wondered how big an exception came with that handful of words. But his world and hers had been different—evidently, very different—for a century and a half. She couldn't expect him to fill her in on all that history in one lump. She did ask, "So you have teachers who think they're little tin gods, too?"

"You'd better believe it," he answered. "Every alternate that has teachers has some like that. They've got the power, and the students don't, and they enjoy rubbing it in. Human nature doesn't change from one alternate to another. The way it comes out changes because of religion and technology and culture, but people are still pretty much people." He winked at her. "I'm a people, aren't I?"

"I thought so, till now," she answered tartly, and he laughed. She went on, "This is a world—an alternate—where Marxism-Leninism-Stalinism came out on top."

"That's right." Eduardo nodded. "And anybody who can say 'Marxism-Leninism-Stalinism' and make it sound natural the way you do has a pretty good handle on the dialectic, no matter what your dumb teacher thinks."

Annarita smiled, but she continued with her own train thought: "And you come from an alternate where capita' won."

He nodded again. "That's me."

"Are there . . . alternates where the Fascists won?

Eduardo nodded one more time. "Yes, and the bad as you'd think they would be. They're even w. one."

The way he said it was like a fist in the stomach. "Are we really that bad?" Annarita asked in a small voice. Of course she took the only world she knew for granted—how could she do anything else?

"Well . . . You're not so good, not when it comes to treating people the way you ought to," Eduardo answered. "But I'll tell you what the difference is. If somebody here gets out of line, he goes to a camp. If they decide to kill him later, it's just part of doing business, and nobody gets excited about it. In the Fascist alternates, he still goes to a camp. But if they kill him there, they enjoy it."

"Oh." Annarita winced. That got the message across, all right. "And what about in your home timeline?" she asked.

"We don't have camps for people who commit political crimes," Eduardo said. "We don't send important people who commit political crimes to psychiatric hospitals, either. We don't really even arrest people for political crimes, not the way you do here. We don't in Europe and America, anyway—not even in Russia any more, not very much. Asia, Africa, sometimes South America . . . Things are different there. We could be better, heaven knows. But going out to the alternates has shown us we could be worse, too."

"They don't have political arrests in the Soviet Union?" re than anything else, that told Annarita how different from vorld the home timeline was.

t she'd forgotten something. "No, in Russia, I said," Ed- nswered. "There is no Soviet Union in the home time- ember? It broke up in . . . 1991? Or was it 1992? I nber which—it's only a question on a history test for hing that really matters any more. Russia and Be- her for a while, but then they separated again."

had the right amount of . . . has it been that long? to clump up . . . Annarita

...USSR.

...g to imagine Mi-
...an and Inter Milan, the

...not the same place. It's not the same at
...o said—in Russian much more fluent than hers.

She gaped at him. "I didn't know you spoke Russian," she said in that language, pronouncing it as carefully as she could.

"Well, I do," he answered, dropping back into Italian. "Might come in handy here—you never can tell—so I learned it. We have ways of doing that in nothing flat." He snapped his fingers.

"I wish we did!" Annarita thought of all the time she'd spent sitting in class and doing homework and memorizing vocabulary and declensions and conjugations. She thought of all the time she still needed to put in. Learning a language in nothing flat seemed like a party trick—one she didn't know.

"I'm sorry," he said, plainly guessing what was on her mind. "Things kind of, well, stagnated here once the competition with capitalism ended."

Banging noises from outside and then a smoother mechanical hum made them both turn their heads. "At least we've finally got the miserable elevator fixed," Annarita said. That didn't seem much next to picking up Russian with pills or however Eduardo did it, but it was better than nothing.

His smile said he understood what that *finally* meant. Anyone who'd grown up in the Italian People's Republic would ..., of course. But Eduardo, despite speaking perfect Mi-... Italian, was in some ways more foreign than a man from

Mongolia. Still, he ‌
voice as he asked, "How long ‌

"I don't remember exactly—it's bee‌
said. "Years. Years and years. Now we won't have‌
and down all those times every day."

"Good for you," he said, and then, "Sometimes, in the
home timeline, people climb stairs so they can get exercise."

Annarita thought about that for a little while. "Maybe it's
different if you don't have to do it," she said at last, which was
the kindest thing she could come up with.

Her father walked into the apartment. He was grinning.
"*Ciao*," he said. "I just rode the elevator up here. How about
that?"

"Good for you!" Annarita said. She shot Eduardo a glance.
Exercise, indeed! He didn't say a word.

Gianfranco wanted to play *Rails across Europe* all through the
break between school years. That didn't thrill Annarita. He
needed a little longer than he might have to realize it didn't.
And he needed longer still to see that even Eduardo might
rather have been doing something else.

"I thought you enjoyed it," Gianfranco said reproachfully
when the light dawned at last.

"Well, I do . . . some," Eduardo answered. "But we brought
the games here as a means to an end. We wanted to use them to
get people in this alternate to think different. They aren't an
end in themselves, not for us."

"*Rails across Europe* is for me, and I'm not the only one w‌
thinks so," Gianfranco said.

Eduardo gave him a crooked smile. "*Grazie*. It's sup‌

to be interesting. If it weren't, we wouldn't have had any customers, and we wouldn't have been able to change any minds at all."

"You changed mine, that's for sure." Gianfranco looked down at the game board, and at his railroad route marked out in erasable crayon. "This is my only chance to be a capitalist. I'm not even an elevator repairman."

"What's that supposed to mean?" Eduardo asked.

"You should have heard those guys—Rocco and whoever the other one was—go on," Gianfranco said. "They were in it for the money, nothing else but. If racing baby buggies paid better, they'd do that instead. You could tell. I even called them capitalists, and they didn't get mad."

"Really?" Eduardo said.

"*Sì*." Gianfranco crossed his heart to show he was telling the truth. There was one of the gestures that hung on to show Italian society was less godless than the government said and wished it was.

"Who exactly were these people? Rocco and his pal, you say?" Eduardo seemed more interested than Gianfranco had thought he would.

"What do you mean, who? They were a couple of repairmen, that's all." Like a lot of people in the so-called workers' paradise, Gianfranco looked down his nose at men and women who really did work with their hands. He didn't know he did, and he would have denied it had anyone called him on it, but it was true.

Eduardo had other things on his mind. "Is there any way to find out exactly who they were? It could be important. They might be . . . friends of mine."

That took a moment to sink in. When it did, Gianfranco blinked. "You mean, people from your home timeline?"

"I don't know," Eduardo said. "I sure would like to, though." He made a fist, then brought it down gently on the table by the game board. Gianfranco got the idea that he would rather have banged it down as hard as he could. "Maybe they were looking for me. If they were, if they came to the right building and didn't find me . . . It makes you want to scream, you know?"

"Plenty of people here like money, too, you know," Gianfranco said.

"Oh, sure. Maybe I'm building castles in the air, just because I want to so much." Now Eduardo's smile was sheepish. "But I can hope, can't I? And nobody ever said the authorities closed down our shop in San Marino."

"Ah, so that's where it is. You never told me before," Gianfranco said.

San Marino, southeast of Milan near Rimini on the Adriatic coast, covered only a few square kilometers. It was entirely surrounded by Italy. But it was an independent country, and had been for more than 1,500 years. It was also, Gianfranco realized, a good place for a shop like The Gladiator. Things were looser in San Marino than in Italy. The government was Marxist-Leninist-Stalinist, of course, but it wasn't *very* Marxist-Leninist-Stalinist. San Marino depended on vacationers and tourists. It took money, and the importance of money, more seriously than Italy did.

"That's where it is, all right," Eduardo agreed. "How do I go about finding out who these repairmen were?"

Gianfranco gaped. "*I* don't know." He'd never had to worry about anything like that before.

"They didn't just fall out of the sky," Eduardo said patiently. "Somebody in this building would have hired them, right? Maybe the manager, maybe the janitor, but somebody. Whoever it is, he'll know their firm, won't he?"

"I guess so." Gianfranco knew he sounded vague. "Or would somebody in the city government have sent them out when our turn finally came up?"

Eduardo said a couple of things that should have set fire to the table. Somehow, they didn't. "It could be," he said when he calmed down a little. "Things work like that here, heaven knows. D'you think your father could find out for me if it is? He's got the connections to do it if anybody does."

"Well, yeah," Gianfranco said. "But why do I tell him that you want to know? Or even that I want to know, if you don't want him knowing you do?"

Some of the things Eduardo said this time made what had come out before sound like love poetry by comparison. He needed longer to get control of his temper. At last, he said, "Well, you're right. I wish you weren't, but you are. You don't want to become an apprentice elevator repairman all of a sudden, eh?"

"No," Gianfranco said with such dignity as he could muster. Sure enough, he didn't think much of working with his hands. He was an apparatchik's son, all right.

"Too bad." Eduardo sounded as if he meant it. But he also had some of his usual sarcastic edge back. Before, he'd been too upset for sarcasm. He went on, "You'd sure make things simpler if you did."

"Simpler for you, maybe," Gianfranco said.

"*Sì*, simpler for me." Eduardo spread his hands. "Whenever somebody says something like that, what else is he going to mean?" Yes, he was closer to his normal self.

"Sorry," Gianfranco said. "But if I start asking too many weird questions, my father isn't the only one who'll wonder why. Before too long, some informer or other will get word to the Security Police. Then they'll start asking questions of their own."

"Do you know who's likely to be an informer?" Eduardo asked.

"I can guess some people who may be," Gianfranco answered. "Some, though, nobody'd guess in a million years. That's how things work."

How many people talked to the Security Police? No civilian knew for sure. Gianfranco would have bet no one official at the Security Police had the number at his fingertips. Handlers dealt with informers. But there were millions of them—he was sure of that. Brothers spied on sisters. Wives spied on husbands. Bosses informed on their workers—and the other way round. How huge were the archives with all those accusations, all those denunciations? Wouldn't they fill up the whole country sooner or later? *Probably sooner,* he thought.

Eduardo sighed. "All right. Do what you can without sticking your neck out. If you can find out, wonderful. If you can't . . ." He sighed again, louder. "If you can't, maybe it's time to go to San Marino."

"It's a nice place. People say so, anyway—I've been to Rimini, but never there," Gianfranco said.

"I wouldn't be going to sightsee," Eduardo reminded him.

Gianfranco nodded. He understood that. And if Eduardo found what he was looking for, he would disappear. Gianfranco understood that, too. And he himself would stay stuck in this dull old world after Eduardo had given him a glimpse—no, half a glimpse—of something so much better. Where was the justice in that?

Ten

The chief janitor of the apartment building was a large, impressive man named Marcantonio Moretti. He scratched his bushy, Stalin-style mustache as he nodded to Annarita. "Yes, it is very good to have the elevator running again," he said.

"And it's so smooth! Just like a dream!" Annarita wasn't in the drama society at Hoxha Polytechnic, but she knew how to lay it on with a trowel.

"*Grazie*," Comrade Moretti said, as if he'd done the work himself. He hadn't, of course. He didn't do much work of any sort. He was the chief janitor because his brother-in-law was a medium-important official in Milan's Bureau of City Maintenance. Under Communism, capitalism, or any old kind of ism at all, whom you knew mattered at least as much as what you could actually do.

"Who were the repairmen who did the job? They ought to get commendations for the Stakhanovite work they did," Annarita said. If people really worked like Stakhanovites or anything close to it, the elevator would have got fixed as soon as it broke down. Maybe it wouldn't have broken down in the first place. But how long had they had to wait? Much, much, too long— Annarita knew that.

"Well, I don't exactly remember," Moretti said instead of saying he had no idea, though that had to be just as true.

"I'd really like to find out," Annarita said.

Comrade Moretti scratched his mustache again. Had Gianfranco said something like that, the chief janitor would have run him out of his office. Annarita was much prettier than Gianfranco. That shouldn't have had anything to do with anything, which wasn't the same as saying it didn't.

"Hey, Ernesto!" Moretti yelled.

"What's up?" Ernesto Albosta called from the back room. A moment later, the assistant janitor came out. He wasn't impressive. He was short and skinny and slouchy and had crooked teeth. He wore ratty overalls and a cap pulled down low on his forehead. But Moretti was only the front man for the housekeeping staff. If you needed something fixed, Albosta was the one to see. If you needed to find something out, Albosta was the one to ask.

"Who were the guys who did the elevator?" Moretti asked.

"I don't know where the devil they found 'em," Albosta answered. "They're not even a Milanese outfit. The fix was in somewhere—you can bet on that."

"So where are they from, then? Bergamo? Como? Piacenza?" Moretti named three cities not far away.

But Ernesto Albosta shook his head each time. "Farther off than that. I think Rimini. Yeah, that's right—they're called By the Arch Repairs, from the Roman one in the middle of town there." He spread his hands. "How's an outfit from over by the Adriatic supposed to get work here? Somebody knows where the bodies are buried, all right."

"Sounds like it," Moretti agreed. "Now I'm going to wonder if we've got to worry about the elevator dying on us in two weeks. If it does, I guarantee you we'll never see those worthless bums again."

"Got that right," Albosta said, and slouched away scratching himself.

Marcantonio Moretti nodded to Annarita. "Now you know," he said, as if he'd known himself.

"Yes. Thank you." Annarita got out of his office as fast as she could while staying polite.

Now she knew—but she wondered *what* she knew. She couldn't remember whether the repair truck had plates from Italy or San Marino. In detective stories, people always noticed stuff like that. She'd paid no attention, though.

Still, there was a fair chance those had been Eduardo's friends looking for him. They hadn't found him. Were they still in Milan, checking other places where he might be? Or had they given up and gone away? She couldn't begin to guess.

Neither could Eduardo when she told him what she'd learned. "That's . . . too bad," he said. She got the idea he'd clamped down on something stronger. He sighed. "I have to go to San Marino, then, and hope they're not watching the border."

"My family and the Mazzillis are going to Rimini on vacation in a couple of weeks," Annarita said. "San Marino would be easier as a day trip from there than it would going straight from Milan."

"Is Rimini here full of Germans and Scandinavians trying to get sunburn and skin cancer on the beach?" Eduardo asked.

"*Sì.* Some of them hardly wear any clothes at all." Annarita sniffed. "You can probably have a good time even if you don't get up to San Marino."

"Nothing wrong with looking. When you do more than look, that's when life gets complicated," Eduardo said. "Maybe you and Gianfranco can come up to San Marino with me. What could look more innocent than a guy with his cousin and her boyfriend?"

What could give me better cover? he meant. Annarita understood that. She didn't mind. What her parents would think . . . was bound to be a different story. Of course, if she didn't tell them ahead of time, they wouldn't have a chance to find reasons to say no.

Italy slowed to a crawl in August. It didn't get as hot in Milan as it did farther south, but it was muggier here. Everybody who was anybody got out of town for a while. Doing business often took time—Gianfranco thought about the elevator in his building. Trying to do business in August was a fool's errand.

"It will be good to get to the beach," his father said as they packed for vacation.

"If we can get to the beach," his mother said darkly. "All those foreigners there in as little as the law allows . . ."

"Well, we've got the hotel reservations. The place is only a couple of blocks from the sand," his father said. "It's where we stayed last year. You liked it then, Bella."

"I wasn't talking about the hotel," Gianfranco's mother said.

Gianfranco kept his mouth shut. Anything he said in a discussion like this could and would be used against him. If the swim trunks he packed were his skimpiest pair, then they were, that was all. He didn't have to mention it.

"Have a good trip," Ernesto Albosta said as Gianfranco's family and the Crosettis brought their bags down to the lobby. The elevator made that much easier. Albosta sounded mournful, and no wonder. He was stuck in town in August. Marcantonio Moretti, by contrast, was on holiday somewhere a little north of Rome.

The Crosettis drove a little Fiat. Their bags barely fit into the trunk. They and Cousin Silvio barely fit into the car. Gianfranco's father had a Mercedes. Gianfranco had always taken that for granted. His father had waited a long time to get the car. Nobody, not even a Communist Party official, could avoid that. But when he got it, he got the best.

On the autostrada, the Mercedes soon left the Fiat behind. The highway ran east and a little south, past towns and farms that had been there since time out of mind. Whizzing past those brick buildings in the countryside, Gianfranco wondered how much history they'd seen. A century and a half earlier, Germans and Americans would have fought over them. A century and a half before that, they might have watched Napoleon's army march past. Before that . . . Well, how old were they? He had no idea.

When he asked his father, he got a shrug for an answer. "Annarita might know about stuff like that," his father said. "Me, I don't much care. I'm a practical man, I am."

"If you want to be practical, keep your eyes on the road," his mother said.

"Haven't hit anything yet, have I?"

"Sometimes I think you're trying to."

When they started going on like that, Gianfranco stopped listening. He'd heard it too many times before. They rolled along the autostrada, and then stopped rolling and started crawling. Gianfranco's father said several things that made his mother cluck. "It doesn't count if you're in the car," his father said defensively.

"Oh? Since when?" His mother didn't believe a word of it.

"It's an old rule I just made up," his father said. His mother snorted.

At last, they got past the slowdown. Three small cars were scrap metal, and a truck had some good-sized dents. Everybody put the pedal to the metal on the autostrada. When accidents happened, they were often bad ones. "I hope the people are all right," Gianfranco's mother said. He hoped so, too, but he wouldn't have bet on it.

A little past Bologna, his father pulled off the road for a rest stop: snacks, espresso, and a pause to use the bathrooms. The Mazzillis were just getting into their car when the Crosettis pulled into the same parking lot. "Fancy meeting you here!" Gianfranco called, waving.

"That was a nasty wreck," Annarita's father answered. "See you at the hotel."

"You sure will." Gianfranco's father unlocked the car. Anybody who lived in a big city learned to lock it all the time. Otherwise, enterprising people took things according to their abilities and their needs. The Mazzillis got in and got back on the highway.

A Roman triumphal arch sat right in the middle of Rimini's main square. Somewhere not far away would be that repair shop. Cars went under the arch as if it were built as an overpass. Italy had a long, long past. Every so often, it stuck out an elbow and poked the present. South of Rome, there were still stretches of the Appian Way with the paving Roman legionaries had marched on. It must have been easier on their feet than it was on the springs of modern cars and trucks.

Finding a place to park in a strange town was always an adventure. At last, Gianfranco's father managed. It was only a block and a half from the hotel, so he felt entitled to be proud of himself. Everybody was in a good mood carrying luggage to the lobby.

Gianfranco's father gave their name there. The clerk looked down his nose at them and said, "Do I have a record of your reservation? I don't see you here. I have Crosettis from Milan, but no Mazzillis."

Gianfranco gulped. His mother gasped. His father said, "Do you know who I am? I'm the second Party secretary in the Milanese Bureau of Records. Now let me talk to your manager right this minute. Is he a Party member?"

That wasn't likely. The clerk, looking worried now instead of enjoying himself, shook his head. "No, uh, Comrade. Hold on. I'll get him."

As if by magic, the manager found the "missing" reservation. The Mazzillis went to their room. "He wanted to squeeze money out of us," Gianfranco's father said as soon as the door closed behind them. "Well, he picked the wrong people to annoy, he did. Gianfranco, go back to the lobby and wait for the Crosettis. Don't let him play games with them."

"But he said he already had their reservation," his mother said.

"He said that to us," his father answered. "He'll probably tell them he has ours but not theirs. Or he will unless Gianfranco's there to give him the lie."

When Gianfranco got to the lobby, the clerk was saying he had no reservation for a big blond man who spoke Italian with a guttural accent. "But this is an outrage!" the blond man spluttered. "Most inefficient!"

A few minutes earlier, Gianfranco would have thought so, too. Now he decided the hotel was very efficient—at gouging its customers. The blond man demanded to see the manager, too. He didn't have the clout Gianfranco's father did. He also didn't seem to realize the manager expected to get paid off. At last, the manager proposed a fee for fixing the reservation. Fuming, the blond man paid.

Gianfranco read soccer scores and game reports in a newspaper. He waited for about twenty minutes before the Crosettis came in. Then he walked over to them and started chatting. They had no trouble with their reservation. The clerk gave him a dirty look. He smiled back as if he couldn't imagine why.

"This ought to be fun," Eduardo said.

"Are you talking about the beach or the mountains?" Annarita's father asked.

"Oh, the beach," Eduardo answered. San Marino lay in the mountains. Gianfranco could see how that wouldn't be fun for the man from another world. It would be work—or it might be disaster, if the authorities had closed down the other shop his people ran here.

What would he do then? What *could* he do then? Settle down here and try to stay out of the Security Police's way? Hope his people would come back and look for him? Gianfranco didn't see what other choice he had. He would probably feel like a sailor shipwrecked on some distant shore who knew he would never see home again.

But those repairmen, Rocco and his pal, came from around here, too. Maybe they also came from Eduardo's world. And maybe they didn't. If the other shop was shut, Eduardo would have to find out.

"Yes, the beach will be nice," Dr. Crosetti said. "Remember, use plenty of sunscreen. Some people think a nice tan is worth anything, but you pay for it down the road. Not just skin cancer, but a hide like a rhino's, too."

Gianfranco and Annarita and Eduardo all looked at one another. It wasn't that her father was wrong. From everything Gianfranco had ever heard, Dr. Crosetti was right. Still . . . A doctor could take a lot of fun out of a vacation.

Annarita didn't think the beach was so nice. The competition was too fierce. The tall, fair girls from the north fascinated Italian men. Blondes had intrigued Mediterranean men since Greek and Roman days, and the tradition lived on. And the girls from Germany and Scandinavia flaunted what they had. Their suits, what there was of them, made Annarita's seem dowdy by comparison.

They didn't worry about skin cancer, either. Some of them were turning brown. Some were turning golden. Some were just turning red, the red of a roast before it went into the oven. They didn't care. They laughed about it. "So good to see the sun," one of them said in throaty Italian. The sun was sure seeing—and baking—a lot of her.

Most of them lay on their towels or strolled along the sand. A few went into the Adriatic. It was warm—or warm enough—in August, though it would cool down once summer ended. It wasn't like Hawaii or even North Africa, where you could swim the year around.

When Annarita remarked on that, her father nodded and looked east, towards Albania. "No, but it stays hot all the time on the far side of the water," he said.

Albania was not a happy place. As far as Annarita could

tell, it had seldom been a happy place. Enver Hoxha, after whom her school was named, had backed China against the USSR after Stalin died. When the Soviet Union won the Cold War, it paid Albania back by pretending the sorry little country wasn't there. No aid went in. Nothing but trouble came out.

These days, the government in Tirane was pro-Moscow. The hills seethed with pro-Chinese guerrillas, and with bandits who didn't like anybody further removed than their own first cousins. Several fraternal Socialist countries, Italy among them, had soldiers in Albania trying to put down the bandits and the rebels. They weren't having much luck.

A couple of tall blond men walked by, talking in a language full of consonants and flat vowels. Norwegian? Swedish? Annarita couldn't tell. Big blond men did nothing for her. From what she could see, the northern men didn't find small, dark women especially wonderful, either. Oh, well.

"*Dio mio!*" Eduardo pointed. "A cormorant just flew by."

"He's fishing," Annarita's father said. "He must have some luck around here, or he would have starved by now."

"Well, I expect I'll go fishing pretty soon, too," Eduardo said. "Fishing for answers, I mean."

"I'd rather see the mountains than the beach," Annarita said. She liked the idea of the sea, not least because she lived hundreds of kilometers away from the real thing. The idea of the sea in her mind, though, didn't include a beach packed with scantily clad foreigners.

Her father sighed. "I wish Cousin Silvio were going up to San Marino by himself," he said. He and her mother knew. They weren't happy, but they weren't—quite—saying no.

"If we can help him get there without any trouble, we should," Annarita said.

"I'm not thinking about what happens if he gets there without any trouble," her father said. "I'm thinking about what happens if there is some. You have no idea what being a zek is like. And it's worse for a woman, believe me."

"Whatever happens, it won't land on Annarita and Gianfranco," Eduardo said. "I'll tell the authorities they didn't know anything about it."

"If something goes wrong, what happens after that will be up to the gentlemen in the jackboots. You won't have anything to say about it," Dr. Crosetti retorted. But he still didn't tell Annarita she couldn't go.

Maybe he got distracted. A blond girl with a tiny suit and a dancer's arched-back, catlike strut certainly seemed to distract Eduardo. Annarita's father also noticed her. He would have had to be blind, or more likely dead, not to. Most of the time, Annarita would have despised her on sight. But if she helped keep the argument from taking off, maybe she wasn't so bad after all.

Gianfranco didn't have much legroom in the back of the Crosettis' Fiat. He'd probably feel folded up like an accordion by the time they got to San Marino. He also wished Annarita would have sat back here with him, not in front with Eduardo. The other way did look more natural, but he wished she were back here anyhow.

"We ready?" Eduardo asked. When nobody told him no, he put the car in gear and drove off toward the mountain republic.

He shifted gears clumsily. "You're used to an automatic transmission, aren't you?" Gianfranco said.

"Does it show that much?" Eduardo said. Again, nobody

told him no. He sighed. "I'm afraid I am. Not many stick shifts in the home timeline. Hardly any, in fact."

The Mazzillis' Mercedes had an automatic. That made it special here. Everything in the home timeline seemed better than the way the Italian People's Republic did the same thing.

"Watch out for the traffic lights," Annarita warned.

Eduardo laughed. "Don't worry about that. I know all about red lights and green lights—we've got plenty of them back home."

He stopped when he was supposed to. Once or twice, he stopped when a local would have charged on through. Maybe he didn't want to take any chances. Or maybe they just didn't have any guts in the home timeline. Gianfranco almost got on him about it, but thought better at the last moment.

"Now we see what's what, or some of what's what," Eduardo said as they neared the border crossing. Italians needed only their internal passports to enter San Marino. It wasn't foreign enough to require the other kind. Approval to travel to real foreign countries was harder to come by.

"Papers." The guard on duty sounded bored. Gianfranco hoped he was. He sure seemed to be. He glanced at the three internal passports, stamped them, and handed them back. "Go on. Enjoy your stay."

"*Grazie*, Comrade," Eduardo said politely. The guard shrugged and waved him forward.

He didn't just go forward. He went up. The city of San Marino sat at the top of a mountain. One side was a sheer drop of most of a kilometer. The other side was only very steep. The fortress at the heart of the town had never fallen. Gianfranco could see why not.

With so many ups and downs, where where you supposed to

find a flat place, or even a fairly flat place, to park your car? That, though, the people who ran San Marino had taken care of. There was an enormous parking lot near the bottom of the city. It was crowded when Eduardo drove into it, but not impossibly crowded.

"Whew!" he said when he turned the key and the motor died. "To drive a stick in a country like this, you need one foot on the gas, one foot on the brake, and one foot on the clutch."

Gianfranco thought about a tripod man. "Your seat wouldn't be very comfortable then," he said.

"Mm, no, I suppose not," Eduardo agreed.

"What's San Marino like in the, uh, home timeline?" Annarita asked. "Have you been there? Been here? However you say it?"

"Yes, I've been here," Eduardo answered. "It doesn't look a whole lot different. Most of the buildings are old enough to go back before the breakpoint, so they're pretty much the same. This lot isn't there, though."

"In that case, where do people park?" Gianfranco asked as they got out of the Fiat.

Eduardo locked the car. "Everywhere."

Annarita found a different question: "Why isn't this parking lot there?"

Eduardo looked around. Nobody stood close by. There probably wouldn't be any microphones hidden in a place like this. You'd have to wait forever before you heard anything good. He nodded to himself and said, "In the home timeline, they didn't have who knows how many zeks to use up carving a big flat lot out of the mountainside."

"You think that's how they did it here?" Gianfranco asked.

"I know that's how they did it here." Eduardo pointed back

toward the entrance to the lot. "There's a little sign over there that says, *This lot built with the help of the Italian Department of Corrective Labor.*"

"Oh." Gianfranco nodded. "I didn't see that." *Corrective Labor* meant zeks, all right. Instead of using bulldozers and dynamite, you gave the political prisoners picks and shovels and turned them loose. If you felt especially mean, you also gave them impossible work norms. Then you punished them for not meeting those norms. The Russians and the Chinese went through zeks by the million. Italy was more economical, but even so. . . .

"Come on." Eduardo pointed again, this time towards a stairway. "Let's go."

Gianfranco's shoes crunched on the gravel of the parking lot. He felt as if he were walking on dead men's bones. And maybe he was.

Annarita quickly found there were two ways to get around in San Marino. Both had drawbacks. The streets didn't go straight up the mountainside. They climbed gently, going sideways, then doubled back and went sideways in the other direction. If you followed them, you could get where you were going, but you'd take a while.

If you wanted a more direct route, you could climb stairways between levels. There were lots of them. They were tall and steep and tiring. "This is the first time I wish the repairmen hadn't fixed the elevator," she said as she trudged up and up and up. "I've got out of practice."

"If you're going anywhere here, it helps if you're part mountain goat," Gianfranco said.

"When mountain goats stop, though, other goats don't try to sell them stuff," Eduardo said. "Or I don't think they do, anyway."

You couldn't say that about the people of San Marino. Yes, it was a Marxist-Leninist-Stalinist state. Annarita didn't think there was a country in the world that wasn't— except the Vatican, which was even smaller than San Marino. But it winked at capitalism's sins.

Shops and hotels filled the gray stone buildings that lined the streets. Some of the shops sold cheap glass trinkets—octopi with staring eyes, yellow lions, dragons. Some sold postage stamps, new and old. San Marino had been printing fancy stamps for collectors since the early days of the twentieth century. Some sold reproductions of antiquities, others the real thing. You could buy recordings of musicians from all over Europe, a lot of them bootlegs the local authorities pretended not to notice. You could buy . . . anything you had the money for. If you got hungry or thirsty while shopping, you could take care of that, too.

Annarita could see why Eduardo's people had put a shop here. It stood out much less than The Gladiator did even in a busy arcade like the Galleria del Popolo. "What's the name of your place here?" Annarita asked.

"The Triple Six," he answered. That was the best throw you could make in most of the games the shops sold.

"Where is it?" Gianfranco asked, panting a little. Yes, the stairs here put the ones in the apartment building to shame.

"I've never been here before, but I know it's up near the top." Eduardo pointed up toward the castle that crowned the mountain. Gianfranco didn't quite groan, but his face looked mutinous. Annarita's legs felt mutinous.

"Maybe we could stop for a little while before we get there," Gianfranco said.

"Well, maybe we could." Eduardo pointed again, this time towards a little shop that sold cold drinks and snacks. "How about a Fanta? You'll move faster with some sugar in you."

"Now you're talking!" Gianfranco said. Annarita nodded.

You didn't sit down inside. Instead, you stood at tall tables. No doubt that helped move people in and out and made more money for the fellow in the white apron who served up the sodas. It wasn't the kind of place that had, or wanted, regulars.

In keeping with San Marino's eagerness to draw tourists, it dressed its policemen in comic-opera uniforms. Three of them marched past the snack shop. Several people photographed the procession. "They look like a bunch of clowns," Gianfranco said.

Eduardo shook his head. "They *dress* like a bunch of clowns. It's not the same thing. Look at their guns. Look at their faces."

He had a point, Annarita decided. No matter what they wore, the policemen carried assault rifles like the ones the Italian Army used: great-grandchildren of the classic AK-47. And, under their silly hats, the men looked tough and capable. Unless you were a fool or you had a death wish, you wouldn't want them angry at you.

They paused, then moved towards a man who lurched along the sidewalk. When they held out their hands for his papers— a request understood from San Marino to San Francisco—he didn't hand them over. Instead, he shouted a mouthful of Slavic consonants at them.

"Ooh—he's a Russian," Gianfranco said softly. Even the

police had to be careful with citizens of the strongest country in the world.

"He looks like one," Annarita said. And he did: his broad face was very fair, and he wore clothes that didn't fit very well and weren't very stylish. Russians relied on muscle. Most of them didn't worry about style.

"You wouldn't see many Italians drunk this early in the morning," Eduardo said, which was also true. Lots of people joked about the way Russians drank. Russians joked about it themselves, which didn't stop them from doing it.

The policemen stayed polite, but they didn't go away. One of them said something. The Russian tourist shook his head. "*Nye kulturny!*" he shouted. Annarita winced. She wondered if the policemen knew that *uncultured* was a much worse insult in Russian than it would have been in Italian. But it turned out not to matter—the tourist knocked one of their hats to the ground and stomped on it.

A second later, he was on the ground himself. The Sammarinese policemen gave him a thorough thumping, then yanked him upright and started to haul him away. The one who'd lost his hat picked it up, carefully pushed out the dent the Russian gave it, and set it back on his head at the right jaunty angle.

"You idiots, you can't do this to me!" the tourist shouted in Russian. None of the local policemen showed any sign of following him. She wondered if she ought to translate, but decided that would only make matters worse. A moment later, as if to prove her right, the tourist yelled the same thing in bad Italian.

"Idiots, are we?" said the policeman whose hat the Russian had knocked off. "See how stupid you think this is." He punched the tourist in the nose. By the drunk man's howl, he thought it smarted.

"*Bozhemoi!*" he shouted, and snuffled, because blood was running down his face. Then he remembered to use Italian: "When the Soviet consul hears about this, all you bums will need new jobs—if they don't send you to a gulag in Siberia to teach you not to mess around with your betters."

A different policeman punched him this time. "Shut up," he said coldly. "We jug drunk Russians about three times a day. If we wanted to waste our time on you, we could send you to one of our camps for assaulting a police officer. Keep running your mouth and you'll talk us into it."

The tourist said something that had to be *mat'*. Annarita didn't follow all of it. What she could understand made her ears heat up. Then the Russian went back to Italian: "You donkeys don't know who I am. You don't know what I am. I am a colonel in the Committee for State Security. You're fighting out of your weight."

Annarita gulped. The KGB was the outfit that taught the Security Police everything they knew. But the Security Police had the power of the Italian government behind them. The KGB had the power of the Soviet Union behind *it*. Lots of people said the KGB *was* the real power in the Soviet Union. The feared and fearsome outfit could without a doubt make policemen in San Marino very unhappy if it wanted to.

"If you are—if you aren't just a lying Russian lush—you're a disgrace to your service," one of the policemen retorted. "Come down to the station, and we'll find out what you are. And you'll find out you can't mess with police officers no matter what kind of big cheese you think you are."

They dragged him away. "He'll get off," Gianfranco said gloomily. "Russians always do."

"He shouldn't. He was drunk and disorderly," Annarita said. "But you're right—he *is* a Russian. And if he does belong to the KGB, they'll pull strings for him."

"They shouldn't be able to do things like that." Gianfranco looked at Eduardo. Plainly, he was waiting for Eduardo to tell him things like that never happened in the home timeline.

Eduardo sighed instead. "You'll find people with influence wherever you go," he said. "Whether that has to do with money or politics or power really doesn't matter. It's the influence that counts."

"*Blat*," Annarita said. The Russian slang meant nothing to Gianfranco. "It means influence," she explained.

Eduardo nodded, then asked, "You guys done?" Gianfranco was. Annarita quickly finished her soda. Eduardo straightened up and took his elbows off the table. "Come on, then. Let's do some more mountain climbing."

He wasn't kidding. Up they went. It wasn't like climbing stairs in an apartment building. It was more like climbing them in a skyscraper. Annarita knew her legs would start feeling it soon. She laughed. Why was she kidding herself? Her legs already felt it.

At last, after what seemed like a very long time, they made it to the top of the mountain. The street there led to the castle and, signs promised, the museum inside. "Well, I'm ready for another Fanta," Gianfranco said. Eduardo gave him a look. "Just kidding," he added hastily.

Maybe he was, maybe he wasn't. Annarita wasn't sure. Eduardo didn't push it. They ambled along the street, looking at the shops like any other tourists. If you wanted to take home a plaster castle to remember San Marino by, this was the place to get one—or silver jewelry, or clothes, or anything else you happened to crave. They might not call it capitalism here, but that was what it amounted to.

And there was a sign with three dice on it, each showing a six. People were going in and out of that shop, the same as they were with the ones to either side of it. "It's open!" Gianfranco said joyfully.

Annarita thought Eduardo should have looked delighted. He looked worried instead. "*Sì*," he said in a low voice. "It's open. Let's walk by and get a better look."

It looked just like The Gladiator. The same games and books and military models were on display in the front window. Most of the people going in were guys between Gianfranco's age and Eduardo's. Most of them had the same look. Annarita needed a moment to put her finger on it, but she did. None of them would have been in the popular crowd at school. They wore their clothes carelessly. Their hair needed combing. She would have bet most of them got good grades—and the ones who didn't weren't dumb. They just didn't care about school. Gianfranco was like that, or had been till he got interested.

"You ought to go in and say hello to your friends," he said now.

"I suppose." Eduardo sounded worried, too. "Why don't you kids find another shop to go into? If something's wrong and they nab me, with luck they won't grab you, too. You can call your folks down in Rimini, and they'll come get you."

They would have to come in the Mazzillis' car. Gianfranco's father wouldn't be happy about that. Annarita didn't suppose she could blame him. He didn't know Cousin Silvio was a wanted criminal.

She wanted to look at a dress shop while Eduardo went into Three Sixes, but she knew Gianfranco wouldn't be caught dead in there. She chose a record shop instead. Some of the music it sold you could find anywhere. Some, though, only circulated underground most places. Governments had come down hard on what they called degenerate noise for almost a century and a half. People still made it, though, and sold it and listened to it. It was almost as subversive as the stuff The Gladiator sold.

Most places, it got sold under the counter, and played by people who trusted their friends not to inform on them. Here, it was right out in the open where anybody could see it and buy it. Elvis, the Beatles, the Doors, Nirvana—classics, if you liked that kind of thing. There were newer groups, too: the Bombardiers, Counterrevolution, Burn This Record.

"Wow!" Gianfranco stared. "We ought to buy some of this stuff. When's the next time we'll see so much together like this?"

"Probably not a good idea right now," Annarita said.

"What? Why not?" Gianfranco might have thought she was crazy.

"If our friend ends up getting in trouble, do you want to be carrying anything that could land *you* in trouble if they snag you?" She didn't need to explain who *they* were. In the Italian People's Republic, as in every fraternal Communist state around the world, there was always a *they*.

"Oh," Gianfranco said in a small voice. "Well, I'm afraid that makes sense. I wish it didn't, but it does."

"Next time we're here, maybe," Annarita said. If they

hadn't arrested the shopkeeper by then. Or if he wasn't working for the Security Police, trapping unreliables. You never could tell.

"When will that be?" Gianfranco challenged.

"Who knows? A year? Two years?" She shrugged. "Probably no longer than that. Rimini's a nice place to go on holiday, and San Marino's easy to get to from there." She began to say more, but then stopped. "Look! Here's, uh, Cousin Silvio."

They both hurried out of the record shop. One look at his face said everything that needed saying. "It's no good?" Gianfranco asked, just to be sure.

"No. It's a trap. Those have to be the Security Police in there," Eduardo said, walking quickly toward the closest stairway. "The place is a snare now, a lure. I didn't expect to recognize anybody in it, but the guy behind the counter didn't know what I was talking about when I said something was as rotten as '86."

"I don't, either," Annarita told him.

"In the home timeline, we were playing Vietnam in the World Cup finals in 2086. The ref missed the most obvious offside in the world, Vietnam scored, and we lost 2-1." Eduardo sounded furious as he explained. "We got robbed, right there in broad daylight. No Italian from my world doesn't know about that. This fellow didn't have a clue, so he's from here, not there. I hope the people from the home timeline got away, that's all."

Eleven

Gianfranco was taller than Eduardo, and had longer legs. But he needed to hustle to keep up with the man from another world as they hurried toward the stairs that led down to the Crosettis' Fiat. "What are you going to do now?" he asked, breathing hard.

"I don't know. I just don't know," Eduardo answered.

"Those maybe-capitalist repairmen?" Annarita suggested. Gianfranco had the same thought at the same time, but she got it out first. It would never do him any good now.

"I suppose so." Eduardo sounded anything but thrilled. "They're probably from the Security Police, too. Heaven help the poor fools who go into Three Sixes. Next thing they know, they'll end up in camps wondering what the devil happened."

"And they're the people Italy really needs!" Gianfranco exclaimed.

"Some of them are, maybe," Eduardo said. "But some of the people Italy needs are the ones who'll stay away from a place like that after the Security Police shut down two others. They'll think something's fishy about this one."

"They'd better," Annarita said. "When the authorities closed down The Gladiator and the shop in Rome, it was all over the news. If you weren't paying attention, you had to be dead."

"Or stupid. Stupid in a particular way," Eduardo said. "Politically stupid."

"Ah," Gianfranco said. Lots of the people who'd been regulars at The Gladiator fit that bill. He probably had himself, and his father was in politics up to his eyebrows. Most people like that were harmless. Even the Security Police recognized as much. But those people left themselves open for trouble when crackdowns came—and crackdowns always came. Everybody had a file. If your file said you went into places where counterrevolutionary sympathizers gathered, that could be all the excuse the authorities needed.

Or maybe they wouldn't need any excuse at all. If they wanted to turn you into a zek, they could turn you into a zek. Who'd stop them?

Nobody. That was the trouble right there.

Going down all those flights of stairs was a lot easier than climbing them had been. When Gianfranco and Annarita and Eduardo got back to the car, the man from another world pulled out his pocket computer. He turned it on, checked something, and breathed a sigh of relief.

"What is it?" Gianfranco asked.

"They haven't put any tracers in here," Eduardo answered. "That's good, anyhow. You live in a place like this for a while, you start thinking everybody's after you all the time. Instead, it's only some of the people some of the time. Happy day."

Usually, Gianfranco took the possibility of being spied on for granted. Why not? He couldn't do anything about it. Nobody could. And chances were that someone he knew, someone he liked and trusted, sent the Security Police reports about him.

You couldn't guess who all the informers were. If you knew, you'd act different around them, and then what would their reports be worth?

Eduardo kept looking around nervously while he was using the marvelous gadget from the home timeline. "Relax," Annarita told him.

He looked at her as if he thought she'd gone round the bend. Gianfranco knew *he* did. "I can't relax," Eduardo said. "What if somebody sees me with this thing?"

"What if somebody does?" Annarita returned. "He'll think it's something fancy that belongs to the Security Police."

Eduardo blinked, then started to laugh. "Maybe you've got something there."

Gianfranco thought Annarita was likely to be right. Ordinary people didn't think about other worlds. They thought about secrets in this one—and they had reason to. Even so, he said, "What if somebody from the Security Police sees him?"

"He'll think Cousin Silvio's in military intelligence, or a Russian or a German." Annarita had all the answers.

She was also liable to be right there. The Security Police looked for secrets within secrets, sure. But they weren't equipped to understand a secret that came from outside this whole world. "They don't know the shops are from the home timeline, do they?" Gianfranco asked as Eduardo started the Fiat.

"Not unless they caught somebody and tortured it out of him," Eduardo said, backing the car out of its space. "I don't think they did. Otherwise, they'd know about me. No, I think everybody else got back to the home timeline just fine."

"What kind of evidence would your people leave behind?" Annarita asked.

"Maybe a computer, if they couldn't grab it and take it with them," Eduardo answered. "But without the right password or voiceprint, it wouldn't do the Security Police any good."

"There wouldn't be any sign of the machine you use to go back and forth?" Gianfranco tried to imagine what that machine would be like. He pictured something that hummed and spat sparks. It probably wasn't like that for real—he had sense enough to realize as much. It was probably quiet and efficient, even boring. But when he thought of a fancy, supersecret machine, he thought of one that belonged in the movies.

"No." Eduardo shook his head. "Just an empty room below ground with lines painted on the floor to warn people to stand back so they don't get in the way when the transposition chamber materialized."

"What would happen if somebody did?" Gianfranco and Annarita asked at the same time.

"Nobody wants to find out." Eduardo shifted gears even more roughly than usual. "It would be a pretty big boom— we're sure of that much. Two things aren't supposed to be in the same place at the same time."

How big was a pretty big boom? Would it blow up the shop? A city block? A whole city? Gianfranco almost asked, but finally decided not to. Any one of those was plenty big enough. He did ask, "You have armies and things in the home timeline, don't you?"

"*Sì.*" Eduardo steered carefully. The road twisted and doubled back on itself as it went down to the border checkpoint. It seemed to Gianfranco that the man from another timeline spoke as carefully as he drove.

Gianfranco persisted anyhow: "If one of your armies fought one of ours, who would win?"

"We would." Eduardo sounded completely sure. "If everything was even, we would, I mean. We're quite a ways ahead of you when it comes to technology. But we couldn't fight a war here or anything. We'd have to try to ship everything in through a few transposition chambers, and that just wouldn't work."

"Logistics." Gianfranco had played war games instead of *Rails across Europe* often enough to know the word.

"What?" Annarita didn't.

That gave him a chance to show off. "It's how you keep an army supplied. Being brave doesn't matter if you run out of bullets."

"Or food," Eduardo added. "Or fuel. Or anything else you need to fight with. Fools talk about strategy. Amateurs talk about tactics. Pros talk about logistics."

"So you're a pro, Gianfranco?" Annarita teased.

"No, of course not," Gianfranco said.

"But he could sound like one on TV," Eduardo said. Gianfranco and Annarita both laughed. So did Eduardo—at himself, Gianfranco thought. When Annarita made a questioning noise, the man from another world explained why: "In the home timeline, that joke is ancient—almost as old as television. Didn't occur to me it could really be funny here. But you haven't heard it before."

"We probably have jokes like that, too," Gianfranco said.

"You do. I heard one at The Gladiator," Eduardo said. "Every day, this guy would take a wheelbarrow full of trash past the factory guard. The guard kept searching the trash, but he never found anything. The guy finally retired. The guard said, 'Look, I know you've been stealing *something* all these years. Too late for me to do anything about it now. So will you tell me what it was?' And the guy looked at him and said—"

"'Wheelbarrows!'" Gianfranco and Annarita chorused the punch line. Sure enough, that joke was old as the hills.

"See what I mean?" Eduardo hit the brakes. "Here comes the checkpoint."

"Your papers." As usual, the guard sounded bored. Gianfranco hoped he looked bored as he handed over his internal passport. Eduardo's false documents had passed muster every time. Why wouldn't they now? And they did. The guard returned them with a nod. But then he said, "Let's see what's in your shopping bags."

Now Eduardo's shoulders stiffened. He couldn't know what Gianfranco and Annarita had bought, or whether they would get in trouble because of it. "Here you are," Annarita said, and gave them to Eduardo to give to the guard.

He looked inside each one, then nodded again and passed them back. "No subversive literature or music," he said. "Too much of that trash has been coming out of San Marino lately. But you're all right. You can go on." He touched a button in his booth. A bar swung up, clearing the road ahead for the Fiat.

They hadn't gone more than a hundred meters before Annarita said, "See what would have happened if we'd bought those records?"

"I said you were right back there in the shop," Gianfranco said.

"What's this?" Eduardo asked. Annarita told him about the shop with the music by bands the authorities didn't like. He said, "The Security Police are liable to be running that place, too. Wouldn't surprise me a bit."

"We thought of that," Annarita said. "It's one more reason we didn't buy anything there. We didn't want to take any kind of chances with you along."

"*Grazie, ragazzi*," Eduardo said. "You took a big enough chance just coming with me."

Gianfranco wanted to say it was nothing. It wasn't, though, not in the Italian People's Republic. "But that was important," Annarita said, which seemed to sum things up pretty well— better than Gianfranco could have, anyhow.

"*Grazie*," Eduardo said again, and drove on down toward Rimini.

Annarita went through the telephone book, looking for the address of the elevator repairmen. Watching her, Eduardo fidgeted. So did her mother and father. Seeing their nerves made her start to realize how big a strain sheltering Eduardo was for them. They hadn't said much about it—they still weren't saying anything—but that didn't make it any less real.

"I'm not finding any Under the Arch Repairs," she said worriedly.

"Didn't you tell me the name of the place was By the Arch?" her father asked.

"I'm an idiot!" Annarita exclaimed, and went to the right place in the book. There it was! Her smile made Eduardo and her parents breathe easier. Yes, this would have been hard enough if he really were their cousin. By now, he'd spent enough time with them that he almost might have been. Almost. Amazing, the power one little word held.

"It's at 27 Avenue of the Glorious Workers' Revolution," she said.

Her father and mother both nodded. Like her, they were used to street names like that. Eduardo made a face. "I wonder what they called it before the revolution," he said. "What-

ever it was, that's probably still its name in the home timeline."

"Is the Galleria del Popolo still the Galleria Vittorio Emanuele
in the home timeline?" Annarita asked.

To her surprise, Eduardo nodded. "*Sì*—it is."

"Does Italy still have a king there?" she asked. She'd only
read about kings in history books. If Eduardo came from a
world where the country had a real one . . . She didn't like that
idea very much.

But he shook his head. "No—I told you that once before,
remember? We've been a republic—a real one, not a people's
republic—for a long time. We don't forget we used to have
kings, though, and we don't pretend they were always villains."

"What do you mean, a real republic and not a people's republic?" her father asked.

"Secret ballots. More than one candidate for each position.
Candidates from more than one party running for each position.
Parties with different ideas about how to solve problems. Parties that turn over power to the other side if they lose an election," Eduardo answered.

The more Annarita thought about that, the better she liked
it. Here, the government did whatever it wanted. Every so
often, voters got the chance to rubber-stamp the people who
already ran things. Ballots were supposed to be secret, but
everybody knew better. You needed to be brave, or a little bit
crazy, to vote no. You needed to be more than a little bit crazy to
run against a government candidate. Annarita didn't know what
would happen to anyone who tried. Probably end up in a camp,
not on the ballot.

She tried to imagine the Communist Party giving up power
after it lost. She couldn't do it. Holding on to power was what

the Communist Party was all about. It said it held on for the sake of the workers and peasants. They weren't the ones who benefited, though. The apparatchiks were.

Eduardo pulled out his pocket computer and called up a map of Rimini. A green dot of light blinked on and off close to the square with the Roman triumphal arch. He pointed. "There's the Avenue of the Glorious Workers' Revolution, and there's number 27." His tone took all the glory away from the name of the street.

Annarita's father got up and looked at the map. "Only a few blocks from where we are," he said. "That's lucky."

"Well, I hope so, anyhow," Eduardo said. "I'll find out in the morning."

"What will you do if it turns out to be no good?" Dr Crosetti asked. It wasn't quite *How long will you stay with us then?*—but it was pretty close.

Eduardo understood that. With a sigh, he said, "I'll look for a job, and I'll look for an apartment. I don't know what else I can do in that case. I just have to try to fit in till my people come back to this alternate—if they ever do."

He would be exiled like no one else. To leave your country behind was bad enough. How much worse would it be to lose your whole world?

"I'm afraid that's a good answer," Annarita's father said. "If you're cast away on a distant island, you have to join the natives."

"It's not quite like that." Eduardo was doing his best to stay polite, only his best wasn't as good as it might have been. If he'd left the *quite* out, things would have been better. It said he thought living in this Italy was nearly as bad as living among savages would have been. Maybe he had his reasons for feeling that way. The computer that fit in the palm of his hand argued that he did. It irked Annarita all the same.

And when had Eduardo ever irked her before? She didn't feel anything about him that should have made Gianfranco jealous. She might have, though, had Eduardo shown any sign of interest in her. She knew she was inclined to give him the benefit of the doubt in just about everything.

Or she had been, anyway. Now? Long ago, some American had written, *Fish and visitors smell in three days*. Eduardo had been as close to a perfect guest as anyone could be. But his welcome was, if not wearing out, at least fraying at the edges. If the repairmen were just repairmen, it was time for him to strike out on his own.

"I hope everything goes the way you want it to," Annarita said.

"Thanks," Eduardo said. "Me, too. It's about my last chance, isn't it?"

Maybe he'd hoped one of the Crosettis would tell him no. But none of them said a word.

Rimini in August hardly seemed like an Italian city. Most of the people on the streets didn't look like Italians. They didn't dress like Italians. They didn't sound like Italians, either. Taverns advertised beer and aquavit, not wine and grappa. Restaurants had strange signs in their windows.

"What's gravlax?" Gianfranco asked Eduardo.

"Smoked salmon," Eduardo answered. "It's pretty good, actually."

"What language is it in?" Gianfranco wondered.

"Swedish, I think, but don't hold me to it," Eduardo said. "Ah, good—there's the arch."

"*Sì*," Gianfranco said. The Roman monument reminded him he was still in his own country. They wouldn't have anything like that in Hamburg or Copenhagen or Stockholm. Sure enough, several blond tourists were taking pictures of the arch. Gianfranco wondered if it commemorated a victory over their ancestors.

Getting across the square wasn't easy or safe. Cars packed it, all of them going wherever they pleased. They ignored the shouts and whistles of the policemen who tried to tell them what to do. Men and women on bicycles and on foot threaded their way among the cars. You needed nerve to cross the square on foot. Drivers blew horns and stuck their heads out the window to yell at anyone who dared get in their way. Gianfranco had no idea why hundreds of people weren't mashed flat every day. But they didn't seem to be.

And if you hung back, you'd never get across. Eduardo started for the far side with as much confidence—and attitude—as anyone who'd grown up here. Gianfranco stuck close to him and hoped for the best.

Some drivers leaned on their horns whether they needed to or not. That made Gianfranco's ears ring. Eduardo knew what to do about it. He got alongside one of them and yelled, "*Beeeep!*" right into the open window as loud as he could.

The man in the car almost jumped out of his skin. "You nuts or something?" he shouted at Eduardo.

"I don't think so," Eduardo said. "Are you?" And he walked away, Gianfranco in his wake. The driver, stuck in traffic, stared after them with eyes bugging out of his head.

"That was wonderful," Gianfranco said.

"Some people think they can act like idiots just because they're behind the wheel," Eduardo said. "Or maybe he's a jerk all the time."

"I wouldn't be surprised," Gianfranco said.

"Neither would I. Some people are, that's all." Eduardo shrugged. "You do your best to get along with them. You try not to let them do too much damage to you. Not much else you can do. If you scream at them all the time, they win, because they've turned you into a jerk."

"I never thought of it like that." Gianfranco knew more jerks at school than he wished he did. "Makes pretty good sense."

"Never underestimate the power of human stupidity." That sounded like a joke, but Eduardo didn't seem to be kidding. He stopped short to keep an Opel from running him down. "Like that moron, for instance."

"He's got a car. We don't. He thinks that makes him the boss," Gianfranco said.

"Well, if he hits us, he's right," Eduardo said. "Oh, they'd throw him in jail, but how much good does that do me if I'm in the hospital?"

"Not enough," Gianfranco said.

"Looks the same way to me."

They made it to the far side of the square without getting maimed. Gianfranco sighed with relief. The streets on the far side were crowded, but at least he and Eduardo had a sidewalk to use again. Cars hardly ever came up onto it with more than two wheels, which gave the two of them a fighting chance to dodge.

"Here's the Avenue of the Glorious Workers' Revolution," Gianfranco said.

"Sure looks glorious, doesn't it?" Eduardo could pack more bite into a handful of words than anyone else Gianfranco knew—except maybe Annarita's father.

The avenue looked anything but. Most of the buildings along it were a couple of hundred years old, dating from the late-nineteenth or early-twentieth century. Some of them might not have been painted in all that time. The sidewalk had cracks. The street had potholes. Big lumps of asphalt repaired some of them. Those stuck up like cobblestones, and were almost as hard on cars as the more numerous holes nobody'd bothered to fix.

"You said it was number 27?" Gianfranco asked.

"That's right." Eduardo nodded. "Now I have to hope everybody in the place isn't on holiday, even if it is legit. It's August, after all."

"What do you do if everybody is?" That hadn't occurred to Gianfranco.

"What *can* I do? I pound my head against the door," Eduardo answered. "Then I come back here when vacation time is over. But I hope I don't have to. Stuff breaks down in August, too. They ought to keep *somebody* around . . . I hope."

"Me, too," Gianfranco said. They went past 164, 161, 158, 153. . . . Most of the businesses were dark. Eduardo muttered under his breath.

He started muttering again a little farther along. This time, Gianfranco could make out the words: "Getting close." And so they were. They walked by 47, 39, 38, 36. . . .

"Look!" Gianfranco pointed at the grimy little sign ahead.

BY THE ARCH REPAIRS, it said, and then, in smaller letters, ELECTRICAL EQUIPMENT OUR SPECIALTY.

"That's the place, all right." Eduardo walked faster. As Gianfranco had in San Marino, he needed to hurry to keep up. "Now we find out what's going on—or we find out nothing's going on."

When Gianfranco saw the dirty window at the front of the shop, he thought nothing was. Then, through the dirt, he saw a lightbulb shining. "Somebody's in there," he said.

"Looks that way." Before going in, Eduardo looked behind him and to both sides. If somebody from the Security Police was watching, he wasn't obvious about it. Eduardo's right hand came down on the latch. It clicked. The door swung open. Gianfranco thought the hinges should have creaked, but they didn't.

Eduardo went in. Gianfranco followed. Eduardo didn't say anything, though he hadn't wanted Gianfranco and Annarita along when he went into Three Sixes.

The guy behind the counter wasn't anyone Gianfranco had seen before. He looked half asleep. A ceiling fan spun lazily, stirring the air without cooling it. Gianfranco was surprised the calendar on the wall wasn't from 1996, or maybe 1896.

"Help you, Comrade?" the repairman asked when Eduardo showed no sign of vanishing in a puff of smoke.

"Well, I don't know," Eduardo said, and that had to be true on levels Gianfranco could barely imagine.

"You've got something that's busted. You want somebody to fix it. If it's a buggy or a gas lamp, you're in the wrong place. If it's got an electric motor in it, maybe we can do you some good." The repairman sounded so reasonable—and so sarcastic at the same time—that Gianfranco wanted to punch him in the nose.

"Well, I don't know," Eduardo repeated. "This isn't something just anybody can take care of." *That* was bound to be true. Maybe nobody in this whole world could take care of it. Certainly nobody *from* this whole world could take care of it.

"And so? Do I look like just anybody?" The fellow in the grimy coveralls drew himself up with touchy pride. The answer there, as far as Gianfranco could see, was *yes*. The repairman was around forty. He was chunky—not fat, but definitely chunky. He should have shaved this morning, but he hadn't. His face wouldn't set the girls' hearts pounding, not with that honker in the middle of it. "So what's your trouble? Home? Industrial? This is a good time to get industrial work done. Not much happens in August most places."

"Why are you open, then?" Gianfranco asked.

"Somebody's gotta be," the repairman said with a resigned shrug. "We take turns with four or five other outfits. It's our year. What can I tell you?" He spread his hands.

"How long have you been in business here?" Eduardo asked. For a moment, Gianfranco didn't get it. Then he did. If this guy's great-grandfather had started the shop, it had nothing to do with the home timeline.

But the man answered, "Just a few years. We're modern, we are. We don't have a bunch of old stuff to unlearn. When we do something, we do it right the first time."

"Were you here the last time the *Azzuri* made it to the World Cup finals?" Eduardo inquired. Gianfranco thought him a fool for asking. The Italian team hadn't got that far since before he was born. Then Gianfranco caught himself. The Blues hadn't got that far *here*. It was different in the home timeline. That story Eduardo told . . .

The repairman suddenly stopped being bored. He thumped his elbows down on the counter and leaned forward. "That lousy ref," he growled. "We were robbed, nothing else but. If Korea hadn't got that goal—"

"Vietnam. It was Vietnam," Eduardo said, his own excitement rising. Gianfranco wondered who was testing whom. He decided they were testing each other. They both needed to.

"*Sì*, you're right. It was." The repairman nodded.

Now Eduardo did some prodding: "It was the plainest hand ball anybody could see—except the blind fool didn't."

"No, no, no. It was an offside. Don't you remember anything?"

Eduardo took a deep breath. "I remember as much as any Italian from the home timeline would."

"So do I." The repairman came out and threw his arms around him and gave him a bear hug. They started dancing, right there in the middle of the shop. To Gianfranco's eyes, they couldn't have looked much sillier if they tried.

"I've been stuck here for months!" Eduardo exclaimed. "Now all I have to do is hop in a transposition chamber and I'm home."

"A transposition chamber? Here?" The repairman's face fell.

"Yes, here," Eduardo said impatiently. "The next closest one's in San Marino, and the Security Police are running that shop."

"Tell me about it!" the repairman said. "That's where we came through, and it's where we were going to go back from. Except now we can't."

Eduardo made as if to pound his head on the counter. "This isn't fair. It just isn't fair," he said. Gianfranco would have been screaming. In a way, Eduardo was, too, but in a quiet tone of voice. He went on, "I finally manage to connect with other people from the home timeline, and what good does it do me? Not even a little bit, because you're as stuck as I am."

"'As I am'? Not 'as we are'?" The man in the coveralls jerked his thumb at Gianfranco. "Who's the kid? And how come you're running your mouth in front of him? If this is some kind of setup—"

"It isn't. He's all right. Odds are the Security Police would have nabbed me after they closed down The Gladiator if he didn't find me a place to stay," Eduardo said.

"Yeah?" The repairman gave Gianfranco a dubious look. "What have you got to say for yourself, kid?"

"Well, to begin with, stop calling me *kid*," Gianfranco said "My name's Gianfranco. And it sounds like you need to get back into the shop in San Marino if you're going to go back to the home timeline."

"Brilliant deduction, Sherlock," the repairman said. "The only trouble is, we need to do it without making the Security Police land on us with both feet. I suppose you've got a way to manage that?" His sarcasm had a nastier edge than Eduardo's, which usually invited you to share the joke. When this guy gibed, the joke was likely to be on you.

But Gianfranco nodded. "I do. Or maybe I do, anyway."

Annarita and Gianfranco walked along the beach, their feet sometimes in the water, sometimes not, as little waves went in and out. A blond man with a dreadful sunburn jogged past. Annarita thought he was intent on putting in as many kilometers as he could before he burned to a crisp. By the look of him, he was almost there. A kid kicked a soccer ball around. He couldn't have been more than eight, but he was already pretty good.

"Do you really think this will work?" Annarita said. If she and Gianfranco couldn't talk safely here, they couldn't anywhere. Of course, that was also possible. And if they couldn't, they'd find out the hard way.

He shrugged. "I don't know. We have a chance. If you've got any better ideas, I'd love to hear them."

Farther up on the sand, two teams were whacking a volleyball back and forth over a net. Most of the men and women were almost as badly burnt as the jogger. They were all laughing and grinning. Annarita couldn't understand why toasting your brains out was supposed to be so much fun. Maybe the Germans and Scandinavians never saw the sun at home, so they had to overdo it when they went on holiday. All the same . . .

She tried to pull her mind back to the business at hand. "Your father won't know what he's getting into, will he?"

"Well, no," Gianfranco admitted. "He wouldn't do it if he did." He looked a challenge at her. "Go on. Tell me I'm wrong."

She couldn't, and she knew it. "How much trouble will he get into if this all works out the way you want it to?"

"Shouldn't be too much," Gianfranco said confidently. "He's a Party official. He'd be doing the best job he knew how to do. Nobody could hold it against him."

"No? Are you sure?" Annarita didn't usually play devil's advocate, but it seemed natural here. "When something goes wrong, people almost always hold it against somebody. That way, they don't have to blame themselves."

"If it goes the way it's supposed to, nobody will even know anything's happened—nobody but us, I mean," Gianfranco said.

"If things always went the way they were supposed to, we'd all be happier. Richer, too, chances are," Annarita said.

"Well, what's our other choice?" Gianfranco asked. "Leaving the people from the home timeline stuck here for good. Do you want to do that?"

His voice held a certain edge. Yes, he was still a little jealous of Eduardo. And maybe he had reason to be if Eduardo *did* get stuck here. Seventeen and thirty made a scandal, but twenty-two and thirty-five could make a match. Annarita didn't know if that would happen. She didn't know if she wanted it to happen. But she did know it wasn't impossible—and so did Gianfranco.

She sighed and picked her words with care: "No, he should go home if he can. But remember that *if he can*. Better Cousin Silvio should get an apartment and a job here than the Security Police should catch him and grill him and throw him in a camp. And they *would* grill him—over a hot fire. Or do you think I'm wrong?"

If he said yes to that, she would know he wasn't thinking very well at all. But he didn't. She gave him credit. "You're not wrong," he answered. "I didn't mean that. I don't want those goons grabbing him—who would? But he's ready to try it. So are the guys from the repair shop. They don't want to spend the rest of their lives here."

So there, Annarita thought. Now she had to nod, even if she didn't much want to. Gianfranco was right. All the men from the home timeline weren't just ready to try to get away. They were eager. Even if this was home to Annarita and Gianfranco, it was something much less pleasant to them. Annarita said the only thing she could: "Do they understand how big a chance they're taking?"

Gianfranco didn't answer right away. His head swiveled towards a statuesque blonde who was tan, not pink, and whose gold suit covered as little of her as was legal, or maybe a little less than that. Annarita didn't kick sand at him. She couldn't have said why not, but she didn't.

When he still didn't answer, she repeated her question—pointedly. "Oh," he said, as if coming back from a long way away. "Well, why wouldn't they?"

"Because they aren't from here. That's the point," Annarita said. "They don't really know how dangerous those people are."

"Well, those people don't know all the tricks they've got, either," Gianfranco replied. "Things should even out."

She wouldn't be able to change his mind. She could see that coming like a rash—one of her father's favorite lines. "The worst thing that can happen to the Security Police is, they get embarrassed. The worst that can happen to Cousin Silvio and the others is a lot worse than that."

"But the best that can happen is, they get away. And then people from the home timeline come back here and figure out some other way to nudge us along toward freedom." Gianfranco's face lit up—and he wasn't looking at a pretty Swedish girl this time. He was seeing something inside his own head, something he liked even better than pretty girls. "One of these days, we can be just like the home timeline ourselves!"

"I don't want to be just like them," Annarita said, and his eyes widened and his mouth shaped an astonished O. He couldn't have been any more shocked if she'd slapped him in the face. She went on, "I don't. I want to be what *we're* supposed to be. We're not the same as they are, and we can't be now. We've grown apart for too long. They do lots of things better than we do. But you know what? I bet we do some things better than they do, too."

Gianfranco didn't believe a word of it. "Like what?"

"Take care of each other, maybe," Annarita said. "And I bet we're a lot better at being happy with what we've got."

"Well, sure we are," Gianfranco said. "Next to them, we haven't got much. We'd better be happy with it."

"Yes, we'd better," Annarita agreed. That seemed to take Gianfranco by surprise. She went on, "Being happy with what you've got—it's not all bad, you know. If you're not happy with what you have, one of the things you can do is take away what somebody else has and keep it yourself. That's part of what capitalists do."

"That's part of what our schoolteachers say capitalists do," Gianfranco retorted. "Have you seen anybody from the home timeline really act that way?"

"Well . . . no," Annarita said slowly. How much of what she'd learned—how much of what everybody in the Italian People's Republic learned—in school was true? How much was just propaganda? She didn't know. She couldn't know, not for sure. If a fish always lived in muddy water, it wouldn't know that water could be clean and clear, either. But she added, "We're not seeing everything that those people do, either. They may have reasons for behaving one way here and some other way back in their home timeline."

Now she watched Gianfranco look thoughtful and a little unhappy, the way she had a moment before. She liked him better for that—it showed his mind wasn't closed. He also spoke slowly when he replied, "I suppose that's true for some of them. But I don't like to think Ed—uh, Cousin Silvio—would."

"No, I don't, either," Annarita said—and if her prompt agreement made Gianfranco jealous, then it did, that was all.

If it did, he didn't show it. She liked him better for that, too. "If he gets back to the home timeline, he can do anything he wants," he said. "But sooner or later—sooner, I hope—his people will come back here. And when they do, we ought to help them any way we can."

Annarita nodded. She almost said, *Well, what can we do?* But she and Gianfranco were doing everything they could now. They'd already kept Eduardo out of the hands of the Security Police for a long time. With some luck, they would help him and his friends back to the home timeline.

With some luck . . . How good *was* Gianfranco's plan? She could see that it *might* work. But she could also see that it might go horribly wrong. And if it did, it would come down on everyone's head. She wasn't even close to sure Gianfranco could see that.

Twelve

Gianfranco's heart pounded as he and his father and two policemen from San Marino in their silly uniforms trudged up the stairs toward the city's top level. One reason his heart pounded was that he'd already climbed a lot of stairs. If you lived in San Marino, you got your exercise whether you wanted it or not.

Still, nerves made his heart thutter, too. He thought Annarita thought he didn't think anything could go wrong. Thinking that was so twisted, it made him smile. But she wasn't right. He knew this might not work. He knew there would be trouble if it didn't—and there might be even if it did. He just didn't see any other scheme that had even a small chance of getting Eduardo and his comrades back where they belonged.

"It is very unfortunate that you let this shop go on operating," his father said to the policemen. "*Very* unfortunate. There was one like it in Rome, and they shut it down. There was one like it in Milan, and we shut it down." By the way he said it, he might have closed down The Gladiator all by himself. He hadn't had anything to do with it, but the Sammarinese policemen didn't need to know that.

"*Sì*, Comrade," they said together. All they knew was that an important—well, a fairly important—Party official from

Italy was up in arms about The Three Sixes. Well, no. They also knew they wanted to get him out of their hair.

But that wouldn't be so easy. Gianfranco's father kept thundering while he climbed. "My own son told me about this place," he said. "My own son! If he could find it, if he knew there was a problem with it, why couldn't you? Why didn't you?"

He didn't say anything about the way Gianfranco had haunted The Gladiator. He was a practical working politician, after all. He knew you talked about what strengthened your case and ignored what didn't.

By the time they all got to the topmost level, Gianfranco's shirt was sticking to him. The policemen looked half wilted, maybe more. Gianfranco and his father wore light, comfortable clothes. Those dumb uniforms were made of wool. They had to feel like bake ovens under the summer sun.

"Why couldn't the stinking shop be lower down?" one of the policemen grumbled.

"We ought to jug the clowns who run it just for being so high up," the other one said. Gianfranco grinned. If they got mad at the people in the shop, that only helped. He was glad they weren't mad at his father—or, if they were, they weren't showing it.

They tramped toward the castle with anger in their eyes. "Now where is this place?" Gianfranco's father asked him. His tone said he was too important a personage to bother looking for the sign himself.

Most of the time, that would have annoyed Gianfranco. Here, he knew his father was talking that way to impress the policemen, so it didn't . . . quite so much.

He pointed. "There it is, Father."

"Right out in the open!" his father exclaimed, as if a hidden gaming shop could have done much business. "Well, we'll put a stop to that!"

He tramped into The Three Sixes, the policemen in his wake. Gianfranco came in, too. He wished he were coming to play *Rails across Europe* or even one of the other games. But if he were, his name would go on a list. Those weren't men from the home timeline behind the counter. They belonged to the Security Police.

Along with assorted tourists, Eduardo and three men from the repair shop in Rimini were inside The Three Sixes. They knew what would happen next, which was more than the tourists did—and more than the men from the Security Police did, either.

"How dare you run an operation like this?" Gianfranco's father thundered. "How *dare* you? This capitalist plot has been suppressed in Rome and Milan, and we'll suppress it here, too!" He sounded a lot more important than he really was.

He sounded convincing, too. Several tourists almost fell over one another getting out of there. Gianfranco guessed that a lot of the ones who stayed didn't speak Italian well enough to understand his father.

The men behind the counter did. One of them said, "Comrade, I'm afraid you don't understand what—"

"I understand much too well!" Gianfranco's father roared. "I understand you're corrupting the youth of Italy—and San Marino, and other places—with these miserable games and lying books. You think you can make the poison sweet, do you? Well, you won't get away with it." He turned to the policemen. "Do your duty!"

"All right, you guys," one of the cops said to the pair behind the counter. "Come along to the station with us. You've got some questions to answer."

"No," said the fellow who'd spoken before.

That was the wrong answer. It couldn't have been wronger if he'd tried for a week. Both policemen drew their pistols faster than a cowboy in an American Western. "Come along with us, I said. Now you're in real trouble."

"You don't know what real trouble is. You don't know who you're messing with, either," said the man behind the counter.

"We're with the Security Police," his pal added.

In Italy, that would have been plenty to get them off the hook. Gianfranco's father looked worried, almost horrified. Gianfranco suspected he did, too—because his father did.

But the Sammarinese policemen laughed. "For one thing, chances are you're lying through your teeth. For another, even if you're not, so what? Do you think you're in Italy or something?"

Both men behind the counter looked daggers at him. "This little tinpot excuse for a country, pretending that it's real—"

That was also the wrong thing to say. It held a lot of truth, which made it even wronger. "Shut up, you jackal in a cheap suit," one of the policemen said. "For half a lira, I'd blow your brains out if you had any. You open your mouth one more time and I may anyhow. Now come along before I get itchy."

"You'll be sorry," the bigmouth in back of the counter said. But he and his friend kept their hands in plain sight and finally got moving.

One of Eduardo's buddies started toward the door that would take them down toward the subbasement where they could call a transposition chamber. He was too eager, though, and moved too soon. The second policeman snapped, "What do you think you're doing? This place is closed, as of right now. Get out of here!"

Now Gianfranco knew exactly what kind of expression he was wearing. Blank dismay—it couldn't be anything else. He'd thought of everything—except that. The police were supposed to be so busy arresting the people who ran The Three Sixes, they wouldn't worry about anything else. Some general or other once said, *No plan survives contact with the enemy*. Whoever he was, he knew what he was talking about.

And then Gianfranco let out a startled gasp, because Eduardo's arm was around his neck and *something* was pressing hard into the small of his back. He hoped it was only a knuckle, but he wasn't sure.

"Don't anybody try anything cute, or the kid gets it!" Eduardo sounded like a twelfth-generation Mafioso.

"My boy!" Gianfranco's father cried.

Without that, the Sammarinese policemen or the Security Police might have done something everybody would have regretted—especially Gianfranco. As things were, they stood frozen in place while Eduardo backed Gianfranco to the door. He waited till his buddies went through, then yanked Gianfranco in after him.

"Down the stairs! Quick!" Eduardo said, locking the door.

"Shouldn't I just wait here?" Gianfranco asked.

"No way," Eduardo said. "Now they really will shoot us if they get a chance. Congratulations. You're a hostage."

"Will you take me to the home timeline?" Gianfranco might have been the most enthusiastic hostage in the history of the world.

"Probably. Come on—hustle!"

Hustle Gianfranco did. He heard thuds behind him, then a gunshot through the door. That made him hustle even more.

Eduardo was right on his heels. He slammed another door behind him. "If this shop is like The Gladiator, this one's tougher," he said.

"It better be," Gianfranco said. "I don't like getting shot at."

"You just joined a big club," Eduardo told him.

The repairman called Giulio was busy in a room in the basement. Gianfranco got a glimpse of another computer, one with a screen bigger than Eduardo's handheld. "It's on the way, which means it's here," the man from the home timeline said.

"Huh?" Gianfranco said.

Nobody answered him. The repairman named Rocco touched the palm of his hand to a particular section of wall. Eduardo lifted a section of floor that didn't look different from any of the rest. A metal stairway waited below. "Come on!" Eduardo called. He want down last, and again closed the door after them. "That'll keep the Security Police scratching their heads," he said, sounding pleased. "I don't think they found the palm lock at all."

"Devil take the Security Police," Rocco said. "There's the transposition chamber. Let's get out of here. We'll have to fill out a million forms for bringing the kid with us, but what can you do?"

The shiny white chamber looked something like a box, something like a shed. An automatic door slid open. The men from the home timeline hurried inside. So did Gianfranco. The seats looked like the ones airliners used. They even had safety belts. Feeling a little foolish, Gianfranco closed his around his middle.

A man in funny-looking clothes—clothes from the home

timeline?—sat at the front of the chamber. "Anybody else?" he asked.

"No. We're it," Eduardo answered.

"All right." The man spoke to the air: "Door close." The door slid shut. It must have had some kind of computer inside. The man pushed a button. A few lights on the panel in front of him went from red or orange to green. That was all.

But Rocco grinned and thumped Eduardo on the shoulder. "On the way home!"

"*Sì*." Eduardo was grinning, too.

"But we're not moving!" Gianfranco said. Could it be that the Emperor had no clothes?

"It doesn't feel like we're moving, but we are," Eduardo said. "We'll be back in the home timeline in about ten minutes, and when you look at your watch it'll be the same time as it was when you left. Traveling between alternates is a weird business all the way around."

Gianfranco didn't know what time it had been when they left. He didn't know if Eduardo was pulling his leg, either. Pretty soon, though, if any of what the man from the home timeline said was true, he'd get the chance to find out.

Comrade Mazzilli was fit to be tied. Annarita couldn't blame him, not with what he knew. She also couldn't tell him some of the things that would have eased his mind. She and her parents just had to sit there and listen while he blew up in their faces.

"That cousin of yours—he's a snake in the grass!" Gianfranco's father shouted. "He grabbed the boy and took him away, and then—then he disappeared! With Gianfranco!"

"I don't know how he could have done that, Cristoforo," Annarita's father said, as soothingly as he could.

It didn't help. "I don't know how, either, but I saw it with my own eyes!" Comrade Mazzilli yelled. "Those thugs dragged poor Gianfranco down some stairs. There's no way out down there, no tunnels or anything, but the Sammarinese and the Security Police—it really was the Security Police running that shop—couldn't find 'em. They jumped into a rabbit hole with my poor boy!"

He and Gianfranco's mother were in agony. "I'm sure Silvio wouldn't hurt him," Annarita said. "I don't think Silvio would hurt anybody."

"Fat lot you know about him. You're lucky he didn't grab you, too," Gianfranco's father said. "So what can we expect now? A ransom note?" Kidnappings for money didn't happen very often, but they happened.

"I don't think it's like that, Cristoforo," Annarita's father said.

"*Then where are they?*" Comrade Mazzilli bellowed. "They have to be somewhere, but where?"

In the home timeline, I hope, Annarita thought. *I wish Eduardo would have kidnapped me.* Gianfranco would be hard to put up with when he got back—if he got back. Would he decide to stay in the home timeline if it really was so much better than this one? Would the people there want him to stay or make him stay? That would be bad—not for him, but for everyone here. How could the Crosettis and Mazzillis go on sharing a kitchen and bathroom if the Mazzillis thought a Crosetti cousin made their boy disappear?

"The Security Police say it's the best vanishing act they ever saw," Comrade Mazzilli went on, not shouting quite so loud. "They say stage magicians can't do any better. But what good does that do me? It might as well be real magic, because Gianfranco's really gone!"

"He'll turn up. I'm sure he will." Annarita's father had plenty of practice reassuring patients. He used that same skill on Cristoforo Mazzilli now. But he needed reassuring himself— he glanced at Annarita before he said anything. Annarita gave him a small, encouraging nod. That was all she could do.

And Gianfranco's father refused to be reassured. "I don't know how you can be so certain," he said. "Not unless you're part of the plot yourself, I mean."

"Cristoforo, if you don't know better than that, if you really mean it, we *are* going to have a problem," Dr. Crosetti said heavily. Sure enough, a world of trouble was in the air.

"Sì, Comrade Mazzilli. That's just ridiculous," Annarita said.

"I've already got a problem. And everything that's happened is ridiculous—and it all revolves around your miserable cousin," Gianfranco's father said. But then he sighed and shook his head. "No, I don't mean it. I've know all of you too long to believe such a thing. I was upset. I *am* upset. I have *reason* to be upset." His voice got louder again with every sentence. But nobody could tell him he was wrong, not without giving away all the secrets that had to stay secret.

Annarita wondered whether he would believe the truth if he heard it. Even if they'd had it, they couldn't very well have shown him Eduardo's pocket computer, a miracle machine that couldn't possibly come from this world. The best thing Gianfranco's father could do was decide Eduardo had conned them before kidnapping him.

"Of course you do." Annarita's father was still trying his

best to be soothing. "Yes, of course you do. But right now you have to wait. The police from San Marino and the Security Police must be working hard on the case."

"Fat lot of good *they'll* do." Comrade Mazzilli didn't seem impressed with the forces of law and order. "For heaven's sake, those . . . people snatched Gianfranco right under their pointy noses. You think they'll find him? They couldn't find water if they fell out of a boat!"

"Are you going to play detective by yourself?" Dr. Crosetti asked reasonably.

"Well, no," Gianfranco's father said. "But waiting? I'll be climbing the walls—that's what I'll be doing. And so would you." Without waiting for an answer, he pounded out of the Crosettis' hotel room.

Annarita's father let out a long, weary sigh. "I don't ever want to go through that again—and it's a thousand times worse for poor Cristoforo than it is for us. He's afraid Gianfranco's gone for good, and I'm pretty sure he's not."

"Just pretty sure?" Annarita asked.

"Yes, just pretty sure," her father answered. "We know what Eduardo told us. We know what he showed us. But we don't know what he didn't tell us and didn't show us. How much of what we heard was true? How much of it covered up things he didn't want us to know?"

"You don't really believe that!" Annarita said, the way her father had when Comrade Mazzilli accused him of being part of Eduardo's plot—which, in a way, he was.

"I don't want to believe it," he said now. "But I hope more than I can tell you that Gianfranco comes back safe and sound—and soon."

For as long as he'd known about visiting the home timeline, Gianfranco had thought visiting it would be a lot like going to heaven. It seemed more like a visit to purgatory. He could see heaven from there, but the people in charge of the place didn't want to let him go out and touch it.

They didn't make any bones about why, either. "The less you know, the less you'll be able to tell the Security Police," said one of their officials in an accent that sounded just like his own.

"Are you nuts?" he squawked. "I won't tell those clowns anything. And they don't know anything about crosstime travel. They think I've been kidnapped for ransom or something. If I wanted to spill my guts, I could have done it a million times by now."

"He's right, Massimo," Eduardo said. "All he had to do was let out a peep, and the Security Police would have put me through the meat grinder. He never said boo. He didn't even give a hint. Nobody ever thought I was anything special, and that's thanks to him."

"And to Annarita and her folks," Gianfranco put in—fair was fair.

"And to them," Eduardo agreed. "But you're here, and they aren't. And your being here is . . . well, a little awkward."

He might have said *a big pain* instead. Obviously, that was what he meant. Massimo said, "Keeping contamination to a minimum is standard Crosstime Traffic policy." He might have been a priest quoting from the Bible—or an apparatchik quoting from *Das Kapital*.

"Cut the kid some slack, will you, please?" Eduardo said. "We owe him a lot. *I* owe him a lot. Do it for me, not for him."

"And since when are you more important than a multinational corporation?" The way Massimo said it told Gianfranco that not everything he'd learned about capitalism was a lie. But then the Crosstime Traffic official unbent enough to add, "Well, we'll see what my superiors think." He sighed. "The least they'll do is drug him so he *can't* spill no matter what those goons try on him."

One of his superiors must have been a human being under his funny-looking suit. Clothes in the home timeline kept making Gianfranco want to giggle. The man gave Gianfranco permission to go around Rimini with somebody along to keep an eye on him. Eduardo was the somebody.

The Roman arch in the middle of the square was the same here as it was in his alternate. The little cars zipping around near it and under it sure weren't, though. There were many more different styles, and they were painted in much brighter colors. And there was another difference. "The exhaust doesn't make my eyes sting!" he said.

"That's right," Eduardo said. "They burn hydrogen, not gasoline—or gasoline and motor oil, like German Trabants." He made a face—Trabants were nasty. "The exhaust is water vapor, not a bunch of stinking, poisonous chemicals."

"I've heard talk about using hydrogen back home," Gianfranco said. "It's nothing but talk, though."

"They probably won't try to do it till they run out of oil," Eduardo said. "And that's liable to be too late."

"How will you get me back to my alternate?" Gianfranco asked. "I don't think you can put me back in the basement at The Three Sixes."

"I don't think so, either, even if it would be nice if we could," Eduardo answered. "I don't know anything officially, you understand. My guess would be, they'll take you over to Milan and insert you there."

Gianfranco wasn't sure he liked the sound of that. It made him seem more like a needle than a person. And he said, "What? Back at The Gladiator? Aren't the Security Police still all over it, too?"

"Not any more. We monitor them," Eduardo said. "The shop is still locked up, but that's about it. They don't think anybody else will show up there."

"So if I appear down in the basement in the middle of the night . . ." Gianfranco began.

"You've got it," Eduardo said. "All you'd have to do is come out and go home. Of course, you might want to wear gloves while you're in the shop."

"I don't know why, except maybe when I touch the door to leave," Gianfranco said. "You probably have more fingerprints inside there than I do, but I can't think of many other people who would."

Eduardo laughed. "I can't even tell you you're wrong. You sure wasted a lot of time in there."

"I don't think it was a waste," Gianfranco replied with dignity. "If I hadn't spent so much time there, I never would have got here—even if you did have to kidnap me to get me down the stairs."

"That's not why I did it," Eduardo said. "Things were going wrong. We couldn't get down there unless I grabbed you."

"Whatever you do with me, I hope you do it soon. My family must be going out of their minds," Gianfranco said.

"And they're probably furious at the Crosettis because of me," Eduardo said. "They didn't figure I'd turn out to be such a desperate criminal. But none of what happens next is my call.

It's up to the bosses at Crosstime Traffic. They'll decide when they're good and ready, and that'll be that. Any which way, it's all over for me."

"What do you mean?"

"I won't be going back to that alternate. No chance they'll let me, and I don't think I would even if I could. I've been burned. I'm bound to be on every wanted list in the Italian People's Republic. If I show my nose there, everyone will jump on me with both feet."

"Oh." Gianfranco nodded. "*Sì.* I guess you're right." Eduardo wouldn't be coming back to see Annarita any more, then. That didn't break Gianfranco's heart, even if he did his best not to show it.

The higher-ups at Crosstime Traffic figured out what to do faster than Eduardo had made Gianfranco think they would. That afternoon, he and Eduardo got into an Alfa Romeo to go back to Milan. "Please fasten your seat belt," a woman's voice said after he sat down.

He did. "How does it know?" he asked the guy who was driving, a fellow in his mid-twenties named Moreno. Whether that was first name or last Gianfranco never found out.

"Sensor in the seat, and another one in the lock mechanism." Moreno spoke a French-flavored dialect. Gianfranco had to listen to him closely to follow what he said.

He drove like a maniac. Gianfranco had never imagined going from Rimini to Milan so fast, not unless he flew. He was glad he wore the seat belt. How much good it would do in case of a crash at that speed was a different question. Every time the Alfa hit a bump, Gianfranco almost went through the ceiling.

They were doing better than 160 kilometers an hour when

an unlucky sparrow bounded off the windshield. "That little bird is—"

"Kaput," Moreno finished for him, with a wag of the hand. Gianfranco would have said something like *very unhappy*, which didn't mean Moreno was wrong—there was a tiny splash of blood on the window glass.

The Italian countryside here didn't look much different from the way it did in Gianfranco's world. Milan was a different story. Parts of it hadn't changed. The old buildings—La Scala, the Duomo, the Galleria del Popolo or Galleria Vittorio Emanuele—seemed the same. But massive skyscrapers of glass and steel gave the skyline an alien look. And . . .

"What's *that*?" Gianfranco asked. Whatever it was, it covered a lot of space.

"That's the soccer stadium," Eduardo answered. "One of them, I mean. AC Milan plays there. Inter Milan has a stadium about the same size on the other side of town."

"Oh, my," Gianfranco said. Milan's two big soccer clubs had the same names here as they did in his alternate. But the size of that stadium said soccer was a much bigger business in the home timeline. He wasn't sure whether that was good or bad. "Is the game better here than it is in my Milan?" he asked.

"Sometimes," Eduardo answered. "The big teams here have the best players from all over the world, not just from one country. The seasons are longer here, though, and the players don't always try as hard as they might. When it's good, it's better, I guess. When it's not . . ." He shrugged. Moreno said something rude. Eduardo went on, "The top players get so much money, they don't always want to take chances, either."

Gianfranco started to laugh. "We always hear about the

capitalists exploiting the workers. It sounds like the soccer workers exploit the capitalists, too."

That made Eduardo laugh. "*Sì.* It can happen. But the players make so much, they're capitalists, too."

Moreno had to drive around the Galleria del Popolo several times before he could nab a parking space. (Gianfranco knew that wasn't the right name here, but he still thought of the place that way.) "Traffic here is even worse than it is back home," he said. Moreno swore again.

"We've got more cars," Eduardo said. "We don't have to wait for years before we buy one. We just put down the money and drive away. We don't have to put down very much, either. There's a lot more buying on credit here than in your alternate."

"Doesn't that suck people into debt?" Gianfranco asked as he got out.

"It can," Eduardo said. Moreno zoomed off. Eduardo continued, "Yeah, it can—I'm not going to lie to you. But with most people, it doesn't. And they get to buy things they would have trouble affording if they had to save up the money ahead of time."

"Advertisements everywhere," Gianfranco remarked as they walked through the Galleria. Electric signs and TV screens shouted at him to buy cars and cologne and fasartas and soda. He didn't even know what a fasarta was. He didn't want to ask Eduardo, for fear of seeming ignorant. After a while, though, he did ask, "Doesn't all this drive people crazy?"

"Oh, you'd better believe it," Eduardo said. "Most people try to tune it out. But that just means the people who put the ads together make the new ones even bigger and noisier than the ones that came before. It's a war, like any other war. *Ignore this if you can!* the advertisers say. So people do."

Gianfranco couldn't ignore the ads. He didn't have the practice people here did. In his Italian People's Republic, goods were scarce. There wasn't much competition. If you had something, people rushed out and bought it. Whether it was overcoats or avocados, they didn't know when they would see the like again. But everything seemed to be available all the time here. You had to persuade people to part with their money, make them want to buy your shoes and not Tod's. Gianfranco had no idea who Tod was or whether his—her?—shoes were good or bad. But ads for them were all over the Galleria.

So were ads for Crosstime Traffic. That surprised Gianfranco, though he didn't know why it should have. "You really do work for a capitalist corporation," he said to Eduardo.

"Yes, and I don't think it's evil or gross, either," Eduardo said. "Without Crosstime Traffic, the home timeline would be a mess. Oh, you'll get lots of people who tell you it's a mess anyhow, but it would be a different mess, and a worse one."

He knew what Gianfranco was thinking, all right. In the Italian People's Republic, looking out for a profit first was shameful. It wasn't quite illegal, but you didn't want to get caught doing it. Here . . . nobody cared.

A lot of the buildings in the Galleria looked the same as the ones in Gianfranco's alternate. They *were* the same buildings, like La Scala and the Duomo. They'd gone up before the two worlds split apart, so they existed in both. Strange to think of two sets of the same buildings in different worlds.

Or maybe more than two . . . "How many alternates have the Galleria in them?" Gianfranco asked.

Eduardo looked startled. "I don't know. A lot—that's all I can tell you. All the ones where the breakpoint is after it was built. Some of them, though, you don't want to visit."

"Alternates where the Fascists won?" That was the worst thing Gianfranco could think of.

"Those are bad, but some of them aren't too much worse than yours," Eduardo answered. That gave Gianfranco a look at his own alternate, and at how it seemed to the home timeline, that he hadn't had before. He could have done without it. Eduardo went on, "Those are bad, but the ones where they really went and fought an atomic war are worse."

"Oh." Gianfranco winced. "How many of those are there?"

"Too many. We stay out of most of them," Eduardo said. "They've been knocked too flat to be worth doing business with. They've been knocked too flat to be dangerous, too. Nobody in any of them will find the crosstime secret any time soon."

"I guess not," Gianfranco said. "Do you try to nudge the Fascist alternates the way you've been nudging mine?"

"*Sì*," Eduardo said, and not another word.

"Any luck?"

Eduardo doled out two more words: "Not much." A little defensively, he added, "It's not easy. A world is a big place, and we don't have a lot of resources to put into any one alternate."

"I wasn't complaining. I was just wondering," Gianfranco said. "Boy, the buildings may be the same here, but the shops sure aren't." The one they'd just walked past would have got the shopkeeper flung into a camp in his Milan. Here, nobody but a couple of customers walking in paid any attention to it.

"Different alternates, different customs." Eduardo seemed glad Gianfranco had changed the subject. Was he embarrassed the home timeline couldn't do more with alternates it didn't like? Or was he embarrassed it wasn't trying harder? Its first job was to turn a profit. If it didn't do that, it wouldn't have the money to try to do anything else.

CROSSTIME TRAFFIC. Gianfranco was surprised the sign in the familiar shopfront didn't say The Gladiator. He knew he shouldn't have been, but he was anyway. "What do we do now?" he asked as Eduardo held the door open for him.

"We give you your cover story. We give you the drugs so you'll stick to it no matter what. Then we wait until midnight and send you home," Eduardo answered. "If they catch you inside and ask you how you got there, tell 'em we had a tunnel that runs all the way from Rimini to Milan. That'll shut 'em up."

Gianfranco laughed. "I bet it will."

"What do we do if Gianfranco doesn't come back?" Annarita's mother asked for about the fiftieth time as the family Fiat neared their apartment building. The Crosettis had never had such a miserable end to an August holiday.

"I think we change our names and run off to Australia," Annarita's father said.

"How are we supposed to do that?" Annarita asked, curious in spite of herself.

"Well, if we change our names, everyone will think we're Australians anyway, so there shouldn't be any trouble." Her father made it sound ridiculously easy. But the accent was on *ridiculously*.

"You're not helping," Annarita's mother said. "The Mazzillis are going to hate us forever. We may have to move, and wish we could go to Australia."

"I think Gianfranco will be back," Annarita said.

"He'd better be," her mother said. "Our life becomes impossible if he isn't, and that's nothing next to what happens to the poor Mazzillis. Their only child gone—" She shook her head. "I wouldn't want to keep on living if anything happened to you, Annarita."

"Don't talk like that, Mother," Annarita said. "Just don't. Not about me, and not about Gianfranco, either."

"What worries me is, he's liable to decide he likes it there," her father said. "And if he does, and if they let him, he's liable to decide to stay. A lot of the time, boys that age only think about themselves. What staying there would do to everybody who has to stay here . . . He may not worry about that for a long time."

"I hope you're wrong!" Annarita exclaimed.

"I hope I'm wrong, too," Dr. Crosetti said. "Eduardo and his friends are more likely to care about what happens here than Gianfranco does, though."

Gianfranco was her boyfriend. When her father criticized him, she felt she ought to leap to his defense. But she couldn't. She was too afraid her father was right. All the marvels the home timeline had to offer . . . Yes, they would tempt Gianfranco. They would tempt plenty of people from this alternate. And he was young enough and smart enough to start over there if he wanted to—and if they let him.

"Maybe I should fix something for us to eat," her mother said. "I don't think the Mazzillis will want to have supper with us tonight."

"I'll help," Annarita said.

Chopping vegetables and cooking pasta let her take her mind off her worries for a while. Gianfranco's mother stuck her nose into the kitchen. When she saw Annarita and her mother busy there, she drew back in a hurry. Any other late afternoon, she would have come in and chatted. No, things wouldn't be the same if Gianfranco didn't come back.

They might not be the same even if he did. Annarita frowned when that occurred to her. The Mazzillis would go right on blaming Eduardo for kidnapping him. As far as they knew, Eduardo was the Crosettis' Cousin Silvio. Why *wouldn't* they think everybody in Annarita's family was responsible in some way?

The knife in Annarita's hand flashed as she cut zucchini into slices almost thin enough to see through. "This is a mess," she said. "Nothing but a miserable, stinking mess."

Her mother was slicing even thinner. "You're not wrong. I wish you were. If Comrade Mazzilli weren't who he was, Gianfranco might be able to tell him what was what. But the way things are . . ."

"*Sì*," Annarita said unhappily. Because Comrade Mazzilli was a Communist Party official, Gianfranco had used him to get the Security Police out of the way so Eduardo and his friends could escape. His father wouldn't like that even a little bit. And again, how could you say he was wrong not to like it?

Supper turned out to be a very unhappy meal. The Crosettis ate quickly to get out of the dining room and let the Mazzillis have it. Annarita thought about going on like that day after day, year after year. It could happen. In the Italian People's Republic, moving away from neighbors who didn't like you was often harder than finding some way to put up with them. But it would be anything but pleasant.

"We'll have to take turns going first," Annarita's mother said with a sigh—she must have been thinking along the same lines.

"I wonder how much trouble Comrade Mazzilli can make for us if he really works at it," her father said. There was another interesting question. Because of his Party rank, he might be able to make quite a bit.

If Gianfranco didn't turn up, he'd have every reason to do just that. Annarita had never dreamt helping someone could do such a good job of complicating her life.

Thirteen

The door to the transposition chamber opened. Gianfranco hurried out. He didn't remember anything about being drugged. He wasn't supposed to. But what they'd told him while he was out would kick in when the Security Police started grilling him. So people from the home timeline claimed, anyhow. He hoped like anything they knew what they were talking about.

The lights in the subbasement under The Gladiator came on. Motion sensors, Eduardo had told him. He looked back over his shoulder. One instant, the chamber was there. The next, it was gone—gone for good.

"Stuck here," Gianfranco muttered. "Stuck here forever." He said something that should have set off a smoke detector, if there was one here. He would have been just as happy to stay in the home timeline—probably happier. Only the thought of what was bound to be happening to his family and to Annarita's made him come back—that and the obvious unwillingness of the Crosstime Traffic people to let him do anything else. He hadn't argued much. What was the point, when he could see he would lose? Better to jump if you were going to get pushed anyway.

He went up the stairs to the trap door at the top. He pushed it up and went through into the basement. If there were Security

Police officers in the shop, they would hear him. But Eduardo had promised him there wouldn't be, and he seemed right.

No motion sensors up there, or none that worked. It stayed dark. The Crosstime Traffic people had warned him it would. He held the trap door open for a moment so he could get his bearings with the light shining up from below. Then he shut it and walked toward the next stairway with his hands out in front of him as if he were blind.

Even so, he almost tripped over the bottom step. He groped till he found the bannister, then went up the stairs. They put him in The Gladiator's backmost room. He came out into the room where he'd spent so much time playing games. The tables and chairs were still in place. He proved as much by nearly breaking his neck on a couple of them.

After a good deal of groping, he opened the door to the front of the shop. Then he could see again, thanks to the street lights outside. He waited for somebody from the Security Police to yell, "Don't move!" But he had The Gladiator all to himself.

He covered his fingers with a handkerchief when he opened the outer door. No alarm sounded. He scurried away as fast as he could go anyhow. The Security Police might not be here, but he would have bet they had some way to know when that door opened.

Even after midnight, the Galleria del Popolo wasn't deserted. Bars and restaurants—and maybe some shadier places— stayed open late. Gianfranco smelled fresh cigarette smoke in the air. (Many more people smoked here than in the home timeline.) Behind him, someone called, "Hey, you! What are you doing?" The voice didn't sound as if it belonged to anyone from the Security Police. It sounded more like that of an ordinary person worried about burglars.

No matter whose voice it was, Gianfranco ignored it. He turned a corner, then another, then another. He didn't run—that might have drawn unwelcome notice to him. But he did some pretty fancy walking.

Once he was sure nobody was on his heels, he slowed down, breathing hard. The man back near The Gladiator had worried that he was a criminal. Now he worried about running into a real one. That would be irony, wouldn't it? Go off on an adventure no one in this world could ask, and then get knocked over the head for whatever you had in your wallet? He shivered, though the summer night was mild.

Not many people were on the street. The ones who were seemed as nervous of him as he was of them. That reassured him. He knew he was no sneak thief or robber. All they knew was that he was tall and might be dangerous.

He turned around a couple of times to figure out where he was—he'd gone around those corners at random when he was getting away from The Gladiator. Then he nodded to himself. Milan's skyline looked familiar again. Those skyscrapers that changed it from the home timeline were gone. His apartment building would be . . . over that way.

Off he went. He shrank into a dark doorway when a police car went by. The *carabinieri* inside didn't notice him, or else didn't care. The car rolled down the street.

When he got to the apartment building, he took the stairs. He somehow felt the elevator would draw too much notice. That was probably foolish, but he didn't care. He hadn't got used to the elevator yet anyway.

He looked at his watch. It wasn't even one o'clock yet. Eduardo had known what he was talking about. Time—or rather, duration—really did stand still inside a transposition chamber.

Gianfranco wondered why. From what Eduardo said, chrono-physicists in the home timeline did, too.

Here was the familiar hallway. Here was the familiar—and familial—door. He reached into his pocket. Where the devil were the familiar keys? He'd had them—and now he didn't. They had to be somewhere in the home timeline, or maybe in the transposition chamber. He felt like pounding his head against the wall. Instead, he started pounding on the door.

People joked about the midnight knock on the door. They joked so they wouldn't have to cringe, because those knocks were much too real and much too common. Even so, Annarita didn't think she'd ever heard one . . . till now.

The terror that filled her also amazed her. That a simple sound could cause so much fear seemed impossible. No matter how it seemed, she lay shivering in her bed. She might suddenly have been dropped into crushed ice.

The pounding went on and on. Was it her door? Were they coming for her parents—and for her—because of what had happened to Gianfranco?

She almost screamed when the light in her bedroom came on. There stood her father in his pajamas. "It's not for us," he said. "It's next door."

Half a dozen words that sounded like a reprieve from a death sentence. And, no two ways about it, they might have been just that. There was a joke that ended, "No, Comrade. He lives one floor down." Annarita had always thought it was funny. Now she was living inside it and understanding the relief the poor fellow who said that had to feel.

Then the knocking stopped—the door must have opened.

A split second later, Annarita heard screams and shrieks. At first she thought the Security Police were beating the Mazzillis. Then she made out Gianfranco's name. His mother cried, "You're back!"

Annarita jumped out of bed. She ran over and gave her father a hug. "They played fair with us," she said. "They didn't have to, but they did."

"A good thing, too," her father said. "I just didn't know what to tell the Mazzillis any more."

"Shall we go over there?" Annarita asked. "They can't get mad if the noise woke us up."

"They can find plenty of other reasons to get mad if they want to," Dr. Crosetti said. "But yes, let's go over. At least they can't blame us for getting Gianfranco murdered now. That's a good start."

The Crosettis needed to knock several times before the Mazzillis paid any attention to them. A lot of noise was still coming from inside the apartment. But Gianfranco's father finally opened the door. "Ah," he said. "You must have heard us."

Of course we did. Half of Milan heard you, Annarita thought. Her father only nodded. "We did," he agreed. "We're glad he's back. We're gladder than we know how to tell you."

"Is he all right?" Annarita asked.

"He seems to be," Comrade Mazzilli answered cautiously.

"I'm fine." Gianfranco came to the door. He was grinning from ear to ear. "I couldn't be better."

"How was it?" Annarita talked to him right past his parents.

"Amazing," he answered. "Just amazing."

"How did you get away from the villains?" Gianfranco's mother said. "I was so glad to see you, I didn't even ask yet."

"Oh, they let me go," Gianfranco said. "That was all a bluff to make sure nobody started shooting at them." He made it sound as if Eduardo and his friends hadn't done anything worse than knock on the wrong door.

"How did you—all of you—get away from the Security Police?" Comrade Mazzilli asked. "They swore up and down that there was no way out of the shop."

Gianfranco winked at Annarita. His parents didn't notice— they were out of their minds with joy to have him back safe and sound. But Annarita knew the answer, and they didn't. Gianfranco had had a ride in a transposition chamber. She hadn't imagined she could be so jealous. He couldn't tell his mother and father about the chamber, though. What *would* he say?

He didn't say anything at first—he let out a wordless, scornful snort. "The Security Police aren't as smart as they think they are, then," he declared. His parents both nodded. Everybody liked to believe the Security Police was nothing but a bunch of fools. That mostly wasn't true, but people wanted to believe it was, because it made the Security Police seem less dangerous than they really were. "They must have missed the trap door set into the basement wall," Gianfranco went on. "It opened into a secret room with a tunnel. They put a blindfold on me so I couldn't see where the tunnel went, but we got away."

Annarita had all she could do to keep a straight face. Her father's expression looked a little strained, too. Gianfranco was stealing big chunks of the plot from a TV thriller that was on a couple of weeks before. He'd seen it, and so had the Crosettis. His mother and father evidently hadn't.

"Well!" his father said. "I'm going to tell those bunglers a thing or two—you'd better believe I am. And the first thing I'm going to do is tell them you're here and you're safe, and no thanks to them." He stormed off toward the telephone.

"I'm glad they didn't keep you." Again, Annarita talked past Gianfranco's mother, who would think she meant the kidnappers. Gianfranco would know her *they* included everybody in the home timeline.

He spread his hands. "I couldn't do anything about it any which way."

Her father wasn't just talking on the phone. He was shouting: "Comrade Mazzilli here. What? I woke you up? Too bad! I've got news worth waking you up for, you lazy good-for-nothing. Gianfranco's home! . . . What do you mean, am I sure? You blockhead, he's standing right here in front of me. And a whole fat lot of help getting him back *you* people were, too!"

He listened for a moment, then slammed the phone down. "That's telling them, Father!" Gianfranco said.

"Those idiots said they'd send somebody over to take your statement," Comrade Mazzilli said. "I think they're ashamed of themselves for not knowing what's what. They've got plenty to be ashamed about, too."

"I think we'd better go back to bed," Annarita's father said. "Gianfranco, I can't tell you how glad I am to see you again." That was bound to be nothing but the truth.

"Me, too," Annarita said, which made Gianfranco's face light up in a way her father's words hadn't. "Good night."

"Good night," Gianfranco said with a wry grin. "At least you get to go back to sleep. Me, I've got to talk to the Security Police."

"You're right! I should have told them to come in the morning," his father said. "I'll go call them back."

"Never mind. I'll deal with it now, and then I'll sleep for a week," Gianfranco said.

"Good night," Annarita said again. She and her parents went back to their own apartment. She wondered if she would be able to fall asleep again after the excitement in the middle of the night. As it turned out, she had no trouble at all.

The man from the Security Police scowled at Gianfranco. "Where exactly in the wall was this stinking trap door?" he demanded.

"I don't know," Gianfranco said.

"What do you mean, you don't know? What kind of answer is that?"

"It's the truth," Gianfranco lied.

"How can it be the truth? You went through the miserable thing, didn't you?"

"Sure. Of course."

"Well, then?" the Security Police officer said triumphantly.

"Well, then—what? This guy had an arm around my neck. I was backwards to the wall when I went through the door. If I had eyes in my rear end, I could tell you more."

"Plenty of people keep their brains there." The officer yawned. It was half past three in the morning. He looked like a man who wanted to be asleep in bed, not grilling a kidnapping victim who'd appeared out of thin air. With a sigh, he went on, "So where did you go from there?"

"I don't know, not really," Gianfranco answered. "I already told you, they put a blindfold on me after that."

"Why didn't they just knock you over the head?" No, the

officer wasn't happy about being here in the middle of the
night.

"Beats me," Gianfranco said. "You could ask them yourself
if you'd managed to catch them."

"As far as we can see, they might have disappeared by
magic, not by your stupid trap door," the man from the Security
Police grumbled. He was righter than he knew. One of
Crosstime Traffic's biggest advantages was that nobody from
this alternate really believed in other worlds. Travel from here
to the home timeline might as well have been magic. With another sigh, the officer asked, "When did they let you go?"

"This morning. Yesterday morning, I mean." Gianfranco
yawned. His mother had brought espresso for the Security Police officer and for him. Despite the strong coffee, he was still
very tired. Too much had happened with not enough sleep.

"You should have let us know you were free as soon as they
did," the officer said.

Gianfranco just looked at him. The officer turned red and
made a production out of lighting a cigarette. The Security Police called on you. If you were in your right mind, you didn't
call them. Everybody knew that—even Security Policemen.
The only reason Gianfranco's father, a loyal Party man, had told
them Gianfranco was back was to let them know what a bunch
of blundering idiots they were.

After blowing out a long plume of smoke, the man from the
Security Police asked, "How did you get back to Milan?"

"I stuck out my thumb," Gianfranco answered. "One truck
took me as far as Bologna. I got another lift there, and it took
me here." Hitchhiking was against the law. That didn't mean
people didn't do it, even if it was dangerous. And if he said he'd

taken the train, they could ask who'd seen him at the station and find out if there were records of his ticket. Thumbing a ride didn't leave a paper trail.

The officer tried his best: "What were the names of the men who picked you up? What were they carrying?"

"I think one was Mario and one was Luigi." Gianfranco pulled ordinary names out of the air—or out of what the Crosstime Traffic people had told him while he was under their drugs. "One of them said he was carrying mushrooms. The other guy didn't talk much. He just smoked smelly cigars."

"Right." The Security Policeman sucked in smoke himself. He scribbled notes. Would people start checking to see if a trucker named Luigi—or maybe Mario—who smoked cigars was on the road yesterday? Did Crosstime Traffic have men who looked like Mario and Luigi? He wouldn't have been surprised.

"Anyway, I'm here now and I'm fine," he said.

His father stepped in and added, "No thanks to the Security Police."

"We did what we could, Comrade. We're not done yet," the officer said. "We'll catch those villains—you wait and see."

Gianfranco knew better. His father didn't, but he also didn't seem much impressed. "I'll believe it when I do see it," he said.

"We work for the safety of the state and of its people," the Security Police officer said.

"Shouldn't those be the other way around?" Gianfranco asked.

The officer sent him a hooded look. *Who do you think you are, to doubt that the state comes first?* The man didn't ask that out loud, but he might as well have. In the Italian People's Republic, the question was only too reasonable. The state had come first here for many, many years. But Gianfranco was just back from an Italy where that wasn't so, an Italian Republic that left the people out of its name but took them more seriously than this one did. He hadn't been able to stay there long, but the attitude rubbed off. Maybe the drugs should have fixed that too, so he didn't pop off.

"Can we finish this another time, Comrade?" his father asked the officer. "Gianfranco has to be tired, and so do you. Could you let him have a little rest, now that he can sleep in his own bed again?"

"Well, all right." The man from the Security Police didn't seem sorry to have an excuse to go home—and Gianfranco's father was a Party wheel, even if he wasn't a great big one. The officer got to his feet. "I'll report to my superiors, and we'll see if they have more questions to ask. *Ciao*." He left the apartment.

"*Grazie*, Father," Gianfranco said around another yawn. "I *am* tired."

"No wonder, after everything you've been through," his father answered. Gianfranco had been through more and stranger things than his father imagined. On the other hand, his father's imaginings had to be scarier. "I don't know what I would have done if you didn't come home safe."

"I'm here. I'm fine—except that I'm sleepy," Gianfranco said.

Lying down in his own bed did feel good. But one thought kept him from sleeping for quite a while. He understood all the reasons why he couldn't stay in the home timeline. Even so, coming back here after seeing what freedom was like made him feel as if he'd just got a life sentence to a prison camp he couldn't hope to escape from.

Gianfranco didn't want to talk about things in his apartment or in Annarita's. She knew why, too. The Security Police were too likely to have bugged one of them, or maybe both. He didn't dare tell her the truth if unfriendly ears might also hear it.

And so, as soon as they could, they went for a walk in a little park not far from the apartment building. Annarita thought she was more eager to hear than Gianfranco was to talk. "Well?" she asked.

"Well, he wasn't lying," Gianfranco said.

"I didn't think he was," Annarita replied. "And when you disappeared without a trace, I was sure there was only one place you could have gone. What was that like?"

"You mean the chamber?" he asked. Annarita nodded impatiently. "It was like—nothing," he said. "It was like sitting in a compartment in a railroad car, except it was cleaner and quieter. I couldn't even tell we were moving. We *weren't* moving, not the way the two of us are now when we walk. We were going across instead, but that didn't feel like anything."

"And when you got there?" she said.

"They wear funny clothes," Gianfranco said. "They wear brighter colors than we do, and the cuts are strange. *Everything* is brighter there. More paint, more neon lights. Something's always yelling at you, to buy or to try or to fly. They *are* capitalists. They care more about money than we do. But they have a lot more things they can buy, too, and they don't have to wait for years to get them."

"That's nice." Annarita remembered her family's seemingly endless wait for their little Fiat. "But are they as free as Eduardo said they were?"

"They are. They really are." Gianfranco sounded awed.

"They let me watch TV. I listened to the news, and there were people talking about government programs that didn't work. They were going on about how much money the government had wasted—just telling people. They sounded disgusted. It was like, *Well, here we go again.*"

"That's different, all right," Annarita agreed. Plenty of government programs here didn't work. The government wasted lots of money. Everybody knew that. Everybody took it for granted. But you never heard anything about it on television or the radio. As far as those were concerned, the government could do no wrong. That wasn't a big surprise. It was no surprise at all, in fact. The TV and radio and papers were all instruments of the government. Would they, could they, bite the hand that fed them? Not likely!

No sooner had that thought crossed her mind than Gianfranco said, "And you should have seen the papers!" He clapped a hand to his forehead. "They made the TV seem like nothing. The things they called the Prime Minister! Here, people go to camps for even thinking things like that. *They* put them in print, and nobody gets excited."

"Why not?" Annarita asked.

"Because they take it for granted. I asked Eduardo about that. Here, everybody would have a stroke if you said anything bad about the Party or the General Secretary, right?" Gianfranco waited for Annarita to nod, then went on, "If you can say anything you want, the way you can there, you have to yell really loud to get noticed at all."

"Why wouldn't just telling the truth do the job?" she wondered.

"Maybe it would—if it was real important or really interesting," Gianfranco answered. "But when it comes to politics, who knows for sure what's true? All the different parties try to sell their ideas, the same way companies try to sell cars or soap."

Annarita thought it over. She wasn't sure she liked it. It didn't seem . . . dignified. But she supposed getting lots of different kinds of propaganda was better than getting just one. If you had lots, you could pick and choose among them. With only one, you were stuck. She knew all about that. Everybody in this whole world did.

"Do they all walk around with their little computers all the time?" she asked.

"Do they!" Gianfranco rolled his eyes. "Those things are telephones, too, and they can send messages back and forth on them, and photos, and I don't know what all else. Half the time, people in the home timeline pay more attention to their gadgets than they do to what's going on around them. They'll walk out in the street without even looking. It's a miracle they don't get killed."

People here walked out in the street without looking all the time, too. Sometimes they did get killed. "Are the drivers there any more polite than they are here?" Annarita asked.

Gianfranco shook his head. "Not even a little bit. And with all those cars . . . Well, sometimes it jams up so nobody can move. Then it's all horns and cussing." Annarita laughed. That sounded familiar, all right. Gianfranco added, "But when they can move—well, it's all horns and cussing then, too. All the time, pretty much."

She'd been skirting what she really wanted to know: "Did you like it there? Would you have stayed if you could?"

"In a minute," he answered. "I could breathe without filling out a form first, you know what I mean?" He took her hand. "I would have missed you. I would have missed you like anything. But I would have stayed This"— his wave took in not just the park, not just Milan, but the whole Italian People's Republic— "this is jail. We've got to find some way to change it, to get free."

"How?" Annarita asked.

Gianfranco seemed to shrink in on himself. "I don't know. I just don't know."

Gianfranco didn't want to go back to San Marino. He especially didn't want to go back to The Three Sixes. When the Security Police put him in one of their cars and got on the autostrada heading east, what he wanted stopped mattering. They intended to take him there, and they could do as they pleased. His only choice besides going to San Marino was going to a camp. All things considered, going to San Marino was better.

Of course, he might end up going to San Marino *and* to a camp. If the Security Police couldn't find the trap door in the wall he'd talked about, what would they do to him? He worried about that more with every kilometer by which he drew closer to San Marino. Since the trap door didn't exist, he figured he had reason to worry.

The Three Sixes was still operating when the Security Police led him into the shop. All the people who worked there belonged to the Security Police. The games they sold were copies they'd made themselves of the originals from the home timeline. How much had that cost? If it helped trap enemies of the state, the Security Police seemed to think it was worth it.

They took him down to the basement. "So your trap door is here somewhere?" one of them said. His name was Iacopo, or maybe Iacomo. Gianfranco wasn't sure which, and the Security Police didn't bother with formal introductions.

"That's right," Gianfranco said, knowing it wasn't.

"But you don't know exactly where," Iacopo or Iacomo said.

"I'm sorry, Comrade, but I don't. I had my back to the wall, and I was scared like you wouldn't believe." Gianfranco aimed to stick to his story as long as he could.

"Yes, you said so." The officer didn't sound convinced. "But at least you know which wall it's on, right? Even if you couldn't see that one, you *could* see all the others."

No, this wouldn't be easy or fun. The Security Police had thought about what he told them, and drawn reasonable conclusions from it. He wished they hadn't bothered. But he was a Party official's son. And, even worse from their point of view, the people who nabbed him had vanished into thin air. They didn't know that was the literal truth.

Cautiously, Gianfranco nodded. Even more cautiously, he said, "I guess so."

"All right, then." Iacopo/Iacomo went on sounding reasonable. Gianfranco supposed that was better than having him sound ferocious. It still wasn't good. When Gianfranco still didn't say anything, the officer gestured impatiently. "Well? Which one was it?"

"That one." Gianfranco pointed to the wall where Giulio had had his little room, the one from which he'd summoned the transposition chamber. Gianfranco didn't see a door on that wall now, any more than he saw any sign of the trap door that led down to the subbasement. Maybe that meant . . .

"You heard him. Get to work," Iacopo or Iacomo told the other men from the Security Police.

They did. They started banging on the wall, not just with their fists but with hammers and wrenches, too. After a little while, one of them stopped. "Well, I'll be—!" one of them said. If he would be what he said he would be, he would spend a very long time in a very warm place. "Fry me for a chicken if something's not hollow back there."

Gianfranco had hoped the Security Police would find the hidden office. He also hoped the people from the home timeline hadn't left behind anything that would hurt them. They'd had to get out in a hurry, as he knew too well.

Iacopo/Iacomo seemed to be a fellow with simple, direct ideas. "Knock down the wall," he said. "We'll find out what's in back of it."

The men from the Security Police rolled up their sleeves and got to work with sledgehammers. The racket made Gianfranco stick his fingers in his ears. It also made somebody from upstairs come running down. "What are you guys doing?" he yelled. "People think it's an earthquake."

"Tell them it's plumbers. Tell them anything you want," Iacopo/Iacomo said. "We found a secret passage. I didn't think we would, but we did. The kid here wasn't blowing smoke after all." Gianfranco should have been insulted. He *was* insulted, but not enough to say anything about it. The Security Police officer from upstairs went away. The others kept banging at the wall.

Try as they would, the Security Police had a devil of a time knocking it down. They swore and complained. Then one of them smashed enough concrete to bang his sledgehammer off a steel bar. He swore again, this time in disgust. "It's reinforced concrete!" he yelled. "What's hiding back there?"

They needed cutting torches to get in. They were all fit to

be tied by the time one of them squeezed through the opening and shone a flashlight into the room. "Well?" another one called.

"Well, what?" the man inside said. "Some of the ugliest furniture I've ever seen, that's all."

"Go on in, kid," Iacopo/Iacomo told Gianfranco. "Is this where you were?"

"I guess so," Gianfranco said once he scrambled through the hole in the wall. The furniture—most of it gaudy plastic—must have come from the home timeline. Scorched metal filing cabinets stood against the far wall. The air stank of stale smoke. Another man from the Security Police opened a drawer. He looked inside, then muttered and closed it again.

"What's the matter?" somebody asked him.

"Papers are nothing but ashes. Whatever was in there, they got rid of it," he answered.

"Where did they take you next, Mazzilli?" Iacopo or Iacomo asked.

"I don't know," he said. "This is where they put the blindfold on me."

The Security Police officer coughed, then nodded. "Oh, yeah. You did say that." Now he seemed more ready to believe the things Gianfranco had said, even when they weren't true. That was pretty crazy, but Gianfranco didn't complain. Oh, no. The officer lit a cigarette. With the air already smoky, Gianfranco wondered why he bothered.

"So there's a different passage somewhere on one of these other walls?" another officer asked.

"I guess so. How else could they have got me out of here?" Gianfranco said. He knew the answer to that, but the Security Police didn't. And he didn't think they would ever figure it out.

A new school year. New classes, new teachers. Annarita knew she'd feel crazy for the first couple of weeks while she got used to things. Not needing to worry about the Young Socialists' League was kind of a relief. Normally, she would have thought hard about running for president her senior year. But, after she'd proved wrong about The Gladiator, she was sure Maria Tenace would clobber her if she tried. And so, with a small mental sigh, she decided to sit on the sidelines and let Maria have it.

She decided that, anyway, till people started coming over to her and asking her if she'd run. They all seemed horrified when she said no. "You're going to let Maria just take it?" one girl said. "But she'll make everybody hate her and she'll run the League into the ground."

"I don't want to have a big fight with her," Annarita said. "Life is too short."

"Who says you'd need a fight?" the girl answered. "Nobody can stand her, and I mean nobody." She wasn't any special friend—Annarita hardly knew her. That made Annarita wonder if she ought to change her mind. When three more people told her the same thing, she did change it. She put in her petition of candidacy about an hour before the deadline.

Maria Tenace stormed up to her the next day, literally shaking with fury. "So you think you can get away with it, do you?" Maria shouted, as if the two of them were alone instead of in a crowded hallway. "Well, you'll find out!"

She did have some friends. They started spreading stories about Annarita. Of course they'd heard about Gianfranco's kidnapping over the holiday. They tried to blame it on her. She wondered what she could say. Simplest seemed best: "We took in a cousin who was down on his luck. He did something he shouldn't have. I wish he didn't, but is it my fault he did?"

Would that do any good? She didn't know. All she could do was hope. She wasn't very worried either way. If she won, she won. If she didn't, she would have fewer things to worry about the rest of her senior year.

The election meeting was the most crowded one she'd ever seen. She and Maria flipped a coin to see who'd speak in which order. Annarita won, and chose to go last. Maria launched straight into an attack: "Comrade students, your choice today is simple. It is a battle between the forces of reaction and those of progress. If you want to shamelessly excuse backsliding anti-Socialist thought, you will vote for my opponent. She showed her true colors last year, when she refused to condemn The Gladiator, that hotbed of capitalist propaganda. If you would rather have a true Socialist in charge of the Young Socialists' League, you will choose me instead. I hope you do. *Grazie*."

Annarita got up. "I don't think I'm a reactionary," she said. "I just don't like getting people in trouble before I'm sure they need to be there. Maybe I was wrong about The Gladiator." *But I'll never believe I was.* "At least I know I can be wrong, though. I don't think Maria's ever been wrong in her life—and if you don't believe me, just ask her."

Maria Tenace started to nod. She almost gave herself a whiplash stopping when she realized, a split second too late, that Annarita wasn't complimenting her. Everybody saw. If looks could kill, hers would have knocked Annarita over on the spot.

No secret ballot—the vote was by a show of hands. Annarita thought that would doom her. Who wanted to risk being labeled a reactionary? To her amazement, she won by something close to two to one.

After the election, a boy whose name she didn't even know told her, "I don't want somebody turning me in to the Security Police if I say something she doesn't like. I don't think you'd do that."

"I hope not!" Annarita exclaimed. Somebody slammed the door to the hall where the League was meeting. Several people said it was Maria storming away. Annarita went on, "I wouldn't have walked out if I lost, either."

"No, I don't think you would," the boy said. "Congratulations for winning, though. I'm glad you did."

"Thanks." Annarita was glad she had, too. A year with Maria running things wouldn't have been much fun.

Gianfranco was waiting outside when the meeting broke up. He also congratulated Annarita, adding, "I knew you had it in the bag when the Dragon Lady came out breathing fire." That made Annarita laugh. He finished, "Want to celebrate with a soda in the Galleria?"

"Sure. Why not?" Annarita said.

Two or three more people said they were glad she'd won as she was walking out of Hoxha Polytechnic. Just what she'd done started to sink in then. Any university that saw *President of the Young Socialists' League* on an application would be much more likely to say yes. That wasn't why she'd run, but it wasn't bad.

When they got to the Galleria del Popolo, she didn't just have a soda. She had a soda, with a big scoop of ice cream plopped in. It was wonderful. Gianfranco had one, too. They sat at a sidewalk table watching people go by. Two of the people were Russians, in baggy, square-cut suits very different from what Italian men wore. They were arguing at the top of their lungs. Except for a couple of swear words, she hardly understood anything they said. The summer holiday had left her Russian rusty. She supposed it would get better again.

She eyed Gianfranco. His people-watching wasn't all pretty girl-watching. She appreciated that.

He pointed across the street. "Look! That shopfront that's been empty forever is finally going to get somebody new in it."

"You're right." She squinted, trying to make out what was below the big letters that spelled out OPENING SOON! She didn't have much luck. "Can you read it?"

Gianfranco squinted, too. Then he shook his head. "No. Too small. Shall we go over and look?"

"In a bit," Annarita said. "Not yet."

After they finished their sundaes and talked for a while, they did cross the pedestrian-filled street. The sign read, RARE AND UNUSUAL BOOKS TO INTEREST EVERY TASTE. A SHOP FOR THE PERSON WHO THINKS.

Annarita stared at Gianfranco. He was staring at her, too. "You don't suppose—?" he said.

"I don't know," she said. "We'll just have to find out, won't we?"

HARRY TURTLEDOVE, "the modern master of alternate history," lives in Los Angeles.

ISBN-13: 978-0-7653-5379-5
ISBN-10:   0-7653-5379-2

35379

0 37145 00699 4

UPC
S

The Soviet Union won the Cold War. Now, more than a century later, the world's gone communist—and capitalism is a bad word.

For teenagers Gianfranco and Annarita, life in gray, regimented Milan is a bore. Annarita's a student and a member of the Young Socialists' League. Gianfranco's father is a Party apparatchik. The biggest excitement in their lives is a war-game shop called The Gladiator, which runs tournaments and stocks marvelous games you can't find anywhere else.

One day, without warning, the shop is shut down. Someone's figured out that The Gladiator's games are teaching counter-revolutionary ideas. The Security Police are searching high and low for the proprietors, who've vanished into thin air, leaving finger-prints that aren't in the records of any government on earth.

Only one staffer remains: Gianfranco and Annarita's friend Eduardo. On the run, he reveals to them where he's really from: a timeline where history ran differently. Our timeline, in fact...

"A BARN BURNER." –BOOKLIST

$6.99 [$8.99 CAN]

COVER ART BY
SCOTT M. FISCHER
TOM DOHERTY ASSOCIATES, LLC
WWW.TOR-FORGE.COM
PRINTED IN THE USA

6 46529 99100 1